# A Letter of
# Mary

Other Mystery Novels
by Laurie R. King

Mary Russell Novels

*A Monstrous Regiment of Women*
*The Beekeeper's Apprentice*

Kate Martinelli Novels

*With Child*
*To Play the Fool*
*A Grave Talent*

# A Letter of Mary

A MARY RUSSELL NOVEL

Laurie R. King

St. Martin's Press ❧ New York

Library of Congress Cataloging-in-Publication Data

King, Laurie R.
    A letter of Mary / by Laurie R. King. —1st ed.
        p.        cm.
    "A Thomas Dunne book."
    ISBN 0-312-14670-1
    1. Holmes, Sherlock (Fictitious character)—Fiction.   I. Title.
PS3561.I4813L47    1996
813'.54—dc20                                            96-22424
                                                            CIP

First edition: January 1997

10 9 8 7 6 5 4 3 2 1

FOR MY BROTHER
LEAHCIM DRAWDE NOSDRAHCIR
AND HIS FAMILY

FROM HIS SISTER EIRAUL EEL

# EDITOR'S PREFACE

This is the third in a series of manuscripts taken from a trunk full of odds and ends that was sent to me a few years ago. The puzzle of its origin and why I was its recipient is far from solved. In fact, it becomes more mysterious with each manuscript I publish.

After the first of Mary Russell's stories (*The Beekeeper's Apprentice*) came out, I received a cryptic postcard that said merely: "More to follow." After the second (*A Monstrous Regiment of Women*), the following newspaper clipping arrived in the mail:

### OXFORD PUNT FOUND IN LONDON

A group of Japanese businessmen on a river cruise yesterday caught and towed to Hampton Court a punt which police have determined originated at Folly Bridge in Oxford. In it were found clothing and a pair of glasses. The Thames Authority has no suggestion as yet how a punt could manoeuvre the locks and deeper stretches of river.

I rose to the challenge. A bit of research determined that the clipping was a filler in the London *Times*, dated three weeks before the book's publication date. The subsequent phone calls to England cost me an arm and a leg, but eventually I discovered that the clothing (trousers, sensible shoes, and a blouse) was that of a tall, thin woman, and it had been found carefully folded on the cushions, with the glasses on top. There was no suicide note. The pole was in the boat (a punt is not rowed or motorized, I gather, but shoved along with a wooden pole). Downstream from Oxford, the river becomes too deep for the punter to reach the bottom.

I even found out that the police dusted the thing for prints, which sounded like a joke until my informant told me how much a wooden punt costs nowadays. With a vague idea that this might someday help me find where my trunk had come from, I asked for a set of the prints. It took a while to clear this with the higher authorities, but I did after some months receive a copy of the forensic report, which informed me that they had been made by two people, both with long, thin hands, one of them slightly bigger and thus probably male, the other with a scar across one of the pads. The scarred ones had been found on the glasses.

Interestingly enough, the fingerprints taken from the sides of the punt match those on a filthy clay pipe that was in the trunk with the manuscripts.

I should also mention that the inlaid box described in the following pages does exist, although when it reached me, there was no manuscript inside. It did hold a pair of black-lensed glasses, a dainty handkerchief embroidered with the letter M, and a key.

The key, I have been told, is to a safety-deposit box. There is absolutely no way of knowing where that box is.

—Laurie R. King

*. . . I would terrify you by letters.*

—The Second Letter of Paul to the Corinthians 10:9

# PART ONE

## Tuesday, 14 August 1923–
## Friday, 24 August 1923

*A pen is certainly an excellent instrument to fix a man's attention and to inflame his ambition.*

—John Adams

# ONE

α

*alpha*

The envelope slapped down onto the desk ten inches from my much-abused eyes, instantly obscuring the black lines of Hebrew letters that had begun to quiver an hour before. With the shock of the sudden change, my vision stuttered, attempted a valiant rally, then slid into complete rebellion and would not focus at all.

I leant back in my chair with an ill-stifled groan, peeled my wire-rimmed spectacles from my ears and dropped them onto the stack of notes, and sat for a long minute with the heels of both hands pressed into my eye sockets. The person who had so unceremoniously delivered this grubby interruption moved off across the room, where I heard him sort a series of envelopes *chuk-chuk-chuk* into the wastepaper basket, then stepped into the front hallway to drop a heavy envelope onto the table there (Mrs Hudson's monthly letter from her daughter in Australia, I noted, two days early) before coming back to take up a position beside my desk, one shoulder dug into the bookshelf, eyes gazing, no doubt, out the window at the Downs rolling down to the Channel. I replaced the heels of my hands with the backs of my fingers, cool against the hectic flesh, and addressed my husband.

"Do you know, Holmes, I had a great-uncle in Chicago whose promising medical career was cut short when he began to go blind over his books. It must be extremely frustrating to have one's future betrayed by a tiny web of optical muscles. Though he did go on to make a fortune selling eggs and trousers to the gold miners," I added. "Whom is it from?"

"Shall I read it to you, Russell, so as to save your optic muscles for the *metheg* and your beloved furtive *patach*?" His solicitous words were spoilt by the sardonic, almost querulous edge to his voice. "Alas, I have become a mere secretary to my wife's ambitions. Kindly do not snort, Russell. It is an unbecoming sound. Let me see." I felt his arm come across my desk, and I heard the letter whisper as it was plucked up. "The envelope is from the Hôtel Imperial in Paris, a name which contains distinct overtones of sagging mattresses and ominous nocturnal rustling noises in the wardrobe. It is addressed simply to Mary Russell, no title whatsoever. The hand is worthy of some attention. A woman's writing, surely, though almost masculine in the way the fingers grasp the pen. The writer is obviously highly educated, a 'professional woman,' to use the somewhat misleading modern phrase; I venture to say that this particular lady does not depend on her womanliness for a livelihood. Her *t*'s reveal her to be an impatient person, and there is passion in the sweeps of her uprights, yet her *s*'s and *a*'s speak of precision and the lower edge of each line is as exact as it is authoritative. She also either has great faith in the French and English postal systems or else is so self-assured as to consider the insurance of placing her name or room number on the envelope unnecessary. I lean toward the latter theory."

As this analysis progressed, I recovered my glasses, the better to study my companion where he stood in the bright window, bent over the envelope like a jeweller with some rare uncut stone, and I was hit by one of those odd moments of analytical apartness, when one looks with a stranger's eyes on something infinitely familiar. Physically, Sherlock Holmes had changed little since we had first met on these same Sussex Downs a bit more than eight years before. His hair was slightly thinner, certainly greyer, and his grey eyes had become even more deeply hooded, so that the resemblance to some far-seeing, sharp-beaked raptor was more marked than ever. No, his body had only exaggerated itself; the greatest changes were internal. The fierce passions that had driven him in his early years, years before I was even born, had subsided, and the agonies of frustration he had felt when without a challenge, frustration that had led him to needles filled with cocaine and morphia, were now in abeyance. Or so I had thought.

I watched him as his long fingers caressed the much-travelled envelope and his eyes drew significance from every smudge, every characteristic of paper and ink and stamp, and it occurred to me suddenly that Sherlock Holmes was bored.

The thought was not a happy one. No person, certainly no woman, likes to think that her marriage has lessened the happiness of her partner. I thrust the troublesome idea from me, reached up to rub a twinge from my right shoulder, and spoke with a shade more irritation than was called for.

"My dear Holmes, this verges on *deductio ad absurdum*. Were you to open the envelope and identify the writer, it just might simplify matters."

"All in good time, Russell. I further note a partial set of grimy fingerprints along the back of the envelope, with a matching thumbprint on the front. However, I believe we can discount them, as they have the familiar look of the hands of our very own postal-delivery boy, whose bicycle chain is in constant need of repair."

"Holmes, my furtive *patachs* await me. The letter?"

"Patience is a necessary attribute of the detective's makeup, Russell. And, I should have thought, the scholar's. However, as you say." He turned away, and the sharp zip of a knife through cheap paper was followed by a dull thud as the knife was reintroduced into the frayed wood of the mantelpiece. There was a thin rustle. His voice sounded amused as he began to read. " 'Dear Miss Russell,' it begins, dated four days ago.

Dear Miss Russell,

I trust you will not be offended by my form of address. I am aware that you have married, but I cannot bring myself to assign a woman her husband's name unless I have been told that such is her desire. If you are offended, please forgive my unintentional faux pas.

You will perhaps remember me, Dorothy Ruskin, from your visit to Palestine several years ago. I have remained in that land since then, assisting at three preliminary digs until such time as I can arrange funding for my own excavations. I have been called back home for an interview by my potential sponsors, as well as to see my mother, who seems to be on her deathbed. There is a matter of some interest which I wish to lay before you while I am in England, and I would appreciate it if you would allow me to come and disturb your peace for a few hours. It would have to be on the twenty-second or twenty-third, as I return to Palestine directly my business is completed. Please confirm the day and time by telegram at the address below.

I believe the matter to be of some interest and potentially considerable importance to your chosen field of study, or I would not be bothering you and your husband.

I remain,

Most affectionately yours,
Dorothy Ruskin

"The address below is that of the Hôtel Imperial," Holmes added.

I took the letter from Holmes and quickly skimmed the singular hand that strode across the flimsy hotel paper. "A decent pen, though," I noted absently. "Shall we see her?"

"We? My dear Russell, I am the husband of an emancipated woman who, although she may not yet vote in an election, is at least allowed to see her own friends without male chaperonage."

"Don't be an ass, Holmes. She obviously wants to see both of us, or she would not have written that last sentence. We'll have her for tea, then. Wednesday or Thursday?"

"Wednesday is Mrs Hudson's half day. Miss Ruskin might have a better tea if she came Thursday."

"Thank you, Holmes," I said with asperity. I admit that cooking is not my strong point, but I object to having my nose rubbed in the fact. "I'll write to let her know either day is fine but that Thursday is slightly better. I wonder what she wants."

"Funding for an all-woman archaeological dig, I shouldn't wonder. That would be popular with the British authorities and the Zionists, would it not? And think of the attraction it would have for the pilgrims and the tourists. It's a wonder the Americans haven't thought of it."

"Holmes, enough! Begone! I have work to do."

"Come for a walk."

"Not just now. Perhaps this evening I could take an hour off."

"By this evening, you will be bogged down to the axles in the prophet Isaiah's mud and too irritable to make a decent walking companion. You've been rubbing your bad shoulder for the last forty minutes although it is a warm afternoon, which means you need to get out and breathe some fresh air. Come."

He held out one long hand to me. I looked down at the cramped lines marching across the page, capped my pen, and allowed him to pull me to my feet.

We walked along the cliffs rather than descending the precipitous beach path, and listened to the gulls cry and the waves surge on the shingle below. The good salt air filled my lungs, cleared my head, and took the ache from my collarbone, and eventually my thoughts turned, not to the intricacies of Hebrew grammar but to the implications of the letter that lay on my desk.

"What do you know of the archaeology of Palestine, Holmes?"

"Other than what we discovered when we were there four and a half years ago—which trip, as I recall, was dominated by an extraordinary number of damp and hazardous underground chambers—almost nothing. I suspect that I shall know a great deal more before too much longer."

"You think there is something to Miss Ruskin's letter, then?"

"My dear Russell, I have not been a consulting detective for more than forty years for nothing. I can spot a case sniffing around my door even before it knows itself to be one. Despite what I said about allowing you to see her alone, your Miss Ruskin—yes, I know she is not yours, but she thinks she is—your Miss Ruskin wishes to present a puzzle to the partnership of Holmes and Russell, not merely to Mary Russell, a brilliant young star on the horizon of academic theology. Unless you think my standard degree of megalomania is becoming compounded by senility," he added politely.

"Megalomania, perhaps; senility, never." I stood and watched a small fishing boat lying off shore, and I wondered what to do. The work was going slowly, and I could ill afford to take even half a day away from it. On the other hand, it would be a joy to spend some time with that peculiar old lady, whom I indeed remembered very well. Also, Holmes seemed interested. It would at least provide a distraction until I could decide what needed doing for him. "All right, we'll have her here a day sooner, then, on the Wednesday. I'll suggest the noon train. I'm certain Mrs Hudson can be persuaded to leave something for our tea, so we need not risk our visitor's health. I also think I'll go to Town tomorrow and drop by the British Museum for a while. Will you come?"

"Only if we can stay for the evening. They're playing Tchaikovsky's D at Covent Garden."

"And dinner at Simpson's?" I said lightly, ruthlessly ignoring the internal wail at the waste of time.

"But of course."

"Will you go to the BM with me?"

"Briefly, perhaps. I had a note from the owner of a rather bijou little gallery up the street, inviting me to view the canvas of that Spaniard, Picasso, that I retrieved for them last month. I should be interested to see it in its natural habitat, as it were, to determine if it makes any more sense there than it did in that warehouse on the docks where I found it. Although, frankly, I have my doubts."

"That's fine, then," I said politely. Suddenly, Holmes was not at my side but blocking my way, his hands on my shoulders and his face inches from mine.

"Admit it, Russell. You've been bored."

His words so echoed my own analysis of his mental state that I could only gape at him.

"You've been tucked into your books for a solid year now, ever since we came back from France. You might be able to convince yourself that you're nothing but a scholar, Russell, but you can't fool me. You're as hungry as I am for something to do."

Damn the man, he was right. He was wrong, too, of course—men have a powerful drive to simplify matters, and it would be convenient for him to dismiss the side of my life that did not involve him—but as soon as he said it, I could feel the hunger he was talking about, waking in me. I had in the past discovered the immense appeal of a life on the edge of things—walking a precipice, pitting oneself against a dangerous enemy, throwing one's mind against an impenetrable puzzle.

The waking was brief, as I ruthlessly knocked the phantasy back into its hole. If Dorothy Ruskin had a puzzle, it was not likely to be anything but mild and elderly. I sighed, and then, realising that Holmes was still staring into my face, I had to laugh.

"Holmes, we're a pair of hopeless romantics," I said, and we turned and walked back to the cottage.

# TWO

β

*beta*

Shortly before midday on the appointed Wednesday, I drove my faithful Morris to the station to meet Miss Ruskin's train. It was four and a half years since we had met near Jericho, and though I would have known her anywhere, she had changed. Her chopped-off hair was now completely white. She wore a pair of glasses, the lenses of which were so black as to seem opaque, and she favoured her right leg as she stepped down from the train. She did not see me at first, but stood peering about her, a large khaki canvas bag clutched in one hand. I crossed the platform towards her and corrected myself—some things had changed not at all. Her face was still burnt to brown leather by the desert sun, her posture still that of a soldier on parade, her clothing the same idiosyncratic variation on the early suffragist uniform of loose pantaloons, tailored shirt, jacket, and high boots that I had seen her wear in Palestine. The boots and clothing looked new, and somehow ineffably French, despite their lack of anything resembling fashion.

"Good day, Miss Ruskin," I called out. "Welcome to Sussex."

Her head spun around and the deep voice, accustomed to wide spaces and the command of native diggers, boomed out across the rustic station.

"Miss Russell, is that you? Delighted to see you. Very good of you to have me at such short notice." She grasped my hand in her heavily calloused one. The top of her squashed hat barely reached my chin, but she dominated the entire area. I led her to the car, helped her climb in, started the engine, and enquired about her leg.

"Oh, yes, most annoying. Fell into a trench when the props collapsed. Bad break, spent a month in Jerusalem flat on my back. Stupid luck. Right in the middle of the season, too. Wasted half the year's dig. Use better wood now for the props." She laughed, short coughs of humour that made me grin in response.

"I saw some of your finds in the British Museum recently," I told her. "That Hittite slab was magnificent, and of course the mosaic floor. How on earth did they make those amazing blues?"

She was pleased, and she launched off on a highly technical explanation of the art and craft of mosaics that went far above my head and lasted until I pulled into the circular drive in front of the cottage. Holmes heard the car and came to meet us. Our guest climbed awkwardly out and marched over to greet him, hand extended and talking all the while as we moved inside and through the house.

"Mr Holmes, good to see you, as yourself this time, and in your own home. Though I do admit that you wear the djellaba better than most white men, and the skin dye was very good. You are looking remarkably well. How old are you? Rude question, I know, one of the advantages of getting old—people are forced to overlook rudeness. You are? Only a few years younger than I am, looks more like twenty. Maybe I should have married. A bit late now, don't you think? Miss Russell—all right if I call you that? Or do you prefer Mrs Holmes? Miss Russell, then—d'you know, you've married one of the three sensible men I've ever met. Brains are wasted on most men—do nothing with their minds but play games and make money. Never see what's in front of their noses, too busy making sweeping generalisations. What's that? The other two? Oh, yes, one was a winemaker in Provence, tiny vineyard, a red wine to make you weep. The other's dead now, an Arab sheikh with seven wives. Couldn't write his name, but his children all went to university. Girls, too. I made him. Ha! Ha!" The barking laugh bounced off the walls in the room and set the ears to ringing. We took our lunch outside, under the great copper beech.

During the meal, our guest regaled us with stories of archaeology in Palestine, which was just getting under way now in the postwar years. The British Mandate in Palestine was giving its approval to the beginnings of archaeology as a science and a discipline.

"Shocking, it was, before the war. No sense of the way to do things. Had people out there rummaging about, destroying more than they found, native diggers coming in with these magnificent finds, no way of dating them or knowing where they came from. All that could be done with 'em was to stick 'em in a museum, prop up a card saying SOURCE: UNKNOWN; DATE; UNKNOWN. Utter waste."

"Didn't Petrie say something about museums being morgues, or tombs?" I asked.

"Charnel houses," she corrected me. "He calls them 'ghastly charnel houses of murdered evidence.' Isn't that a fine phrase? Wish I'd written it." She repeated it, relishing the shape of the words in her mouth. "And during the war, my God! I spent those years doing nothing but stopping soldiers from using walls and statues for target practice! Incredible stupidity. Found one encampment using a Bronze Age well as their privy and rubbish tip. Course, the idiots didn't realise their own water supply was connected to it. Should've told 'em, I know, but who am I to interfere in divine justice? Ha! Ha!"

"Surely, though, most of the digs are more carefully run now," I suggested. "Even before the war, Reisner's stratigraphic techniques were becoming more widely used. And doesn't the Department of Antiquities keep an eye on things?" My rapid tutorial at the hands of one of the British Museum's more helpful experts at least enabled me to ask intelligent questions.

"Oh, yes indeed, improving rapidly, things are. Of course, there's no room for amateurs like myself now, though I'll be allowed to make drawings and notes when I get back. There's talk of opening the City of David, really exciting. But still, we get Bedouins wandering in with sacks of amazing things, pottery and bronze statuettes, last month a heart-stopping ivory carving, magnificent thing, part of a processional scene, completely worthless from a historical point of view, of course. He wouldn't tell us where in the desert it came from, so it can't be put in its proper archaeological setting. A pity. Oh, yes, that's more or less why I'm here. Where's my bag?"

I brought it from the sitting room, where she had casually dumped it on a table. She opened it and dug through various books, articles of clothing, and papers, finally coming out with a squarish object wrapped securely in an Arab man's black-and-white head covering.

"Here we are," she said with satisfaction as she displayed a small intricately carved and inlaid wooden box. She laid it in front of me, then bent to replace various objects into the bag.

"I'd like you to look at this and tell me what you think. Already gave it to two so-called experts, both men of course, who each took one look and said it was a fake, couldn't possibly be a first-century papyrus. I'm not so sure. Really I'm not. May be worthless, but thought of you when I wondered whom to give it to. Show it to whomever you like. Do what you can with it. Let me know what you think. Yes, yes, take a look. Any more tea in that pot, Mr Holmes?"

The box fit into one hand and opened smoothly. Inside was nestled, secure in a tissue bed, a small roll of papyrus, deeply discoloured at the top and bottom edges. I touched it delicately with my finger. The tissue rustled slightly.

"Oh, it's quite sturdy. I've had it unrolled, and the two 'experts' didn't coddle it any. One said it was a clever modern forgery, which is absurd, considering how I got it. The other said it was probably from a madwoman during the Crusades. Experts!" She threw up her hands eloquently, eliciting a sympathetic laugh from Holmes. "At any rate, the experts deny it, so we amateurs can do as we please with it. It's all yours. I started on it, but my eyes are no good now for fine work." She took off her dark glasses, and we saw the clouds that edged onto the brilliant blue of her eyes. "The doctors in Paris say it's because of the sun, that if I wear these troublesome things and stay inside all the time, it'll be five years before they have to operate. Told them there was no point in having the years if I couldn't work, but, being men, they didn't understand. Ah well, five years will get me going, if I can get the money to start my dig, and after that I'll retire happy. Which has nothing to do with you, of course, but that's why I'm giving you the manuscript."

I took the delicate roll from its box and gently spread it out on the table. Holmes pinned the right end down with two fingers and I looked at the beginning, which, as the language was Greek, began at the upper left. The spiky script was neat, though the whole eighteen inches were badly stained and the edges deeply worn, in places obscuring the text. I bent over the first words, then paused. Odd; I could not be reading them correctly. I went back to the opening words, got the same results, and finally looked up at Miss Ruskin, perplexed. Her eyes were sparkling with mischief and amusement as she looked over the top of her cup at me.

"You see why the experts denied it, then?"

"That is obvious, but—"

"But why do I doubt them?"

"You couldn't seriously think—"

"Oh, but I do. It is not impossible. I agree it's unlikely, but if you leave aside all preconceived notions of what leadership could have been in the first century, it's not at all impossible. I've been poking my nose into manuscripts like this for half a century, and though it's somewhat out of my period, I'm sorry, this does not smell like a recent forgery or a crusader's wife's dream."

It finally got through to me that she was indeed serious. I stared at her, aghast and spluttering.

"Would you two kindly let me in on this?" interrupted Holmes with admirable patience. I turned to him.

"Just look at how it starts, Holmes."

"You translate it, please. I have worked hard to forget what Greek I once knew."

I looked at the treacherous words, mistrusting my eyes, but they remained the same. Stained and worn, they were, but legible.

"It appears to be a letter," I said slowly, "from a woman named Mariam, or Mary. She refers to herself as an apostle of Joshua, or Jesus, the 'Anointed One,' and it is addressed to her sister, in the town of Magdala."

# THREE

*gamma*

Holmes busied himself with his pipe, his lips twitching slightly, his eyes sparkling like those of Miss Ruskin.

"I see," was his only comment.

"But it's not possible—" I began.

Miss Ruskin firmly cut me off. "It is quite possible. If you read your Greek Testament carefully, ignoring later exclusive definitions of the word *apostle*, it becomes obvious that Mary the Magdalene was indeed an apostle, and in fact she was even sent (which is, after all, what the verb *apostellein* means) to the other—the male—apostles with the news of their Master's resurrection. As late as the twelfth century, she was referred to as 'the apostle to the apostles.' That she fades from view in the Greek Testament itself does not necessarily mean too much. If she remained in Jerusalem as a member of the church there, which after all was regarded as merely one more of Judaism's odder sects, all trace of her could easily have disappeared with the city's destruction in the year 70. If she were still alive then, she would have been an old woman, as she could hardly have been less than twenty when Jesus was put to death around the year 30—but impossible? I would hesitate to use that word, Miss Russell, indeed I would."

I drew several deep breaths and tried to compose my thoughts.

"Miss Ruskin, if there is any chance that this is authentic, it has no place in my hands. I'm no expert in Greek or first-century documents. I'm not even a Christian."

"I told you, it's already been seen by the two foremost experts in the field, and they have both rejected it. You want to send a copy to someone else, that's fine. Send it to anyone you can think of. Publish it in *The Times*, if it makes you happy. But, keep the thing itself, would you? It's mine, and I like the idea of your having it. If you don't feel comfortable with it, lend it to the BM. They'll throw it in a corner for a few centuries until it rots, I suppose, but perhaps some deserving student will uncover it and get a D Phil out of it. Meanwhile, play with it for a while, and as I said, let me know what you come up with. It's yours now. I've done what I could for Mariam."

I allowed the little conundrum to curl itself up and then placed it thoughtfully back into its box with the snug lid.

"How did it come to you? And the box? That's surely not first century?"

"Heavens no. Renaissance Italian, from the style of inlay, but I'm no expert on modern stuff. The two came together, though I added the tissue paper to stop it from rattling about. Got it about four months ago, just before Easter. I was in Jerusalem—had just come back from a visit to Luxor, Howard Carter's dig. Quite a find he's got there, eh? Pity about Carnarvon, though. Any road, I had just been back a day or so when this old Bedouin came to my door with a bundle of odds and ends to sell. Couldn't think why he came to me. They all know I don't buy things like that, don't like to encourage it. I told him so, and I was about to shut the door in his face when he said something about 'Aurens.' That's the name a lot of the Arabs call Ned Lawrence—you know, the Arab revolt Lawrence? Right, well, I knew him a bit when he was working at Carchemish before the war, at Woolley's dig in Syria. Brilliant young man, Lawrence. Pity he got sidetracked into blowing things up, he could have done some fine work. Seems to have lost interest. Oh well, never too late, he's still young. Where was I? Oh, right, the Bedouin. Turned out this Bedouin knew him then, too, and rode with him during the war, destroying bridges and railway lines and what not.

"His English was not too great—this Bedouin's, that is, not Lawrence's, of course—but over numerous cups of coffee, with my Arabic and his English, it turned out that he'd been injured during the war and now was finding it difficult to get work. A lot of these people are being crowded out of their traditional way of life and have no real skills for the modern world. Sad, really. Seems that was his case. So, he was selling his possessions to buy food. Sounds like the standard hard-luck story to convince a gullible European to hand over some cash, but somehow the man didn't strike me that way. Dignified, not begging. And his right hand was indeed scarred and nearly useless. Tragic, that, for an Arab, as you know. So I looked at his things.

"Some of them were rubbish, but there were half a dozen beautiful things: three necklaces, a bracelet, two very old figurines. Told him I couldn't afford what they were worth but that I'd take him to someone who could. At first, he thought I was just putting him off, couldn't believe I was not trying to buy at a cut price, but the next day I took him to a couple of collectors and got them to give him every farthing of their value. Amounted to quite a bit, in the end. He was speechless, wanted to give me some of it, but I couldn't take it, could I? I told him that if he wanted to repay me, he could promise never to be involved with digging up old things for sale. That'd be payment enough. He went off; I went back to my sketches for the dig.

"About a month later, late one night, he appeared again at my door, on site this time, with another bag. Oh Lord, I thought, Not again! But he handed me the bag and said it was for me. There were two things in it. The first was a magnificent embroidered dress, which he said his wife had made for me. The other was this box. He told me it came from his mother, had been in the family for generations, since before the Prophet came. I knew it wasn't that old, and he must have seen something on my face, because he took the box and opened it to show me the manuscript. That was what his family had owned for so long, not the box, he said, which had been his father's. He told me, if I understood him right—he would insist on speaking English, though my Arabic's better than his was—that it had been in a sort of pottery mould or figurine when he was a child. It broke when he was twelve, and the whole family was terrified that something awful would happen—sounds like a sort of household god, doesn't it? They hadn't known there was anything inside the figure. Nothing much happened, though, and after a while his father put the manuscript into a box he had been given by some European. It came to this man when his parents were killed during the war, and as he himself had no children, he and his wife decided to bring it to me. I tried to give it back to him, but he was deeply offended, so in the end I took it. Haven't seen him since."

The three of us sat contemplating the appealing little object that sat on the table amidst empty cups and the remains of the cheese tray. It was about six inches long, slightly less than that in depth, and about five in height, and the finely textured blond wood of its thick sides and lid was intricately carved with a miniature frieze of animals and vegetation. A tiny palm tree arched over a lion the size of my thumbnail; its inlaid amber eyes twinkled haughtily in a shaft of sunlight. There was a chip out of one of the box's corners, and two of the giraffe's shiny jet spots were missing, but on the whole, it was remarkably free of blemish.

"I think, Miss Ruskin, that the box alone is an overly valuable gift."

"I suppose it is of value, but it pleases me to give it to you. Can't keep it—too many things disappear when one is on a dig—and can't bring myself to sell it. It is yours."

" 'Thank you' sounds inadequate, but if you wanted to be sure it has a good home, it has found one. I shall cherish it."

An enigmatic smile played briefly over her lips, as at a secret joke, but she said, only, "That's all I wanted."

"Shall we have a glass of wine to celebrate it? Holmes?"

He went off to the house, and I tore my eyes away from the beguiling present.

"Can you stay for supper?" I asked. "Your telegram didn't say when you had to be back, and the housekeeper has left us a nice rabbit pie, so you wouldn't have to face my cooking."

"No, I can't. I'd like to, but I have to be back in London by nine—dinner with a new sponsor. Have to talk up the glory that was Jerusalem to the rich fool. Plenty of time for a glass of your wine, though, and a stroll over your hills." She sighed happily. "We used to come down to the coast every summer when I was a child. The air hasn't changed a bit, or the light."

We took our glasses and walked over the hills to the sea, and when we returned to the cottage, Holmes asked her if she wanted to see the beehives. She said yes, so he found her a bee hat and gloves and overalls, things he himself rarely used. She was at first nervous, then determined, and finally fascinated as he opened a hive and showed her the levels of occupation, the queen's quarters, the neat texture of the honeycombs, the logical, ruthless social structure of the colony. She asked numerous intelligent questions, and she seemed both relieved and reluctant to see the internal workings disappear again behind their wooden walls.

"Had a nasty experience with bees one time," she said abruptly, and pulled off the voluminous hat. "Lived in the country. My sister and I were close then, played lots of games. One was to leave coded messages, in the Greek alphabet sometimes, or little treasures—bits of food—inside this abandoned cistern. Must've been mediaeval," she reflected. "Storing root crops. We called it 'Apocalypse,' had to lift the cover off, you see? Happy times. Golden summers. One day, my sister hid a chocolate bar in Apocalypse, went back for it the next day, and a swarm of bees had moved in. Both of us badly stung, terrified. Apocalypse filled in. Seemed like the closing of paradise."

"They were probably wasps," commented Holmes.

"Do you think so? Good heavens, you may be right. Just think, all those years of hating bees, dispelled in an afternoon. Didn't know you were an alienist, Mr Holmes, among your other skills." She chuckled.

We made our way back to the terrace, where I served a substantial tea while she entertained us with stories of the bureaucrats in Cairo during the war.

Finally, she stood up to go. She paused at the car and looked over the front of the cottage.

"I can't think when I've enjoyed an afternoon more." She sighed.

"If you have another free day before you go, it would be a great pleasure to have you again," I suggested.

"Oh, won't be possible, I'm afraid." Her eyes were hidden again behind the black glasses, but her smile seemed somewhat wistful.

The drive into town was slowed by the number of farm vehicles about on a summer afternoon, but I had allowed plenty of time, and we talked easily about books and the uncluttered and unrecoverable pleasures of life as an Oxford undergraduate. Then she abruptly changed the topic.

"I like your Mr Holmes. Very like Ned Lawrence, d'you know? Both of 'em positively quivering with passion, always under iron control, both stuffed full of ability and common sense and that backwards approach to a problem that marks a true genius, and at the same time this incongruous tendency to mystify, a compulsion almost to obfuscate and to conceal themselves behind an air of myth and mystery. Ned's extravagances," she added thoughtfully, "are almost certainly due to his small stature and the domination of his mother and will bring him to a sticky end. He'll never have the hands of your man, though."

I was quite floored by this tumble of insight and information so placidly given, and I could only pluck feebly at the last phrase.

"Hands?" Was this some idiosyncratic equine reference to Holmes' height?

"Um. He has the most striking hands I've ever seen on a man. The first thing I noticed about him, back in Palestine. Strong, but more than that. Elegant. Nervous. No, not nervous exactly; acutely sensitive. Aristocratic working-class hands." She grimaced and waved away this uncharacteristic search among the nuances of adjectives. "Remember the Chinese ball?"

"The Chinese—oh yes, the ivory puzzle." I did remember it, a carved ball of ivory so old, it was nearly yellow. It could only be opened by precise pressure at three different points simultaneously. She had handed the ball to Holmes, and he had held it lightly in the palm of his left hand, occasionally caressing it with the fingertips of the other. (Holmes, unlike myself, is right-handed.) The conversation had gone on; Holmes had talked with great animation about his travels in Tibet and the amazing feats of physical control he had witnessed amongst the lamas, and his tour through Mecca, while he occasionally reached down to touch the ball. The magician's apprentice knows to watch the hands, though, and I was gratified to witness the gentle arrangement of thumb and two fingers that loosed the lock and sent the ball's treasure, a lustrous black pearl, rolling gently into the palm of his hand.

"So clever, those hands. It took me six months to figure out that ball, and he did it in twenty minutes. Oh, are we here, then?" She sounded disappointed. "Thank you for the afternoon, and do enjoy Mariam. I'll be interested to know what you think of her. Did I give you my address in Jerusalem? No? Oh, dash it, here comes the train. Where are those cards— in here somewhere." She thrust at me two handfuls of motley papers—a couple of handbills, some typescript, letters, sweet wrappers, telegram flimsies, notes scribbled on the corners of newspapers—as well as three journals, a book, and two glasses cases (one empty), before she emerged with a bent white cardboard rectangle. I poured the papers back into her bag, took the card, and helped her up into the carriage.

"Good-bye, my dear Miss Russell. Come see me again in Palestine!" She seemed on the edge of saying something else, but the whistle blew, the moment passed, and she contented herself with leaning forward and kissing my cheek. I stepped down from the train, and she was gone.

On the way home, I was in time to be greeted by a neighbour's dairy herd being brought down the narrow lane for the night. I took the car out of gear to wait and looked down at my hands. Competent, practical hands, with large knuckles, square nails, rough cuticles, ink stains, and a dusting of freckles. The two outer fingers of the weaker right hand were slightly twisted, a thin white scar almost invisible at their base, near the palm, one remnant of the automobile accident that had taken the lives of my parents and my brother and had left me with a multitude of scars, visible and otherwise, following weeks in the hospital, further weeks in hypnotic psychotherapy, and years in the grip of guilt-inspired nightmares. The hands on the steering wheel were those of a student who farmed during the holidays, ordinary hands that could hold a pen or a hay fork with equal facility.

Holmes' hands, however, were indeed extraordinary. Disembodied, they could as easily have belonged to an artist or surgeon, or a pianist. Or even a successful safe cracksman. As a young man, he had some considerable talent as a boxer, though the thought of putting those hands to such a use made me cringe. Fencing, yes—the nicks and cuts he had picked up left only scars—but to use those sensitive instruments as a means of pummelling another human being into insensibility seemed to me like using a Waterford vase to crack nuts. However, Holmes was never one to believe that any part of himself could be damaged by misuse, which only goes to show that even the most intelligent of men is capable of considerable feeblemindedness.

At any rate, his hands had survived unbroken. As Miss Ruskin had seen, his hands were direct extensions of his mind, the long, inquisitive fingers meandering about over surfaces, lightly touching a shelf or a shoe, until without apparent interference from his brain, they arrived at the key clue, the crux of the investigation. His bony hands were the outer manifestation of his inner self, whether they were probing a lock, tamping shreds of tobacco into his pipe, coaxing a complex theme from his Stradivarius, handling the reins of a fractious horse, or performing a delicate experiment in the laboratory. I had only to look at them to know the state of his mind, how an investigation or experiment was proceeding, and how he thought it might turn out. A person's life is betrayed by the hands, in the calluses and marks and twists of skin and bone. The life of Sherlock Holmes lay in his long, strong, sensitive hands. It was a life that was dear to me.

I looked up, to find the road clear of all but a few gently steaming cow-pats, and the farmer's small son staring curiously at me over the gate. I put the car into gear and drove home.

# FOUR

## δ

### delta

F or such a short and apparently uneventful episode, the visit of this passionate amateur archaeologist left behind it a disconcerting emptiness. It took a deliberate and conscious effort to return to our normal work, I to my books, Holmes into a laboratory that emitted a variety of odours late into the night, most of them sulpherous, all of them foul. I indulged myself in an hour of deciphering Mariam's letter before returning to the manly declarations of the prophet Isaiah, waved vaguely at Mrs Hudson's greeting and later at her "Good night, Mary," and worked until my vision failed around midnight. I closed my books and found myself looking at the box. Whose hands had so lovingly formed that zebra? I wondered. What Italian craftsman, so far from an obviously well-known and beloved African landscape, had carved this piece of perfection? I rested my eyes on it until they started to droop, then picked up the box and held it while I went through the house, checking the windows and doors. I then climbed the stairs.

Holmes did not look up from his workbench, just grunted when I mentioned the hour. I went down the hallway to the bath. He had not appeared when I returned. I put the box on the bedside table and turned off the lamp, then stood for some minutes in the wash of silver light from the moon, three days from full, and watched the ghostly Downs tumble in frozen motion to the sea. I left the curtains drawn back and took myself solitary to bed, and as I lay back onto the pillow, I realised that Holmes had not read the newspapers for at least three days.

The observation sounds trivial, a minor disturbance on the surface of our lives, but it was no less ominous than a stream's roil that, to the experienced eye, shouts of the great boulder below. Marriage attunes a person to

Laurie R. King

nuances in behaviour, the small vital signs that signal a person's well-being. With Holmes, one of those indicators was his approach to the London papers.

In his earlier life, the daily papers had been absolutely essential to his work. Dr Watson's accounts are as littered with references to the papers as their sitting room was with the actual product, and without the facts and speculations of the reporters and the personal messages of the agony columns, Holmes would have been deprived of a sense as important as touch or smell.

Now, however, his newspaper habits varied a great deal, depending on whether the case he was on concerned the politics of France, the movements of the art world, or the inner financial doings of the City. Or, indeed, if there was a case at all. He regularly drove the local newsagent to distraction, and vice versa. For weeks on end, Holmes was content with a single edition of one of the London papers, and the Sussex *Express* for Mrs Hudson. When he was on a case, however, he insisted on nothing less than every edition of every paper, as soon as it could reach him, and for days the normal serenity of our isolated home would be broken by the nearly continuous arrivals and departures of the newsagent's boy, a compulsively garrulous lad with skin like a battlefield and a wall-piercing adenoidal voice.

During one of my absences the previous spring, Holmes had inexplicably changed from one of the more lurid popular papers to *The Times*, which to my mind has always been eminently suited to morning tea and a discreet scattering of toast crumbs. However, *The Times* is a morning paper, and it has to travel from London to Eastbourne, from that town to our village, and thence to us. It never reached us much before noon, and often considerably later, if the pimply-faced bicyclist had a puncture or encountered a friend.

If Holmes was at home when the newspaper arrived, he would react in one of two ways, which I had come to watch carefully, as a bellwether of his inner mind. Some days, he would spot the boy coming down the lane and rush down the stairs to snatch it out of whatever hand happened to carry it through the door, hurl himself into the frayed basket chair in front of the fireplace, and bury his head in it, moaning and exclaiming for the better part of an hour. Other days, he would ignore it entirely. It would lie, folded and reproachful, on the table next to the front door. He would pass it by without a glance, drop letters to be posted on top of it, pull a pair of gloves from the drawer beneath it, until eventually, that evening or even the following morning, he would retrieve it, glance through it in a desultory fashion, and discard it in disgust.

32

Those were the days I dreaded, the days when he was deliberately re-sisting the pull of London and all it had been to him. He was also unfail-ingly polite and sweet-tempered on those days—always a signal of great danger. An unread paper meant an unsettled mind, and to this day the sight of a fresh, folded newspaper on a polished surface brings a twinge of ap-prehension. And for three days, he had only glanced at his newspaper over breakfast.

I lay awake and looked at the box on the table beside the bed, seeing the indistinct sparkle of the moon reflected off the blue eyes of a diminu-tive monkey perched on a miniature wall, and I felt, frankly, peeved at the intrusion of yet another concern into an already-full schedule.

Holmes had little love for the, as he saw it, irrational pseudodiscipline of theology. He judged it a tragic waste of my mental energies, described it as a more debilitating addiction than cocaine, and bemoaned his inability to wean me from it. I ignored him as best I could, accepted this as the one area of serious mutual incomprehension, and only occasionally wondered if I had chosen it largely to maintain my identity against the tide of Holmes' forceful personality.

Twice since our marriage, cases had come up that demanded my atten-tion as well as his. I had only recently realised that it was not past him to invent something of the sort in order to remove me from academia's clutches. Not this one, of course; it was too elaborate even for his devious mind. He would, however, take full advantage of it, now that an edge had been driven under my single-mindedness, to prise me from my work. A walk along the cliffs was not apt to be the only interruption Dorothy Ruskin's letter brought.

I stared unseeing at the tiny blur of blue light and slid gently into sleep. Oddly enough, my dreams were pleasant.


The next day, Thursday, *The Times* arrived at one o'clock in the afternoon. It still lay folded when I turned off the lights and went upstairs, and it had not moved when I came back through the house on Friday for an early cup of tea. Two hours later, Holmes came down for breakfast and picked it up absently as he passed. So it was that nearly forty hours had elapsed between the time I saw Miss Ruskin off on the train and the time Holmes gave a cry of surprise and sat up straight over the paper, his cup of tea forgotten in one hand. I looked up from the decapitation of my own egg and saw him staring at the page.

"What is it? Holmes?" I stood up and went to see what had caught his attention so dramatically. It was a police notice, a small leaded box, inserted awkwardly into a middle page, no doubt just as the paper was going to press.

### IDENTITY SOUGHT OF
### LONDON ACCIDENT VICTIM

Police are asking for the assistance of any person who might identify a woman killed in a traffic accident late yesterday evening. The victim was an elderly woman with deeply bronzed skin and blue eyes, wearing brown pantaloons and coat, a white blouse, and heavy, laced boots. If any reader thinks he may know the identity of this person, he is asked please to contact his local police station.

I sat down heavily next to Holmes.

"No. Oh surely not. Dear God. What night would that have been? Wednesday? She had a dinner engagement at nine o'clock."

In answer, Holmes put his cup absently into his toast and went to the telephone. After much waiting and shouting over the bad connexion, he established that the woman had not yet been identified. The voice at the other end squawked at him as he hung up the earpiece. I took my eyes from Miss Ruskin's wooden box, which inexplicably seemed to have followed me downstairs, and got to my feet, feeling very cold. My voice seemed to come from elsewhere.

"Shall we drive into Town, then?" I asked him. "Or wait for the noon train?"

"Go get the car out, Russell. I'll put a few things together and talk with Mrs Hudson."

I went and changed into clothes suitable for London, and fifteen minutes later I sat in front of the cottage in the running car. Holmes came around the side of the house, scraping something from the back of his hand with a fingernail, and climbed in. We drove to London in a car filled with heavy silence.

# FIVE

*epsilon*

It was she. She looked, as the dead always do, unreal, and she lay absurdly small and grey on the cold table in the morgue. Her face was relatively undamaged, though the side of her head was a horribly wrong shape, and the faint remnant of a grimace was the only sign that this waxy tanned stuff had once been animated. The rest of her body lay misshapen under the drape, and when Holmes lifted it to examine her injuries, I turned away and studied a row of tools and machines whose purpose I did not want to know, and I listened to him asking his questions while I determinedly ignored my roiling stomach.

"An automobile. She fell down in front of it, then?"

"Yes, sir. Tripped over something and fell right into the street. As you can see, she had cataracts, so her night vision must've been bad. The PC was at the other end of his beat, didn't get there until he heard the screams of one of the witnesses. There were two, a young couple on their way home about twelve-fifteen Thursday morning. They were none too sober, though, and couldn't remember much other than the lady falling and the car squealing off. No registration number, a big black saloon car they said, but then they also said that they saw an old beggar on the street corner, which is hardly likely at that hour, on a quiet street, is it?" The young policeman's laugh rang out against the hard walls, and I fled to the WC down the hall.

When I came out sometime later, I found Holmes by himself in an office that adjoined the morgue. He was seated at a desk, before a neat pile of clothing, clothes that I had last seen upon the woman who now lay on the slab. Beside the clothes lay a large manila envelope, the flap of which had been opened and not yet tied closed again; next to the envelope was a piece of white typing paper, on which were arranged three steel hairpins and a metal button. I knew without looking that the objects would bear evidence of some kind, most likely that of the paint left by the car that had hit her. He looked up from his close examination of one of her boots when I came in.

"Better?"

"Thanks. I was all right, but it was a choice between leaving or hitting that giggling fool over the head with some unspeakable instrument. Can we go now, or are there more forms to sign?"

"Sit down for a moment, Russell, and have a look at her boots."

I did not sit down. I stood looking at him, and I saw the familiar, subtle signs of excitement in the flash of his deep-set grey eyes, the small smile on his lips, the way his fingertips wandered over the leather. The object in his hand had somehow transformed Miss Dorothy Ruskin from a friend who had died into a factor in a case, and I had a brief vision of him on the open hillside, with the wind in his sparse hair, saying that a case was sniffing about his door. It had not come with the woman's arrival, not for him any-way, but it looked very much as if it had come now, and I wanted nothing to do with it. I wanted to go home and walk the cliffs and mourn the loss of a good woman, not pick up the boot she had worn.

"What am I going to see on those boots, Holmes?"

Wordlessly, he held out the right one and his powerful glass. Reluctantly, I carried them over to the window. The boots were quite new, the toes only slightly scuffed, the soles barely worn. They were the sort that have holes for the laces along the foot, turning at the ankle into two long rows of pro-truding hooks—sturdy, comfortable, easy to lace up. I had a similar pair at home, though mine were of softer leather and had the new crêpe rubber soles. And no bloodstains. I held the glass over the lowest pair of hooks. Unlike the others, these were slightly crooked, and each had a minute nick at the underside, matching a hair-thin line in the leather which extended an inch on either side of the hooks. I concentrated on it, and the magni-fier brought it into focus: Some thin, sharp edge had cut into the leather, caught from below against the two lowest hooks.

The other boot appeared at my side, and I took it. This was the left one, and it had a similar, almost invisible line, this time running at an angle across the toe, nearly obscured by the scuffs that lay beneath it. I placed the boots parallel to the edge of the desk and handed Holmes back his glass. The basement window looked up onto the street level, and I watched sev-eral pairs of feet walk by before I spoke.

"I don't suppose she could have had those marks on her boots when she was with us?"

Holmes paused in the task of securely folding the hairpins and button into the sheet of paper before replacing them in the large evidence envelope. "Is something the matter with your eyes, Russell? Those cuts are on top of everything else. There isn't even much dust in them."

"If she was tripped, then the car was deliberate." I took a deep breath and rubbed my shoulder. "Murder. I must say I wondered, a hit-and-run accident at that time of night. And her bag missing. It seemed unlikely."

"I should think so, Russell. I am relieved to hear that my efforts in your training have not been entirely in vain. I will go and ask the location of the corner where she was killed."

"And the witnesses?"

"And their addresses. Wait here."

We managed to shake off the helpful young laughing police constable and took a cab to the corner where Miss Ruskin had died. The early afternoon traffic was considerably greater than it had been at 12:15 in the morning, and we added to it as we stood on the corner and crouched down and examined walls and attracted onlookers. It was quite an ordinary corner, with a red pillar box on one side, a new electrical lamp standard on the other, and a blunt office building of dirty yellow bricks set back from the cobblestones by a wide pavement. I chose the pillar box and dropped to my knees in the lee of it, my back to the intersection so as to avoid being trodden on. Omnibuses, automobiles, motor lorries, and horse-drawn wagons rumbled past continuously two feet from my head as I bent down and ran my fingertips delicately over the bottom few inches of painted metal. The box had been painted in the relatively recent past. A woman stopped to post a thick stack of letters, and she stared down at me. I smiled politely, then reached farther around the base, staring blankly into the passing wheels, and my fingers encountered what I had hoped they would not.

I moved around to the other side, knelt with my cheek touching the kerb, and squinted up at the delicate, clean cut that lay approximately six inches up the base. It travelled about a third of the pillar box's circumference and was deepest on the side away from the lamppost.

I rose, threaded my way over to where Holmes was squatting, and told him what I had found. The difference with his find, I saw, was that the equivalent cut in the base of his lamppost completely encircled it. It was also not so deep, and on the far side, away from the pillar box, Holmes' finger traced a length of two parallel indentations. He stretched himself out on the pavement, creating a considerable obstacle, and pulled out his glass. After a minute, he grunted.

"A very fine wire, plied or wrapped. Perhaps even a heavy fishing line. Made up as a beggar, he sat against the wall, with the wire dropped in a loop around the pillar box, across the corner, and twice around the lamp-post for extra leverage. The car was waiting just down the street, and when Miss Ruskin came along, the old beggar tightened the wire so it was held about six inches off the ground. She went down, the car came along, and in the confusion afterwards, nobody noticed the man clip the wire, take her bag, and slip away between the buildings. They'll find the car eventually, I expect, a stolen one abandoned somewhere. Let us see what the wall tells us."

Oblivious of the low curses and scandalised looks, Holmes picked himself up from the pavement and made his way to the wall. He hunkered down, with his glass dangling loosely from one hand, and studied the ground.

"About here, I expect. Yes, you see the threads?" I angled my head against the bricks until I could make out a faint fuzz on the rough surface. He fished a pair of surgical tweezers from an inner pocket, picked from the wall an invisible fibre, and held it in front of his magnifying glass. "It appears to be an unpleasant shade of green-grey wool. And here's a dark blue wool, longer staple, at head level for a man of average size. There was indeed a man sitting here begging—or sitting and waiting at any rate—that night, despite the young constable's dismissal of the drunken witnesses. Hold the envelopes, would you? There. No point in looking for fingerprints—he was certainly wearing heavy gloves or the trip wire would surely have cut him and left some nice blood samples, of which there are none. No hair, no cigarette ashes. Curse it! Yesterday we might have found something of value."

We stood up and the crowd of curious onlookers began self-consciously to move off. I finished marking the envelopes and slipped them into a pocket.

"Russell, a bit of footwork now. We need the restaurant she was coming from and the hotel she was going to. I shall take the former and meet you back here in an hour. Right?"

"You really don't think the police will have done this?" I asked plaintively.

"The official forces place an elderly accident victim far down the list in urgency. Having inserted a notice in the papers, they will wait for a response, or so that jovial gentleman in the morgue informed me. At the moment, there is an all-out push against a rash of pickpockets, and if the local police have got around to asking, they have not yet found anything. Surely we can do better than that."

I was forced to agree. We split up, Holmes to retrace Miss Ruskin's steps, I to continue on, in hopes of encountering her destination.

# SIX

ζ

*zeta*

I was fortunate, in that the area was not wall-to-wall with hotels and short-term boardinghouses. The sixth one was distinctly second-rate, with pretensions, but my enquiry about an old lady in pantaloons and tall boots paid off. The man at the desk flicked his eyes over me appraisingly, and obviously he did not know what to make of my combination of wire-rimmed glasses, thick, old-fashioned hairstyle, tailored trousers and jacket, expensive silk blouse, and a gold band on my right hand, with no hat, no gloves, and flat shoes. He was forced to abandon all assumptions and treat me matter-of-factly, which was, of course, one of the reasons I dressed as I did.

"Yes, madam, the lady checked in on Monday afternoon. I saw her on Tuesday, in the afternoon, but I was off duty on Wednesday and Thursday."

"Is her key in?"

"Yes, madam, as well as a letter."

"Oh, I wonder if that's why she didn't meet me today at the restaurant? May I?" My tone and my waiting hand made it no question. He automatically held it out for my inspection, and I deftly took it from him. It had a Cambridge postal mark on it. I thrust it into my handbag and smiled at him. "Yes, it's mine. Very worrying, though. I hope she's all right. Do you mind if I have a look in her room, to make sure she's not ill, or perhaps left a note for me? She's very absentminded." I smiled vacuously at this non sequitur and held out my hand again for the key. The man had been off for two days but even so, it was astonishing that he had not yet heard that a woman had died half a mile away. The police could sometimes be terribly slow if they had no reason to suspect anything out of the ordinary about an accident.

The man hesitated, but just then a taxi disgorged a family with several small American noisemakers and numerous bags, and he dropped the key into my hand and turned to the harried-looking father. I made haste to disappear.

The lock on room seventeen was much used, but it showed no obvious signs of being recently forced or picked. I let myself into a perfectly ordinary room, with sagging bed, battered dressing table, and bath down the hall. Not knowing Miss Ruskin's habits, I could not know how her room might have looked when she walked out of it on Wednesday, and too, the maid would have been in to clean it. I pulled on a pair of cotton gloves and wandered over to the bed, whistling softly through my teeth—a habit that severely tries my husband, friends, and anyone working near me in a library. Nothing in the drawers next to the bed. The little travelling alarm clock on the table had stopped at 7:10, and I picked it up cautiously to give it a gentle shake. It began ticking again—it had just run down.

Comb on top of the dressing table, several white hairs in it. No cosmetics. A small jar of hand lotion, in which a probing hairpin found no hidden objects. I opened the wardrobe, and the first thing I saw was her khaki bag on a shelf inside. So she had come back here before her dinner appointment, long enough to leave her bag, if not to change her clothes. I lifted one handle and shone my pocket torch at the jumble within, but I couldn't see anything inside that looked immediately different from the glimpses I had had on Wednesday. Wait, though—both glasses cases were occupied. Of course—it had been nearly dark by the time she left the hotel for her appointment, so she would not have needed protective lenses. I let the handle fall. Clothes hanging up, nothing much in the pockets, an overcoat, another pair of shoes, lighter than her boots, but still quite sensible. Two much-travelled valises lay to one side, containing a tangle of clothes, objects, and papers that could as easily have been left in that condition by their owner as violently searched.

I went to the minuscule table next to the window. A pile of papers occupied one corner—the typed reports of a dig, along with several pages of artefact sketches and section drawings—next to three books, two on archaeological techniques and a recent one on Bible theory, and a large square magnifying glass. She would have no worry now about her cataracts, I thought, and suddenly I felt a harsh, red anger wash over me as the fact of her murder became real. I reached down and jerked open a drawer, looking blankly at its emptiness. I sat down, feeling equally empty, and stared out the window. A good woman, whom I liked a great deal and knew almost nothing about, had been carefully, deliberately, brutally murdered.

Why? I took the letter from my handbag and contemplated the crime of interfering with His Majesty's postal service.

My thoughts were interrupted by the sound of a key in the door. I stood up quickly and shoved the purloined letter into a pocket, but it was not an irate desk clerk; it was the maid, a neat young woman with shiny brown hair, mop and cleaning rags in hand. She saw me and started to back out the door.

"I'm very sorry, miss . . . madam. I thought the room was empty. I'll come back later."

"No, please, do come in. Please. Could you—do you have a minute? To answer a few questions? Would you mind closing the door? Thank you. I just was curious about my aunt, who is staying in this room. She didn't show up for a luncheon date, and I wondered if you had perhaps seen her today?"

"No, madam. I haven't seen anyone in this room for about a week. There was a nice young man here then, but no lady."

"This would have been in the last few days. Tell me, on Wednesday, was there much of a mess? Or Thursday? The reason I ask is that she sometimes gets very untidy, and I like to give a little extra to the help then."

She was an honest young woman, and she barely hesitated before answering.

"No, madam, not really a mess. On Tuesday, it was untidy, but nowhere near as bad as some. Wednesday, too, not as untidy. But yesterday, why, you'd barely know anyone had been in. To tell you the truth, I didn't even make up the bed yesterday, just straightened it a bit, 'cause I was in a touch of a hurry, as Nell didn't show up and we was shorthanded, like. I just straightened the bed and the papers and picked up some things from the floor."

I couldn't think of a way to make the next question anything other than what it was.

"Had she moved many things around between Wednesday and yesterday?"

She looked at me sharply then, and I could see that she was as quick as she was honest. She studied me for a minute, and her face changed as she put together the drift of my questions with the news that the desk clerk had lacked.

"Are you—why are you asking me this? Who are you?"

"I'm a friend, not a niece. And yes, she died Wednesday night."

The young woman sat down suddenly on the tightly made bed and stared at me.

"The old lady who was run over?" she whispered. "I didn't know . . . I never thought . . . They just said an old woman. . . ." The standard response: not someone I know.

"Yes. I saw her earlier that day, and I want to know what she was doing the rest of the day. Her family wants to know." It was a small lie, and might even have been the truth. Fortunately, she believed me. I returned to my question. "She came back here on Wednesday evening, but I don't know for how long. Did the room look as though she had been here for long?"

This appeal to her professional expertise had its effect. She stood up and surveyed the room.

"On Wednesday, now, I made the bed, dusted, straightened the wardrobe. Put out fresh towels. There was a cup on the dressing table. I took that away. The papers were all over the table, so I tidied them, put the pencils in the drawer. That was about all. Then yesterday—let me think. Did the bed. It looked like she'd made it up herself, but it wasn't smooth like I likes to see it, so I tightened it up. I replaced one towel that was next to the washbasin in the corner. Closed the wardrobe—it was standing open. Picked up the magnifying glass—it had fallen under the desk. That was about all."

"The papers and books weren't moved?"

"No, they were right here on Wednesday." She glanced at them, then looked more closely. "That's funny. Oh, I suppose she must have read them and put them back herself. There was a page on the top with some funny drawings—of this little, like a statue of a fat woman, with no clothes. I remember it had big, you know." She sketched a gesture of abundance at her front and blushed. "And I looked at the page under it, too, just curious, you know. You won't tell Mr Lockhart? The manager?"

"Of course not. What was under the drawing of the figurine?"

"Another drawing, of a horse and a kind of cart."

I looked at the papers, but the top four sheets were all typescript. I thumbed through the stack carefully and halfway down the pile found the page with three drawings of a fertility figure, and several pages further on the drawing of the war chariot. I held them thoughtfully.

"In the same place, you say? But she had looked through them and put them back straight."

"Funny, isn't it? She wasn't that tidy with them Tuesday and Wednesday."

"Yes, well, perhaps she was embarrassed when she realised what a mess she'd left."

"Maybe," she said dubiously. Working as a maid in an hotel no doubt made one sceptical of the human generosity of spirit.

"Well, thank you, Miss . . ."

"I'm Sally, madam, Sally Wells."

"And if her family want to reach you again, what days do you work?"

"I have Saturday afternoon and all Sunday free, madam. Oh, madam, that's not necessary. No, I couldn't take that. Well, maybe part of it. Thank you, madam."

"It's I who thank you, Miss Wells. For the family, that is. You've been most helpful. No, I don't think you need clean in here for the next two or three days, until we can remove her things. And it would be best if you could remain . . . discreet, until then. It wouldn't do to have people trooping in and out of here. I knew you'd understand. Thank you again, Miss Wells."

Downstairs, I dropped the key on the desk and asked how long Miss Ruskin had paid for the room.

"I believe she was planning on leaving us this afternoon, madam."

"The room will be needed until Sunday," I said firmly, and took a bank note from my bag. "Will that cover it?"

"Yes, indeed it will, madam, but—"

"Good, then I'd like the room left as it is until then, please. No one is to enter it."

"Very good, madam," he said dubiously. "May I ask, did madam find her aunt?"

"Oh yes, I found her, I'm afraid. Now there's the problem of what to do about her."

"I beg your pardon?"

"Nothing. Good day."

I ignored his uncertain protests and questions, turned, and walked quickly out onto the street. As I approached the corner where Dorothy Ruskin had died, I saw the spare figure of Holmes, leaning against the ugly yellow wall from which he had extracted the wool fibres. He was reading a newspaper, the *Morning Post* by the look of it. At the sight of his shoulders, my heart lifted—he, too, had been successful. I waited for a gap in the traffic and stepped briskly down from the pavement.

Halfway across, my momentum faltered. Within the space of two steps, I came to a frozen halt, mesmerised by the sight before my eyes. The vertical edge of the approaching kerb was splattered by what looked like a glaze of reddish brown paint but which I knew with utter certainty most horribly was not. The street and the paving stones had been scrubbed down, but the edge had been overlooked, and the sun caught with nauseating clarity the thick blobs of colour, broken in the middle by lines where the sluicing water had made runnels, fading after a few feet to smears and splashes and drips. The strip of stained paving loomed up huge across my vision, and for a brief instant I seemed to glimpse white hair falling in a circle of streetlight, starting to rise, a flare of headlamps and a dimly seen figure crouched against the wall, heard a roar of sudden acceleration and the squeal of tires and the heavy wet sound of metal meeting flesh, and the roar built into a dizzying, pounding noise in my ears that took over all sight, thought, awareness.

I have never fainted in my life, but I would have done so on that street corner had it not been for the abrupt pain of an iron grasp on my arm and Holmes speaking fiercely in my ear.

"Good Lord, Russell, are you trying to reenact the accident? Come, you need to sit down. There's a café down the street."

Movement, faces peering, a deep and shaky breath and the roaring sound fading, Holmes' grip on my upper arm.

"Now sit down. I'll return in a minute."

Seated. Seeing the intricacy of white threads, interwoven, over, under, over in the cloth; two small perfect crumbs; the distorted face of an immensely pale blond woman in spectacles from the bowl of a spoon. I closed my eyes.

The gentle iron fingers returned, on my shoulder; a rattle of china came from in front of me. "Drink this." A hot cup was between my inexplicably cold fingers; scalding rich coffee and the fumes of brandy hit my throat and head in a rush of life. I sat for some minutes, eyes closed and two strong fingers steady on the back of my wrist. The urge to tremble lessened, then passed. I took a deep breath, glanced over at my companion, and reached for the coffee spoon to give my hands something to do.

"Did you have any of your breakfast this morning, Russell?" I shook my head briefly. "I thought not. Here, eat. Then we can talk."

Plates began to appear, and I forced some warm bread and oniony soup into my throat, and after a few swallows it was easier. Over the cheese, I looked up with a crooked smile.

"I'm sorry, Holmes. I saw . . . there was blood on the kerbstone."

"Yes, I noticed. There is no need to apologise."

"I feel extremely foolish."

"The violent death of a good person is a severely disturbing thing, Russell," he said calmly. "Now, what did you find?"

In a moment, with an effort, I matched his tone.

"Her room. A maid, who told me without telling me that the room had been searched, carefully, between Wednesday evening and Thursday morning. Papers disturbed, bed undone and remade, that kind of thing. And, a letter." I pulled it from my pocket and gave it to him. "I couldn't decide whether or not to open it. You decide."

He did not answer, only put it carefully in an inside pocket. He put his hand in the air and asked the waiter for a bill and a cab.

"Where are we going now, Holmes?" I felt weak but was not about to let him know.

"A visit to Mycroft's rooms is, I believe, in order."

I was surprised. I had expected him to answer by saying Scotland Yard, or one of the half-dozen bolt-holes he kept throughout the city—but Mycroft? His corpulent, indolent older brother might indeed throw some light on the matter at hand, were it to be connected with the arcana of international politics rather than mere civil crime. However, we had as yet no indication that this might be the case, and until we did, I could see no point in consulting him.

I voiced my objections, and when I had finished, I added, "And aside from that, Mycroft will not be at home for some hours yet."

Unruffled, Holmes laid a generous tip on the white cloth and escorted me to the door with that formality that masks an iron command.

He was silent in the taxi. I watched him covertly while the food and the purposeful movement of the taxi did their work and everyday reality took root, and by the time the housekeeper had let us into Mycroft's unoccupied rooms, I had recovered sufficiently to begin worrying about the effect this episode would have on Holmes. I sank into a soft chair and let Holmes pull up his chair and take out his tobacco. I cleared my throat.

"I really am most sorry for that lapse, Holmes," I said quietly. "As you know, it is difficult for me to be indifferent when it comes to an automobile accident. I'm afraid that my imagination got the better of me for a moment."

"Enough, Russell. Everyone is allowed a weakness, even a woman of the twentieth century. You have no need to convince me that you are no squeamish and fainting female. Now, if you are quite finished laying your abject humility at my feet, perhaps you would be so good as to give me the details of your investigation. Then I think you may be interested in mine."

A thin haze of blue smoke filled the room by the time I finished. We sat for a few minutes, and then he stirred.

"That her papers were rifled is, of course, suggestive. I thought that might be the case. And I agree: It is most likely that the room was searched after she died. Had there been a chance of her returning to the room, they would have been more careful about returning the papers to their proper order. I think you might at some point have another look at her bag, to see if your memory of its contents on Wednesday differs from what remains in the hotel. Not immediately. Would you like a glass of wine, or some tea? No?" He rose and went over to the cabinet, rattled bottles, and added a swoosh from the old-fashioned gasogene to his glass, then came back and stretched his long legs out to the cold fireplace. "I, too, was not entirely unsuccessful. It did take me some time to uncover the restaurant, which was in an alleyway eight streets down. I walked past it twice. Fortunately, the maître d' had been on duty Wednesday night as well, and he remembered our lady. And the gentleman she dined with was a regular. Fellow by the name of Colonel Edwards, and the man even gave me the address, for a small consideration. The colonel and Miss Ruskin were at the restaurant for nearly three hours, and it was the waiter's impression that they were having a rather intense discussion that seemed to focus on some papers she had brought. He said that the colonel appeared to be very upset and even had to leave the room for a while, ostensibly to make a telephone call, but more, the waiter thought, to have a drink by himself and get back under control. Miss Ruskin, he said, was, if anything, amused rather than angry. Also, he told me that the colonel seemed unaware that his guest was to be a woman and that he was very taken aback when they first met. Incidentally, the man remembers that she had a large brown leather briefcase, which she took with her when she left. He even noted the brass letters *DR* on the top, because they were his initials, as well."

"So, whoever ran her down paused long enough to take her papers with them. Or rather, the beggar did, I suppose, rather than the driver. Those two witnesses must have been very drunk indeed." My own brain seemed sluggish, and my eyes felt hot and tired.

"Russell, I have a proposal to make." I eyed him through the smoke and the failing light. "I propose that you allow me to interview the colonel and whichever of our young couple I can lay my hands on, while you stay here, take a rest, and talk to Mycroft about it all when he comes in."

I began automatically to object, then reconsidered. Action for the sake of proving myself capable was at least as ridiculous as abject humility. It was a measure of my state of mind that I agreed to his proposal without much argument.

# SEVEN

*eta*

Despite my intentions of using the time for careful introspection, I ended up inspecting no more than the backs of my eyelids. I woke at dusk from macabre dreams of leather briefcases and clouded blue eyes on a marble slab, to find myself on the bed in Mycroft's guest room, the sound of voices coming from the sitting room. I washed my face many times with cold and hot water, pushed the pins back into my hair, and went out to join my husband and his brother.

"Good evening, Russell. I hope you slept well."

"Not terribly. Hello, brother Mycroft. You're looking well."

"Good evening, Mary. A glass of sherry, or some tea?"

"It's late for tea, but I am thirsty. Do you mind?"

"Not at all." He rang the bell. "Sherlock was telling me about your mysterious visitor and the day's adventures. Most intriguing."

"Good Lord, was it only this morning that we read about it? It seems a week ago."

The housekeeper came to the door, and Holmes went to ask her for tea. He returned to the chair between Mycroft and me and reached for the inevitable pipe. Mycroft took a cigar from an elaborate chased silver humidor.

"Do you mind, Mary? Thank you." He set to the ritual of clipping and raising a cloud of perfumed smoke and finally had it going to his satisfaction.

"How does it take you, Sherlock? Could it have been simple robbery? Might she have had something of value?"

"Insufficient data, I fear, Mycroft. Russell—ah, here's your tea. No, don't get up. There. Biscuit?" I declined. "Do have one of those sandwiches, at least. They may be your supper. Russell, I did succeed in reaching Colonel

Edwards, just before he left for a weekend shoot in Berkshire, but he gave me a few minutes. He and Miss Ruskin spent the time reviewing her proposed dig, looking through photographs of the site and the location of the exploratory trenches. He was 'favourably impressed,' and he intends—or perhaps I should say intended—to recommend that his organisation support the project."

"What organisation is that?"

"Something called the Friends of Palestine, a group of retired military officers and churchmen. They raise money to support various projects, mostly in the Holy Land. From what he said, I gather it's a combination of drinks club and Bible-study group."

"Men only?"

"Men only. In fact, he admitted that he was surprised when D. Ruskin turned out to be a woman."

"Didn't do his homework, then."

"Apparently not. He did appear to be genuinely shocked at hearing of her death, though it didn't put him off his weekend. He has a garage normally inhabited by three cars, only two present this evening, neither showing signs of any recent repairs. According to the driver—calls himself the chauffeur—the third car is a roadster that belongs to the colonel's son, who is in the machine on his way to Scotland at the moment, some sort of informal motoring competition called a rally. Sounds a considerable danger to livestock and unsuspecting Scots pedestrians. The tyre marks are of an appropriate width for a roadster rather than a saloon car, and several marks on the wall on that side indicate black paint from a low-slung mud guard and a driver who is either exceedingly careless or often intoxicated."

"Speaking of intoxicated, any trace of the witnesses?"

"Miss Chessman and Mr O'Rourke left directly from their respective offices to catch a train for her parents' house near Tonbridge. Her neighbour, who should know better than to trust an old man asking questions, said that Miss Chessman was severely upset over an accident she had witnessed in the wee hours of Thursday morning. Or, to use the neighbour's au courant phrasing, she was severely traumatised by the event and was, in her neighbour's judgement, not far from a nervous breakdown. What I suppose Watson would term 'brain fever.' End of relevant data."

"And the letter?"

"Ah yes, the letter. This must go into the hands of Scotland Yard very soon. Will Chief Inspector Lestrade and his colleagues believe that Sherlock Holmes has possessed the thing and not opened it? Never. Therefore, we may as well steam it open. Is there hot water left in that pot?" I picked it up and sloshed it about by way of an answer. "Good. Toss the biscuits out and pour the water into their bowl. Have you done this before, Russell? Yes, of course you have. Then you know that impatience is not the thing. Too much steam, too fast, warps the paper and tells a tale. Slow, see? Here comes the end. Good-quality glue and paper make it easy. That knife, please, Mycroft— Wipe off the butter first, man! That's better. Come, now, just a bit more—there. I think I'll use tweezers on this, in case the Yard decides to look for prints. Probably useless—the paper's a bit on the rough side—but mustn't take the chance of confusing their poor little heads. Move the tray, please, Russell. Thank you."

Holmes laid the letter down on the table, and we all bent over it. He automatically noted the more obvious characteristics.

"Woman's hand, fussy. Dated Wednesday, would have arrived yesterday. Not old enough to be from the mother, who must be in her nineties. Perhaps a sister."

We read:

Dear Dorothy,

It was so very lovely to see you over the weekend. It made a deep impression on Mama (you may not be able to tell, but I can). I hope you can return before you have to leave, though I will understand if you cannot.

I am writing because shortly after you left, two gentlemen came here looking for you, something regarding a donation to your project in the Holy Land. They told me their names, but I'm afraid I can't remember them, as they were very long and foreign. Perhaps I should have written them down, but I was a bit flustered and could hear Mama calling from upstairs. But you must know them, as they knew you. They were both very dark and tall and looked a bit like the photographs you sent of the people who worked on your excavations, those same sharp noses. Very proper, though—educated gentlemen in proper suits. One of them had a name that sounded something like *mud*. At any rate, I wanted you to know in case they hadn't reached you. They seemed particularly anxious to see you before you left and seemed disappointed they had missed you. I told them that you were going down to Sussex to see Mr Holmes and his wife and that a telephone call there might be possible. I also told them the address of your hotel in London.

I'm afraid I gave them rather short shrift, as Mama was waiting for her bath. I hope they didn't think me rude, and I hope they give you lots of money, which they obviously have, as they drove off in an enormous shiny black saloon car, complete with uniformed driver.

Please write to tell me what the Holmeses were like. I imagine an extraordinary couple. But then, we may see you on Saturday, with any luck.

Your loving sister,
Erica

"Oh God, Holmes, I can't bear the thought of telling that woman that her sister was—that her sister is dead. Isn't it time to turn this over to the police?"

However, Holmes was not listening. He frowned over the pages in his hand, then thrust them at his brother.

"What do you make of the writing, Mycroft?"

"I admit that you are my superior in graphological analysis, Sherlock, but this is not exactly what I might have expected, either from the contents of the letter or from a sister of the woman you described. The lack of education in words and writing indicates only that Miss Ruskin achieved what she did through the sheer force of her mind, but still, I should have expected a greater degree of intelligence and independence here."

"But she's clever—look at those overstrokes!"

"Clever, yes, but with an undercurrent of anger that wells up in the full stops."

"And the hooks on the t-bars, why, I don't believe I've seen such tenacity since the time—"

"Holmes!"

"Yes, Russell?"

"We have to give this to the police. To Scotland Yard."

"She's quite right, Sherlock," said Mycroft. "Much as it goes against your grain, it is their job, and they might take it amiss were you to withhold it from them. They have become quite competent at legwork, you know. I can also make enquiries over the weekend. Fellow at the club knows everything and everyone in the Middle East. He may have some idea of what's going on."

I was tempted to ask how a fellow member of a club dedicated to noncommunication and misanthropy had managed to make known his peculiar talents, but I was distracted by Holmes, who had risen and was pawing vigorously through a desk drawer, finally to emerge with paper, pen, and a pot of glue. He shrugged as he bent to daub the flap of the envelope.

"Very well, if two minds greater than mine own agree, I can only plead force majeure. Russell, would you be so good as to write a note to Lestrade to accompany this virtuously unopened letter?" He paused to examine his handiwork, then bent to reapply a microscopic quantity of glue to a recalcitrant bubble, and continued. "You will tell him that we happened to come across it and thought it might have come from the sister whom Miss Ruskin mentioned during her visit to us. Also stress that he is to do nothing about contacting the lady until he has seen us, and invite him to join us in Sussex at his earliest convenience. Throw in whatever threats or entreaties you consider appropriate, and tell him I said it would do him good to get out of London." He ran a nail along the edge and angled the envelope to the light critically. "You should also mention that a Yard photographer might prove a useful companion. I can do any necessary fingerprints myself."

I looked up from my paper.

"Sorry?"

He lifted his eyes, and his face went carefully, dreadfully blank. He glanced at Mycroft, then looked down at the somewhat overworked envelope in his hands.

"What a noble mind is here o'erthrown," he remarked conversationally, and keeping his voice light, added, "Russell, that theology of yours is rotting your brain even more rapidly than I had anticipated. You did read the sister's letter."

"But you don't think . . ." I trailed off as he raised his face to mine, a face awful in judgement and disappointment.

"What else am I to think, Russell? She visits us, she dies violently, her papers are searched, and her briefcase is stolen. Someone has asked after us and been given our address. It is possible they found what they sought, but if not, can we be anything but their next goal? I only hope that when they didn't find what they were looking for, they didn't vent their irritation on the furniture."

I felt my brain begin sluggishly to move, and my heart sank.

"The box. Oh, Holmes, I left it on the dining room table."

"You left it there, Russell. I did not."

"You moved it? Why?"

"No particular reason. Call it tidiness."

"You? Tidy?"

"Don't be rude, Russell. I put it away."

"Where? No, let me guess." He winced. "Sorry, poor choice of words. Let me deduce. When I went to get the car, you went out the back and came around the house. The toolshed?"

"How utterly unimaginative," Holmes said, offended.

"Sorry, again. The hole in the beech? No—oh, of course. You were scraping off a stinger—you shoved it into one of the beehives." How ridiculous, the relief engendered by a mere nod.

"Not shoved, Russell, gently placed. The third hive from the end is making queen cells at a tremendous rate, so I thought I might give them something else to think about. They've also been very active of late, and most people would think twice about putting a hand in there, even at night."

"Except you. But do you mean to tell me that you anticipated . . . visitors, even this morning?"

"Merely a precaution."

My warming brain gave another, more alarming lurch.

"Mrs Hudson! Good Lord, she's there alone. We must warn her!"

"She is not there. I telephoned from the café and told her to take a day or two away. She's with her nephew in Guildford."

"You knew then? Already?"

"We do not know that anything has taken place. We are merely talking about likelihoods," he said with asperity, and placed the envelope in a breast pocket. I began to laugh.

"My dear Holmes, if I hear you use the word *senility* again, I shall stuff it down your throat. You are still too fast for me. I didn't see the possibilities until I read the letter."

He did not laugh, merely looked at his brother.

"You see why I married her, Mycroft? The exquisite juxtaposition of ladylike threats and backhanded compliments proved irresistible." He turned back to me, and his voice and face hardened. "Russell, if you were occasionally to raise your sight from your Hebrew verbs doubly weak and irregular and your iota subscripts, you might take more notice of the world around you. Your preoccupation with your studies could kill you."

He was dead serious, and Mycroft's fat face mirrored the grim expression of his brother. My voice was small in response.

"Yes, I see. Could we go home now?"

"Do you wish to equip yourselves with some of what the Americans would call 'firepower' before you go?" suggested Mycroft with the air of a housewife offering provisions for a journey. "Or, given an hour, I could arrange an escort."

"No escort, thank you, Mycroft. I've never much fancied myself as a leader of men, and this is no time to begin. Your old revolver would be a welcome addition, on the stray chance that Mr 'Mud' or one of his companions has chosen to wait for us to appear. I should doubt it, but still . . ."

"Quite," his brother said with an admirable lack of concern, and heaved himself upright. He padded out of the room and returned a short time later with a huge and, I was relieved to see, well-oiled pistol, which he handed to Holmes along with a box of ammunition sufficient to withstand a minor invasion of the southern coast. Holmes gave the weapon a cursory inspection and inserted it and the box with difficulty into his pockets.

We took our leave of Mycroft, found a taxi, retrieved the car, left the letter and its covering note at Scotland Yard, and plunged into the darkening countryside of south England, our noses turned for home.

Shortly after midnight, the car's headlamps caught the final signpost. The hedgerows pressed close on either side. A fox with something white in its jaws flickered away into the dark. For the last hour, Holmes had been either stiffly asleep or engaged in a silent contemplation of events. In either case, I interrupted him.

"Do you wish to collect Patrick and another gun as we go past the farm?" My own farm, and its manager, lay a few miles before the cottage. "Or, we could stay there tonight. . . ."

"Do you wish to do that, Russell?"

Damn the man, he would not even use a sarcastic tone for the question, only stating it simply as a request for information. One of the most difficult things about marriage, I was finding, was the absolute honesty it demanded. I thought for a mile or so.

"No, I don't. I admit to a certain, shall we say, uneasiness about walking into a dark cottage. That blood on the kerb . . . disturbed me. But it is my house now, and I find myself distinctly resentful at the thought of being made afraid to enter it. No, I do not wish to stay at the farm tonight. However, I should like to stop and pick up a shotgun. It would give me great pleasure to deposit a load of bird shot into the backside of anyone who had anything to do with Miss Ruskin's death."

The seat beside me began to shake oddly, and I looked over, to see the gleam of white teeth: Holmes laughing silently.

"That's my Russell. Let us stop and find you a mighty blunderbuss, and go liberate our castle."

There was, of course, no one there. With a pounding pulse, fighting down the all-too-vivid memories of the night four years earlier when Holmes and I had nearly died in an ambush inside this house, I stood tensely for what seemed to be hours, watching two of the cottage's doors while Holmes entered the third. No prey was flushed, and soon the entire cottage was blazing with light and Holmes was standing at the front door. Fingers clumsy with relief, I broke the shotgun and went to join him.

Since that morning, I had seen the dead body of a woman I respected and liked, had found evidence of the fact that her death was murder, seen her blood on the street, batted back and forth about London, and spent several hours driving country roads, topped off with twenty minutes outside of a dark house tensely awaiting the sounds of violence. It was now far after midnight, and I stood at the door and looked in at the desolation and the ruin that was my home.

Not one book remained on its shelf. Chairs were turned upside down, their springs exposed, vomiting stuffing onto the floor. Desk drawers had been methodically emptied out onto the middle of the floor, where the carpets had been pulled up. Most of the baseboard was lying loose, prised away from the wall by a crowbar I recognised from the toolshed. Pictures off the walls, the contents of baskets and boxes jumbled together, sewing thread and tobacco, case notes, newspaper clippings, and firewood all lay in a huge mound in the centre of the room. Even the curtains had been ripped from their rods and tossed carelessly on top. I had not been in San Francisco during the great earthquake, but I had seen photographs of the results of that catastrophe, and that was precisely what the room looked like. A huge impersonal giant had shaken the room vigorously, and left it.

"So. I take it they did not find what they were looking for and took it out, as you said, on the furnishings." I was numb, too shocked to be upset, and my voice was matter-of-fact. I was also feeling the first stirrings of rage, a deep, hot bubble that grew and seethed and steadied me. This is my home, I kept thinking. How dare they do this to my home? I moved around the room, stepping over a fireplace poker and some manuscript pages from the book Holmes was writing. I picked up a few books, straightened bent pages, placed them on the shelf. I reached down and took a photograph of my mother from under the coal scuttle. It had been roughly wrenched from its frame and then dropped. I put it on another shelf. Footsteps came from upstairs and Holmes appeared at the doorway, white feathers clinging to his trouser legs.

"For heaven's sake, what are you doing, Russell? That is evidence, and we'll need to look at it in the morning. Not tonight. It would be exceedingly foolish to examine the place without light, and the house batteries would run down before we got halfway through. It will have to wait until morning. It also looks as though we shall need to make use of your farm after all. There are no beds remaining here."

# PART TWO

# Saturday, 25 August 1923–
# Monday, 27 August 1923

*We lay aside letters never to read them again, and at last destroy them out of discretion, and so disappears the most beautiful, the most immediate breath of life, irrecoverably for ourselves and for others.*

—Goethe

# EIGHT

*theta*

Saturday morning dawned clear, but I did not witness it. Long hours later, the growing strength of the light outside penetrated even the north-facing room I was in and tugged at my brain, and I began to crawl towards consciousness. I rolled over to greet the occupant of the other side of the bed and nearly fell out onto the floor. Holmes was missing. This in itself was not unusual, but that the other half of the bed seemed to be missing as well woke me. I raised myself up on my elbows and surveyed the room.

For a moment, my surroundings fell on a blank mind. This was my old room, the north garret room in the house dominated by my aunt, my only refuge from her presence. This was my old narrow bed. Why was I here? Where was Holmes?

Holmes. Beds. Gutted mattresses. Upturned bookshelves and Dorothy Ruskin. I flung back the bedclothes and found my watch. Nearly eight o'clock! Ignoring yesterday's unsuitable clothes, I pulled old friends from drawers and wardrobe, jabbed pins into my hair, and ran downstairs, to find Patrick frying bacon on the old black cookstove.

"Good morning, Miss Mary," he said, using his name for me since I was fifteen. "I drove Mr Holmes over to the cottage at first light. He asked would you please take some hot coffee when you go, and my camera. The thermos bottle is on the table," he added. "I'm just making you some bacon sandwiches, and Tillie boiled up some eggs before she left. Give me a ring if you need anything else," he shouted after me.

If anything, the cottage looked worse by light of day. Holmes had used his hours well, though, and when I came in, I found various chalk marks on the floor and walls in preparation for the police photographer. I greeted him with a greasy sandwich, and we found two relatively undamaged chairs.

"Has Lestrade rung yet?" I asked.

"He should be here in an hour or thereabouts. They received another telephone call, from one of Miss Ruskin's friends at the British Museum who had seen the police notice, but Lestrade agreed to keep the case in his hands until he'd seen me."

"He'll hold back from notifying the sister?"

"He was unhappy and sceptical, but he said he would not give it to Cambridgeshire until he'd seen the body and heard what I had to say."

The body. Life achieving a distance from the ugly fact of violent death. The thought must have shown on my face.

"Best to keep the mind clear, Russell. Emotion can confuse matters all too easily."

"I know." I pushed it away and waved my sandwich at the room. "How could Lestrade be sceptical with this?"

"Unfortunately, it looks like simple burglary with a touch of vandalism thrown in."

"Burglary? Oh God, what did they take? Not your violin? And the safe?" The violin was a Stradivarius, bought ages before from an ignorant junkman at a ridiculously low price. The safe, well hidden, held a number of small valuables and appallingly toxic substances.

"No, the violin they took from its case and threw down, before ripping out the lining of the case. A scratch is all. They missed the safe. They did get your mother's silver, Mrs Hudson's jewellery, and some treasury notes that were in a drawer. Fortunately, the vandalism was not too vicious, mostly throwing things about."

I brushed off the crumbs and swallowed the last of my coffee from a cracked cup.

"To work, then. Shall I take a few photographs before I start putting things away?"

"Lestrade might appreciate it. You'll have to give them to him to develop, though. Not much has survived of the darkroom."

Seventy-five minutes later, I had restored a quarter of the books to their places, dragged two disembowelled chairs out into the garden, nailed up a piece of wood across the broken kitchen window, and was starting on the baseboards when the inspector's car drove up.

"Where do all these flipping hay wagons come from?" he shouted jovially from the open door, and then: "My, my, my, what have we here? Making yourself unpopular with the village toughs, Mr Holmes?"

"Hello, Lestrade. Good to see you again." Holmes climbed down from the ladder and dusted off his hands. I said nothing, as I had a mouthful of nails, but nodded and went back to plying my hammer on the baseboard.

"Mr Holmes, you said you had evidence of a murder for me to look at. Have you a dead body under that pile of rubbish?"

"Not here, Lestrade, this is purely secondary. If you'd like to have your man set to in the kitchen, when he's through we can offer you a cup of tea. I've marked the few possible prints, though I think we'll find that our visitors last night wore gloves. Here, Lestrade, take this chair; it still has four legs." He did not see, or ignored, the look of patient humour that passed between the two men and the photographer's shrug before he took his bulky equipment into Mrs Hudson's normally spotless kitchen.

Lestrade settled gingerly into the chair and pulled out a notebook. Holmes returned to his armfuls of papers, I to my nails.

"Right, then, Mr Holmes. Would you care to tell me what this mess of yours has to do with Miss Dorothy Ruskin, and what the deuces a 'demeter archaeopteryx' is?"

Holmes looked at Lestrade as if the man had begun to spout Hamlet's soliloquy, and then suddenly his face cleared.

"Ah yes, the telephone connexion was a bit rough, wasn't it? No, the phrase was 'amateur archaeologist,' Lestrade. Miss Ruskin's passion, the archaeology of the Holy Land."

"I see," said Lestrade, who quite obviously did not. He went on, with the air of licking a pencil. "And Miss Ruskin was a friend of yours?"

"More of Russell's, I should say. She came to see us Wednesday, gave Russell a box and a manuscript, stayed to tea. She then returned to London and got herself killed." His voice drifted off as he studied one of the pages in his hand. Lestrade waited with growing impatience.

"And then?" he finally prompted.

"Eh? Oh, yes. We know only the outlines of 'what then.' She returned to her hotel room, exchanged her bag for her briefcase and went to dinner with a man who didn't know her, left the restaurant, walked into a simple but effective trap, and died. Her briefcase was stolen and early on Thursday her hotel room searched, and the following evening they came here and searched this house, with rather more enthusiasm and violence than they had talent."

"They?"

"You are looking for at least three individuals," Holmes said absently, his attention again absorbed by the paper. "Two of them stand five feet nine or ten inches, thirteen stone or thereabouts; at least one of them has black hair, both are right-handed, and one of them fancies himself as a flashy dresser, with a tendency towards the extreme in footwear, but betrays himself by purchasing inferior-quality goods—hence the dents in the floor"—he gestured vaguely towards a clear patch of boards—"and by the fact that he bites his fingernails. The other is a man of simpler tastes, wearing new boots with rounded toes, a brown tweed suit, and—kindly note, Russell—a dark blue woollen knit cap. One of them sports a neck scarf of white cashmere and a camel-hair overcoat—probably Pointed Toes. Of the third party, the director of the operation, I can say only that he has unfashionably long grey hair and displayed an entirely unwarranted confidence in the abilities of his confederates by remaining in the car while the house was being ransacked." He rattled off the final information in an uninterested rush and turned to wave the paper at me. "I say, Russell, do you remember that forgery case we handled two years ago? I'm suddenly struck by the fact—"

"Mr Holmes!" Lestrade bristled in irritation, and Holmes looked at him in surprise.

"Yes, Lestrade?"

"Who are these men?"

"I've just told you."

"But who are they?"

"My dear Lestrade, I bowed beneath the concerted authority of the only two people in the world, aside from my sovereign, who have any influence over me, under the insistence that Scotland Yard ought to be given a chance to prove themselves capable of hunting down the murderers of Dorothy Ruskin. I have told you who they are. You need only find them." He turned imperiously away from the near-frantic police detective, shot me a glance that was perilously close to a wink, and dropped to the floor amidst his papers, his right knee tucked under his chin.

Lestrade looked torn between tearing his thinning hair in despair and storming angrily out. I relented and explained what he had seen but not truly observed.

"They were looking for a piece of paper, Inspector Lestrade. When they didn't find it amongst her things, they came here, possibly assuming that she was bringing it to us."

"What sort of paper?"

"That, we don't know yet."

"Then how do you know it was a piece of paper?"

Holmes made a rude noise. I ignored him.

"The way they searched, both here and in her hotel room. The books were shaken out before being dumped, the pictures taken from their frames, carpets pulled up, our various files carefully gone through and a number of pages stolen."

"But you said she left you some papers?"

"A single manuscript page, but it's made of papyrus. It wouldn't have fit into a book without being folded, which would damage it."

"Would they have known that?"

"Lestrade," exclaimed Holmes from his nest of débris on the floor, "that was a most perceptive question. Russell, I do believe a cup of tea would come most welcome to all concerned and that Mr Ellis is finished in the kitchen. Would you be so good . . ."

I accepted my charge and waded out to the kitchen, where I scraped a handful of tea leaves and some sugar from the floor, found a kettle, though no lid, and four mostly unbroken cups. By the time I had found the bread under a saucepan and trimmed the grimy outside from a piece of cheese, the situation was beginning to amuse me. I hunted for an unbroken jar of relish or pickle, discovered triumphantly a large bottle of pickled onions, and thus assembled a rather strange but quite edible meal.

"Holmes?" I called.

"Yes, Russell."

"I'd like to get this cleared up before Mrs Hudson returns. She'll be back tomorrow, you said?"

"Yes."

"Shall I ring Tillie and see if she can send over a pair of her girls to help? Or would you prefer to keep this out of the mouths of the village gossips?"

"I'd rather, if you think we can do it ourselves."

"Probably a good idea. I could ask Patrick to come over with Tillie tonight for a while. That might help, and they wouldn't talk."

I poured the boiling water over the leaves, ignoring a few stray sultanas that clung to the tea, and took the tray into the sitting room. I didn't like the look on Lestrade's face, and I glanced quickly at Holmes for confirmation.

"Yes, Russell, the good inspector has his doubts."

"Now, Mr Holmes, that's not entirely true. If you say there's something in this, I'll believe you. What I said was that I'm going to have trouble convincing my superiors that there's a case here. An old lady has an accident and your house is turned upside down, but deliberate murder? It's a damned awkward—pardon me, Miss Russell—it's an awkward way of committing murder, with a car. Takes some explaining to do."

"I say, Lestrade, you are coming along nicely. That's twice in the past half hour," Holmes began, but I smothered his words with anger.

"Somebody killed her, you can't deny that, and drove off."

"Oh yes, no doubt about that, and that's where it'll lie unless I can take it further. Look, it's like this. We're badly overstretched at the moment, and we've had no fewer than three cases in the last year that have cost us the earth in time and money, with nothing to show—one turned out to be suicide, one an accident, and the third we finally just had to let go for lack of any hard evidence. There's been no little criticism about the Yard, and from up high, too. We're all walking about on tiptoes down there."

"You will go talk with her sister, though?"

"Now, that's another thing. Why all this bother about her sister? It's not right, my delaying her being notified like this. Normally, one of the Cambridge force'd go and tell her. And aside from that, how'd you know the letter was from her? There was only her address on the envelope. Opening letters, now, Mr Holmes, that's an offence. Interfering with the post."

"Why, Lestrade, who else could it have been from but the sister she'd been staying with? We weren't interfering with it; on the contrary, we were making absolutely certain that you received it. In fact, you owe us a favour for bringing it to your attention so promptly."

The younger man fell on this red herring, led astray by Holmes' deliberate air of bland innocence. His narrow face pulled in suspiciously.

"What sort of a favour?"

"I want you to take Russell with you when you go to see Erica Ruskin."

I was surprised but said nothing.

"I can't do that, Mr Holmes."

"Of course you can. Besides, you should have a woman there. Women are so much better at comforting the bereaved, don't you find?" He shot me a warning look, and I closed my mouth so hard, my teeth hurt. "Lestrade, you know you'd have to take another person with you anyway. Russell's not strictly to the rules, but call her a consultant."

Lestrade looked as if he'd rather call me something less polite, and I could see that he was not impressed with my father's smudged shirt and the rat's nest of hair atop my grimy face. He was momentarily forgetting that he had seen me in a number of guises, ranging from a lady of the evening to a blind beggar and a chic young heiress, and once as Dr Watson. No, come to think of it, he had come in later on that particular case. Nonetheless, surely he should trust me to dress the part.

"I will change my clothes and look presentable, Inspector, if you will give me twenty minutes," I said mildly.

"Better get started, Russell," said Holmes. "The good gentlemen are nearly finished here."

"Now just one minute. I haven't said I'd go to see the woman, now have I? I've got work up to my ears already. Why should I jaunt on up to the wilds of Cambridgeshire and fight the hay wagons just so your wife can watch me give an old lady some bad news about her sister? Be reasonable, Mr Holmes."

"She was murdered, Lestrade," Holmes said evenly.

"So you say."

"Precisely. So I say." The two men measured each other over the gouged tabletop, until finally Lestrade let out an explosive breath.

"Oh, very well, Mr Holmes. For you, I'll go, and I'll take her with me. But I don't have time to come back down to this godforsaken wilderness. She'll have to get back on her own."

"I believe I can manage the train, Inspector. Twenty minutes."

Precisely nineteen minutes later, I walked into the sitting room in what Holmes calls my "young lady" guise. The blouse was a bit crumpled, but the unfashionable skirt looked as dowdy as ever and my hair was wrapped tightly around my head and covered with a cloche hat. I pushed a thin note-book and pencil into my ridiculous bag. Lestrade glanced at his watch and stood up.

"Right. Ellis should be finished with the toolshed."

"Send me prints of the photographs, would you, Lestrade? Russell, did you give your films to Mr Ellis?"

"I did. See you later, Holmes. Watch out for the marmalade on the pantry floor."

I turned to leave and nearly walked into Lestrade, who was bent over in a contortion, peering fiercely at the patch of boards Holmes had earlier in-dicated. He straightened hurriedly and left. I followed him to the door, then stopped to look back at the room. A swath of bare floor cut through the débris. Holmes stood amidst the ruins, rolling up the sleeves of his collar-less shirt.

"Don't look so grim, Russell."

"Ring Patrick, Holmes."

"I'll have him meet you at the station."

Tony Ellis had finished with the photography and was loading his equip-ment into the back of the car. Lestrade handed him a bag. I was surprised to see that he had no driver.

"I'll drive back, Tony. Miss Russell is coming with us."

Mr Ellis glanced at me but said nothing as he went to the front of the car and cranked the starting handle for Lestrade. After several attempts, the elderly engine shuddered to life, and he came around and climbed into the narrow back seat. He looked absolutely exhausted, and I was not surprised when I heard snores erupting from the back before we had gained the main road.

"Your Mr Ellis seems to have made a night of it," I commented, though, truth to tell, there was no sign of alcohol about him.

"He's been working for nearly thirty-six hours. We were over in Kent yesterday night when your message reached me. We'd started off with the car, so now we're stuck with it. Can't exactly tuck it into the overhead rack, can you? Ellis offered to come down with me—he doubles as a driver when we're shorthanded."

"Generous of him to volunteer."

"He wanted to meet Mr Holmes."

"Ah. Have you also been on duty since yesterday morning?"

"Yes, but he drove last night. Don't worry, I won't fall asleep at the wheel."

"I was not worried, though if you wish me to take over at any point, I'm quite a decent driver." I made the offer, although he did not seem the sort who would care to be driven by a woman.

"Miss Russell—is that what I should call you, by the way?"

"Yes, that's fine."

"I wonder if you'd mind telling me the whole story from your point of view, to cover the, er, gaps left by Mr Holmes?"

"Certainly. Where would you like me to begin? With her letter to me?"

"Tell me about her. What was she like, how did you meet her, what do you know of her work in Palestine? Anything along those lines."

"Miss Ruskin was one of those odd women this country occasionally throws out, like Gertrude Bell or Mary Kingsley. Fascinated by the exotic, oblivious of comfort or convention, largely self-educated, an incongruous mixture of utter, inflexible certainty and immense insecurity around her peers, so that in normal social intercourse, she usually spoke in brief, brusque phrases. Left off pronouns. Loud voice. In writing or when she was involved in explaining her work, she could be very eloquent. Devastatingly observant. Dauntingly vital. Immensely intelligent, and wise, as well. It's hard to think of her as dead, even having seen her body. I shall miss her."

Lestrade was a good listener, and his questions were apposite. I talked; he prompted. We stopped in Southwark to push Tony Ellis out at the terrace house he shared with his three brothers, then drove on to Scotland Yard, where Lestrade left the photographic film to be developed. He also made what seemed to me a feeble attempt to abandon the automobile, but when a consultation with the schedules revealed a nearly two-hour wait

at King's Cross, he decided not to descend to forms of transport less demanding of constant attention, and despite the lack of a driver, he kept
the car. A motorphile who cannot afford a machine of his own, I diagnosed
with resignation.

There was a pause in conversation as he steered between the carts, drays,
lorries, taxis, omnibuses, trams, and the thousand other forms of moving
targets, but when eventually we had fought free, unscathed, of the greater
concentration of traffic, he resumed as if without interruption.

"This manuscript, what did you call it?"

"It's called a papyrus. We should have shown it to you, but it's in a safe
place and Holmes thought it best to leave it hidden. The manuscript itself
is a little roll of papyrus, which is a kind of thick paper made from beaten
reeds, very commonly used in ancient Egypt and the whole Middle East,
apparently, though very little of it has survived. Miss Ruskin consulted authorities on it, but they decided it was not an authentic first-century document, partly because there's so little extant Palestinian papyrus. However,
she thought that as it was sealed inside a glazed figurine, it could have resisted wear that long. I haven't had a chance to examine it closely, but there
were definite signs of red pottery dust embedded in the fibres. It was put
into the box quite recently, in the last twenty years."

"Tell me about the box."

I described it, the animals, inlay, date, and probable origin.

"I'd like to take it to the British Museum to have a friend look at it, but
it's undoubtedly quite valuable. It's in excellent condition, though how it
got to a Bedouin tribesman from Italy will take some figuring."

"And the manuscript itself, what's it worth?"

"I have no way of knowing."

"Guess."

"Surely you know better than to ask that of a student of Sherlock
Holmes," I chided.

"Miss Russell, I am asking for a rough estimate of the thing's value, not
a bid at auction. What is it worth?"

"Half a million guineas?"

"*What?*" he choked, and nearly had us in the ditch.

"The road, please, Inspector," I said urgently, and then: "You're certain
you don't want me to drive? Very well. The thing could as easily be worth
ten pounds, I have at present no means of evaluating it. But you asked two
questions—one of its worth, and the other of its value. The two are related,
although not the same. If it is not authentic, as merely a curiosity, the manuscript is nearly worthless and of little value. If, however—and it's a very

large if—if it is authentically what it appears to be, whoever owned it could set the price. Only a handful of individuals in the world could afford it. And its value . . . Its value as an agent of change? Good Lord, if the papyrus came to be generally accepted as a voice from the first century, the repercussions would be . . . considerable."

My voice drifted off, and he glanced at me in surprise.

"Perhaps you had best tell me about it. It's a letter, you said?"

I sighed and tried to arrange my thoughts as if I were presenting an academic paper to a colleague. That this particular colleague knew not the first thing about the topic and that I was struggling in far over my head with it did not make the presentation any easier.

"I must begin by emphasising that I am not a qualified judge. I am no expert in Greek or in first-century Christianity. If," I was forced to add parenthetically, "you can even call it Christianity at that point. Miss Ruskin gave me the manuscript knowing this, on, as near as I can gather, a personal whim combined with annoyance at the experts, who rejected it out of hand. She thought it worth more than that, and thought, rightly, that I would find it as tantalising as she did." I took a deep and steadying breath.

"It is a letter, in Koiné rather than classical Greek, with one passage of Aramaic, a form of Hebrew that was commonly spoken at the time. The letter is purportedly written by a woman who calls herself Mary, a common enough name, but she refers to herself as an apostle of Jesus and is writing to her sister in the town of Magdala."

It took several seconds to sink in, but when it had sorted itself out in his mind, he took his astonished gaze off the road again and turned it on me for a disturbingly long time before remembering to steer the car. It was another long moment before he could choose an appropriate reaction, which was, predictably enough, a roar of laughter.

"A letter from Mary Magdalene?" he spluttered. "Of all the . . . Leave it to Sherlock Holmes to come up with something as crazy as that. Next thing, he'll be finding the Holy Grail in a pawnshop. Mary Magdalene! That's a rich one, that is."

I looked out the window at the scenery, row upon row of recently constructed Homes for Heroes that gave off abruptly to fields and cows. Let him wrestle with it, I thought, and set out to count the varieties of toxic wildflower in the passing hedgerows. I had reached eleven before his laughter finally dribbled to a halt, and three more (or should the aquilegia, a garden escapee, be allowed? I debated) before his next question came, spoken like a joke waiting for the punch line.

"What does this letter say?"

I answered as if he had asked a serious question.

"Actually, not an awful lot. There's a section in the middle I'm having difficulties with, partly because of some stains across the script but also because the Greek itself is unclear. It begins with a fairly straightforward greeting, such as the various New Testament letters start with, except that rather than being from 'Paul, an apostle of Jesus Christ by the will of God,' for example, it's from 'Mariam, an apostle of Jesus the Messiah,' and it's written to 'my sister Judith in Magdala.' She is apparently writing from Jerusalem in the last weeks before the city was conquered by Rome and laid waste in the Jewish revolt of the years 68 to 70, when the Temple was last destroyed. She's sending her grandchild to Judith and is herself going away to the south, something about a 'rocky desolation.'

"The rest of it I've only glanced over, but it looked to me like an explanation of why she followed 'the rabbi.' I was planning to tackle that section Friday morning when Holmes saw the notice in *The Times* about Miss Ruskin's death. I'm hoping it gives a hint on why the author should be writing in Greek, since one would rather expect it to be all in Aramaic. It's a nice little puzzle."

Lestrade looked at me, then back at the road.

"Is that so?" he said, and then held his peace for at least five miles. Out of the corner of my eye, I could see his face screw itself up over this utterly foreign dilemma, and suddenly I found myself liking him. Eventually, he gave it up, shook his head, and turned to those parts of the problem that lay within his ken.

"This box. Would you say it's valuable enough to kill for?"

"Insufficient data, as Holmes would say. To an extremely corrupt collector, perhaps, or to a madman, but I shouldn't have thought that the point was merely possessing whatever it was they were after. They must have wanted to be rid of Miss Ruskin as well, or else they would have simply broken in, or held her up, and taken whatever it was they wanted. Either she knew who they were and could identify them to the police or she knew the details of whatever they were wanting and could duplicate the information. Besides, it's not the box itself they were after, as we told you; it was something flat and small, like a piece of paper."

"But you still don't think it could have been the—what d'you call it?"

"Papyrus. I did wonder. Only a lunatic would fold it in half and stick it into a book or behind a framed photograph, but it's possible they didn't know precisely what it looked like. If so, it's not a collector. If it is the manuscript they're after, then we've either got a mad academic on our tails or else someone who wants it suppressed, if not destroyed. Holmes thinks it's more likely that someone believes that Miss Ruskin gave us some other paper entirely, either for safekeeping or investigation. It could be a will or a codicil, or a secret treaty—she was thick with the political types over there, an ideal courier. Even a letter. We don't have it, of course, but I suppose it's a case of Holmes' name causing a dramatic overreaction. Someone had to be very worried in order to risk murder and breaking into an hotel room and then driving to Sussex to ransack a house."

He did not respond to this, and I shifted to look over at him. His rather ferretlike features were without expression as he concentrated on the road ahead.

"But I was forgetting, you have yet to see any tie between her death and our house. Will you go with me later to her hotel room and to the corner where she was killed?"

"Certainly." He took a deep breath. "Miss Russell, let me make myself clear. You know that my father was with Scotland Yard and that he worked with Mr Holmes a number of times. You may not realise it, but he was greatly influenced by the way Mr Holmes worked. He really worshipped Mr Holmes, used to tell us kids stories about how he solved crimes against all odds, just by using his eyes and his head. Even now, he never misses an issue of the *Strand* when it has one of Dr Watson's stories in it. I'm not a child anymore, Miss Russell, but I know how much Scotland Yard owes to Mr Holmes. Things he did that looked crazy thirty, forty years ago are now standard procedure with us. Some of the men laugh at him, make jokes about his pipe smoking and violin and all, but they're laughing at all those stories Dr Watson wrote, and they don't like to admit that their training in footprints and the laboratory's analysis of bloodstains and tobacco ashes comes straight from the work of Sherlock Holmes. Even fingerprints—he was the first in the country to use them in a case. Miss Russell, when he says there was murder and a burglary was connected with it, then I for one believe him. I just have to find a way of laying it in front of my superiors. I must have some firm evidence to connect an apparent hit-and-run accident with your sitting room. No doubt we'll find it eventually, but I'd rather it be sooner than later, when the trail is cold."

This lengthy speech drained him of words for another two miles; then he stirred.

"Sounds to me like your friend handed you a right hornets' nest," he commented.

"My life was full enough without it," I agreed obliquely.

"Not that she could have known," he hastened to add, *nil nisi bonum*.

"I'm not sure. Oh, not the current . . . business, not her death, but she must surely have known that the manuscript would prove a major headache. Owning a thing like that, it's no small responsibility."

"Do you mean you think it's real?" he asked cautiously, unsure whether he had a madwoman in the car beside him or if I was launched on some elaborate Holmesian leg-pull.

"Dorothy Ruskin thought it might be."

"Would she have known?"

"I trust her judgement."

"Oh." I could almost hear the whirs and whine of the desperate reevaluation process going on in his mind. "Responsibility"—his flailing grasp latched onto my word. "What kind of responsibility do you mean? That it's worth . . . so much?" He could not bring himself to vocalise the sum I had only half-facetiously suggested.

"Not the money, no. If the thing were to convince me that it is real, then, you see, I am faced with a decision: Do I spend the rest of my life fighting to convince others of its truth? I told you that if it is what it appears to be, the repercussions would be considerable, but that is putting it mildly. The sure knowledge that one of Jesus' apostles was a woman would shake the Christian world to its foundations. Logically, there's no reason why it should, but realistically, I have no doubt that the emotional reaction would set off a bitter, bloody civil war, from one end of the church to the other. And smack in the centre of it, holding a scrap of papyrus in her hand like a child keeping her dinner from a pack of hungry dogs, would be Mary Russell Holmes. A Jew, to boot."

He looked at me sideways, evaluating the profound distaste in my voice.

"And you call her a friend?"

I had to smile. "Yes, I suppose I do. Not that she expected me to do anything with it—she made it quite clear that she did not mind if I sat on it. It's waited almost nineteen hundred years, after all. What's another fifty? She just wanted me to appreciate it and to keep it safe. That in and of itself seems enough of a problem, at the moment," I added to myself, but he picked it up immediately.

"So you think that your manuscript might be at the bottom of it after all? That someone is trying to get his hands on it?"

"I can easily envisage any number of people who might want to possess such a thing, but at this point, Chief Inspector Lestrade, I am keeping a very open mind," I said firmly. That kept him silent until we entered the village and asked directions of a woman pushing a pram.

# NINE

ι

*iota*

T he house to which we were eventually directed was a small two-storey brick building with a front garden composed of weeds and unpruned roses, a broken front step, and sagging lace curtains at the windows. The bell seemed not to work, but loud knocks brought a shuffling in the hallway and an eye under the door chain.

"Who is that?" The accents were those of Miss Ruskin, but the voice was weak and sounded old.

"Pardon me, I'm looking for Miss Erica Ruskin."

"There's been no Miss Erica Ruskin for nearly forty years, young man. What do you want?"

Lestrade was not daunted.

"I am Chief Inspector Lestrade from Scotland Yard. I'd like to speak with the sister of Miss Dorothy Ruskin, and I was given this address."

Silence fell. The faded blue eye travelled over us, and then the gap narrowed, the chain was slipped, and the door opened.

Dorothy Ruskin had been short, but she would have towered above her sister in both stature and personality. This woman barely cleared five feet, and though she had her sister's erect spine, there was none of her authority and purpose. For an instant, the ghost of Dorothy Ruskin looked at me from the eyelids and nose before me; then it faded and there was only a stranger.

"I am Mrs Erica Rogers, Chief Inspector. Dorothy's sister. Is she in some sort of trouble?"

"May we come in, Mrs Rogers? This is Miss Russell, my assistant." We had agreed that I would take notes and use my eyes, as his "assistant."

"Come in?" She examined us suspiciously head to toe, and I smothered an impulse to check my buttons and pat my hairpins. However, we apparently met her standards and were admitted. "I suppose you can come in. In there, the first door."

The door opened into a small, crowded sitting room, thick with gewgaws and whatnots, sepia photographs, reproductions of popular trite Victorian paintings, porcelain figurines, and souvenirs of Brighton and Blackpool. The air was musty and stale, dim despite the window, and the once good Chinese carpet was worn thin and colourless. There was little dust, and the windows were clean, and it could not have been further from the dirty, mad, and infinitely appealing dwelling inhabited by the sister in distant Palestine.

Mrs Rogers followed us into the room and retrieved a knitting project from one of the pair of heavy leather armchairs, their arms and headrests draped incongruously with delicate lace antimacassers, that occupied either side of the tiny fireplace. She waved Lestrade into the other chair, then looked somewhat helplessly about, as if expecting a third armchair to materialise. I solved her dilemma by moving to a hard wooden stool that sat next to the window, out of her line of sight if she faced Lestrade, and took out my notebook with an air of efficiency. I uncapped my pen and prepared to take my unintelligible notes, the perfect silent partner. Mrs Rogers sank into her chair and looked expectant. Lestrade cleared his throat.

"Mrs Rogers," he began, "I'm afraid I have some unfortunate news for you concerning your sister. She was killed in London on Wednesday night, by an automobile. She had no identification on her, and it took us some time to determine her identity and to find your address."

To my astonishment, she did not react at all, other than a slight tensing of the fingers on her knitting. As if reminded of what her hands held, she withdrew a needle from the ball, pulled loose some yarn, and began absently to knit.

"Thank you for telling me, Chief Inspector," she said calmly.

Lestrade shot a startled glance at me and leant forward slightly in his chair.

"Mrs Rogers, did you hear me?"

"Yes, of course I heard you. I may be falling prey to the infirmities of age, but hardness of hearing is not one of them. You said that my sister was hit by an automobile on Wednesday night. I knew she was dead. I did not know how she died. Thank you for telling me." She looked up then from her work, though the rhythm of the needles remained unchanged. "Will you arrange to have the body sent here for the funeral? I'm afraid I don't know how that should be done."

"Mrs Rogers—" Lestrade stopped. I reflected that it was probably quite rare for his face to be given the opportunity to form an expression of complete incredulity, if only for an instant. She faced him calmly. "Mrs Rogers, how did you know your sister was dead?"

"I knew. I woke up shortly after midnight, and I knew she was dead. I felt her go."

After a long moment, Lestrade snapped his mouth shut and sat back into his chair. He took a deep breath, then let it out slowly. "Mrs Rogers, there is some indication that your sister's death may not have been an accident."

I had my head bent over the notebook, but I watched her hands and the muscles of her face as my pen scratched over the paper. Her fingers faltered for a moment, then resumed their odd, disembodied movements. She said nothing.

"There are certain indications that someone wanted something that was in your sister's possession, Mrs Rogers. Have you any idea what that might have been?"

The old lips twitched and again Dorothy Ruskin passed through the face.

"No, Chief Inspector, I have no idea. I have had little contact with my sister for many years now, and I would have no way of knowing what of her possessions would interest another person."

"I understand that she was here several days ago. Did she say anything to you that might have referred to it, comments about something of value, for example, or a trip to a bank vault?"

"No."

"Did she receive any letters or visitors while she was here?"

"There was a letter from London, a Colonel something. She was planning to meet with him in order to discuss her proposals for an archaeological project, after returning from a meeting with Mr and Mrs Sherlock Holmes in Sussex. Dorothy was—" She stopped suddenly and drew a sharp breath, then whirled to look at me, accusation and—was it fear?—on her old face. "Russell? That's the name that was on a telegram she had."

"Yes, Mrs Rogers," I said, watching her politely. "I am assisting Chief Inspector Lestrade. He also thought my presence might be of use to you, that you perhaps would like to know how your sister had spent her last day."

Her eyes held mine for a long moment, then turned to Lestrade, and finally went back to her hands, which then resumed their work. Her mouth twitched angrily.

"Spying on me, that's what you were doing. Sneaking in here pretending to be sympathetic and asking questions."

"Why should we want to spy on you?" I asked innocently. Her fingers paused, and she went on as if I had not spoken.

"I don't know what Dorothy was doing there in the Holy Land. She never told me, just went off and left me to care for Mama, never a thought for helping out. I am sorry she's dead, but I'm not surprised, and I can't say I'll miss her all that much." She came to the end of the row, jabbed her needle into the ball of yarn, and pushed herself up from the chair. "Now, if it's all the same to you, I have to be checking up on my mother and getting her something to eat. Thank you for coming. I'm not on the telephone, but you know where to reach me when you want to send the body here."

The body.

"Mrs Rogers, I'm sorry, but I must ask you a few questions." She stayed on her feet, so Lestrade was forced reluctantly to stand, as well. I remained where I was. "About the two men who came here on the Wednesday. What time was that?"

"Tuesday. It was Tuesday, in the afternoon. Maybe five."

"She left here on Tuesday morning, then?"

"Monday night," she corrected him. "She took the seven-forty into London. Wanted to have a full day in town, she said. Not like some of us, who can only get free for a few hours."

"Er, yes. And the two men. What did they look like? How old were they?"

"Fiftyish," she said promptly. "They were Arabs, I suppose. Not that I've seen any up close, but Dorothy used to send photographs sometimes. Had funny names."

"Can you remember the names?"

"No, gone clear out of my head. Long, they were—the names."

"And the car they came in? Did you see the registration plate?"

"Not that I remember. It was parked along the side of the house, where your car is. All I could see was that it was long and black."

"And that it had a driver."

"I saw that when they pulled out, from upstairs. There were two heads in the back. Either that or the car was driving itself." She was telling us in no uncertain terms that she was fed up with our presence, and Lestrade gave up. I put my notebook and pen away and walked over to the chair she had occupied. The knitting lay in the chair again, an eight-inch length of fine dark blue wool, ribbing and cables, the bottom of what seemed to be a cardigan.

"You do lovely work, Mrs Rogers. Did you knit the cardigan you have on?" She pulled the front of it together across her thin chest as if to defend herself against my friendly voice.

"Yes. I knit a lot. Now please, I have work to do."

"Of course," said Lestrade. "We will let you know when your sister's body will be released to you, Mrs Rogers. This is my card. If you think of anything more about the two men, or if you have any questions, my telephone number is on it." He laid the white rectangle on the polished table in the hallway, retrieved his hat, and we walked slowly down the grey stones to the car.

"I suppose there must be a wide variety of reactions when a person is told of the death of someone close to them," I suggested without much confidence.

"Oh yes. Tears, hysteria, silence, anger, I've seen all those. Never one quite like that, though."

"An odd woman."

"Very. Odd behaviour, at any rate. You hungry?"

"Not terribly. I could use something to drink, though."


In the end, Lestrade drove back with me to Sussex and spent the night on the floor of our guest room. It was a quiet drive down. I sporadically produced topics of conversation to keep him from falling asleep, lapsing back between times into the contemplation of our visit to Mrs Rogers, the marks of the trip wire (the kerbstone had been washed since yesterday), and the hotel room (which Lestrade left sealed for his prints-and-evidence team).

Holmes was waiting for us, with hot drinks and a remarkably transformed room, tidier than it had been in perhaps ten years. He had even lit a small and not entirely necessary fire, which glowed cheerfully from the grate. Lestrade looked grey with fatigue, and he was given a hot brandy and rapidly dispatched to his rather bare quarters. I was pleased to find feathers contained and new beds in place and said as much to Holmes as I joined him in front of the fireplace.

"Yes, Patrick and Tillie were most helpful. He brought a load of essentials over from your house."

"So I see. These chairs are certainly more comfortable than the seat of Lestrade's car. One of his springs is working its way loose, and I kept expecting to be impaled by it." I sipped my drink, closed my eyes, and sighed in satisfaction. "How can a day spent merely sitting be so tiring?" I mused.

"Don't fall asleep, Russell. Tell me what you found, just an outline, and then I will allow you to retire."

I told him, and though it was hardly an outline, it took no more than half an hour to give a summary of my day. Holmes filled his pipe thoughtfully.

"She was not surprised or upset at the news of her sister's death?" he asked.

"No, just that odd statement that she had felt her sister go shortly after midnight. What do you make of that?"

"I wish I had been there. I find it difficult to work with secondhand information, even when it comes from you."

"So why didn't you go?" I said irritably.

"I am not criticising, Russell. There is nothing wrong with the way you gather information—far from it, in fact. It is only that I still find it difficult to accustom myself to being half of a creature with two brains and four eyes. A superior creature to a single detective, no doubt, but it takes some getting used to."

This easy and unexpected declaration shook me. For more than a third of my life, I had been under the tutelage and guidance of this man, and my existence as an adult had been shaped by him, yet here he was easily acknowledging that *I, too,* was shaping *him.* I did not know how to answer him. After a long moment, without looking at me, he went on.

"I found some interesting things here today, Russell, but that can wait until tomorrow. To answer your question, I do not know what to make of Mrs Rogers's claim to a revelatory experience. Once, I would have discounted it immediately, but now I can only file it away, as it were, under 'suspicious.' You said that she seemed nervous, rather than upset?"

"She dropped one stitch—not when Lestrade told her that her sister had died, but when he said that the death was not an accident—then another one after she realised who I was, and finally she turned a cable the wrong way round before telling us to leave. She'll have to pull it all out to return it to her normal standard of workmanship."

"Suggestive. Anything else?"

"Interesting little things. Trifles, as Sergeant Cuff would say. For one thing, the lady's a fan of yours. There were three copies of the *Strand* tucked into a basket next to her chair, two of them, I'm tolerably certain, were issues with Conan Doyle articles in them—one of the Thor Bridge case from last year, and the Presbury case from this spring. For another, I'd say she's had some sort of a maid until recently. Maybe just day help, but there was a fine layer of dust on top of the polished wood and metalwork. Perhaps two weeks' worth. Finally, her attitude toward her sister was not perhaps as affectionate as her letter might have indicated. There were whatnots on every surface, covering the mantelpiece, the tables, even the windowsills, but only four of them might have come from the Middle East, and those were all pushed behind something else. A very nice Turkish enamelled plate was under an aspidistra, for example, and I saw a lovely little Roman glass scent bottle behind the most disgustingly garish coronation cup I've ever laid eyes on."

"Indicates a certain lack of affection, I agree. Or a severe lapse in taste."

"And, of all the photographs and portraits—there must have been fifty, all in gnarly silver frames—there were only two which might have been of Miss Ruskin. One was a child of about six, and the other was one of those fuzzy romantic photographs of a girl of about eighteen. She was very pretty, by the way, if it was Miss Ruskin."

"I thought she might have been. However, disapproval of one's sister hardly indicts one for her murder."

"Particularly when the person is a frail woman in her sixties, I know. Nevertheless—"

"As you say. We shall set Lestrade on the trail in the morning, and set ourselves to casting about in an attempt to find another trail or flush out a few suspects."

"I believe you're mixing up two quite distinct methods of hunting, Holmes."

"I often do, Russell. It doesn't do to restrict oneself until one is certain of the nature of the game. To bed with you now, before I have to carry you. I have some smoking to do."

I rose wearily. His voice stopped me at the door.

"By the way, Russell, how do you come to know anything about dropped stitches and the method of turning a cable?"

"My dear Holmes, the good Mrs Hudson has instructed me in the rudiments of all the so-called womanly arts. The fact that I do not choose to exercise them does not mean I am in ignorance."

I turned with dignity to my bed, smiling to myself at the soft laughter that followed me up the stairs.

# TEN

# Κ

*kappa*

In the morning, the ambrosia of bacon frying heralded Mrs Hudson's return. By the time I dressed (in the day's clothes rather than a dressing gown, in deference to our guest's sensibilities), Lestrade was up, deep in conversation with Holmes outside on the flagstone patio. It was a magnificent morning, with the heat of late summer already in the sun. Somewhere I could hear the sound of farm machinery.

"Good morning, Russell. Coffee or tea?"

"As the coffee's here, I'll have that. I hope you slept well, Inspector, despite the lack of such luxuries as a bed and clean blankets?"

"I could've slept on the bare boards in my car rug last night, but I was most comfortable on the mattress, thank you."

"Russell, you will be pleased to know that your labours yesterday had the desired effect: The Chief Inspector is convinced. The marks on post and pillar box, plus the marks on Miss Ruskin's boots, equal justification for an investigation. Bacon and eggs are in the chafing dishes. I'll fetch more toast."

"I'd like to see the box she gave you before I go, though, Mr Holmes," called Lestrade at his host's disappearing back.

"So you shall, Lestrade," said Holmes as he took a rack of fresh toast from the hand of Mrs Hudson. "So you shall. I need to check the hives today anyway." He did not explain this apparent non sequitur to Lestrade, and I had my mouth full.

After breakfast, Holmes went down to the hives with his tin smoker and a bag of equipment. Lestrade stayed with me at the table, finishing his coffee, and we watched Holmes make his methodical way up the row of hives, stunning each community into apathy with the smoke and reaching gloveless inside. At one hive, he paused to fix another frame for the honeycombs onto the existing ones. He did the same to the hive in which he had secreted the box, then spent some time bent over its innards with his pocketknife. Lestrade shook his head.

"The best detective England has produced, and he spends his time with bees."

I smiled, having heard this a number of times before.

"He finds that the society of bees helps him understand the society of human beings. I think it's also a bit like the violin—it keeps one level of his mind occupied while freeing up other levels. More coffee?"

I left him to his contemplation of life's oddities and took the plates inside to help Mrs Hudson with the washing up. Soon the men reappeared at the door, a small bulge in the pocket of Holmes' coat and a bee clinging dopily to his hair.

"Kindly leave your lady friend outside, Holmes. She's next to your left ear."

He brushed her off and came inside.

"Let's take it into the laboratory, away from the windows. Lestrade," he said over his shoulder, "are you aware of the presence of three classes of bees in a hive? There are the workers, the females, who, appropriately enough, do all the work. The drones are the lowly males, who keep house and stand about gossiping and occasionally wait upon the queen. And finally, there is the queen herself, a sort of superfemale who is the mother of the entire hive. She spends her life laying eggs and killing any other queen who might hatch out, until she weakens and is herself killed, either by a new queen or by being smothered by a huge clot of her daughters when they see her growing old. If she dies accidentally, and if there are no unhatched queen cells, a worker can lay eggs, but she cannot make a new queen. A very educational society, Lestrade, if a bit daunting for a mere male. By the way, Russell, that new queen we got from your friend in Marston is doing very well. I may weed out a couple of the other hives and try replacing their queen cells with hers. Well, here is Miss Ruskin's little present, Lestrade, for what it's worth."

He drew the lump from his pocket and removed the piece of oiled paper with which he had wrapped the box. Traces of wax showed where the industrious creatures had begun to incorporate this foreign object into their hive, but the box itself was untouched. He gave it to Lestrade, who turned it around in his hands, following with delight the parade of animals, birds, and exotic vegetation. I let him enjoy it for a while before I reached over to pull up the top and show him the papyrus.

"I'll work on finishing the translation and then see if I can find any sort of a code or marks on it. It's very unlikely, but I'll try."

Lestrade reached out and ran a thumb over the inviting surfaces, then glanced at the papyrus curiously.

"I can see why you said it wouldn't fit easily into a book. Good luck with it, Miss Russell. Glad it's you and not me. I'd like a photograph of it and a couple of the box as well, if you would."

"Did the camera appear, Holmes?"

"It did, but in rather too many pieces to be of any use. Patrick's should be good enough for the purpose, though."

"That reminds me, Mr Holmes, can you give me a list of everything they took? We can send it around to the stolen-goods people, have the shops look out for the things. Probably hopeless, but still."

"Quite. I made a list last night, Lestrade. It's on the table by the door. Be careful not to bump the table," he added. "One leg is loose."

"Right." Lestrade handed me the box and glanced at his watch. "Good Lord, I must run. I'm meeting someone at one o'clock. I'll be in touch tomorrow."

"I'll be interested to know what you uncover about Mrs Rogers's background. And I want to see if your print man finds anything in the hotel room."

"In this case, Mr Holmes, it's a print lady," he said primly, and with a tip of his hat to me, he closed the door.

Holmes and I regarded each other, and the noise and the tumult of the last two days gradually settled into the quiet house like dust from a shaken rug.

"So, Holmes."

"So, Russell."

He nodded once, as if in agreement, and we returned to our dreary task, in this case the laboratory, where, by great good fortune, none of the broken beakers and jars had combined to form explosives, corrosives, or poisons. We used heavy gloves, but we still had blood on our hands when the afternoon came and Holmes tipped the last dustpan load into the bin. We pulled off our gloves, inspected the damage, and threw gloves, brush, and the pan itself into the bin and slammed down the lid.

"Lunch al fresco, Russell, is definitely called for. Fresh air and sensible conversation in a place free of broken test tubes, white-haired eccentric ladies, and Scotland Yard inspectors."

We removed ourselves from the cottage to a spot notable only for its lack of scenery and difficulty of approach, then applied ourselves to my thick sandwiches (Mrs Hudson had despaired of teaching me to slice bread and meat thinly) and glasses of honey wine. The summer had been a good one, warm enough to dry hay, wet enough to water the fields. In a month, I should return to Oxford for half of each week. We hadn't much time.

I lay back and watched one thin cloud hang unmoving in the firmament while Holmes put the things back into his rucksack. Dorothy Ruskin, a strong woman who would find it easy to make enemies. Her sister, a widow, left to care for an old woman in a decrepit house. A retired colonel, his absent son, and whomever else she may have met in London. Then there were the two Arabs and their driver in the black saloon car, and whoever had searched our house. I shifted to avoid the sharp edges of a rock beneath my shoulder blade and was jabbed by one corner of the box, which I had thrust into a capacious trouser pocket. I stretched out my leg and fished for the box. I am not an acquisitive person; indeed, some people would say that the fortune I controlled was wasted on me. However, this artefact captivated me in ways I could not begin to explain. I held it up before my eyes. The peacock's tail was lapis lazuli and some green stone. Jade? Turquoise? I rested it on my stomach with my hands over it and closed my eyes to the hot sun.

I must have drifted off, because I was startled when Holmes spoke.

"Shall I abandon you here, Russell, in the arms of Nature's soft nurse?"

I smiled and stretched deliciously on the rocky ground. Holmes caught the box and handed it back to me when I sat up.

"William Shakespeare must have been an insomniac," I declared. "He has an overly affectionate fixation on sleep that borders on obsession. It can only have stemmed from privation."

"A hungry man dreaming of food? You sound like the jargon-spouting neighbour of Sarah Chessman, with her traumatic experiences and neuroses."

"Who better qualified than I for the spouting of psychological jargon?" I muttered, and then sighed and accepted his hand to haul me upright. So much for escapism.

"What next, Holmes?" I asked, grasping the nettle along with his hand.

"I intend to go for a leisurely promenade of the neighbourhood and drink numerous cups of tea and glasses of beer. You, meanwhile, will be bent slaving over your scrap of ancient paper. I trust my eyes and spine will be in considerably better condition than yours by evening," he said complacently.

"You will bring up the topic of our Friday-night visitors in the course of each conversation, I trust?"

He flashed me a brief sideways smile.

"I am relieved to see that your wits are back to their customary state. I admit that on Friday I was somewhat concerned."

"Yes. Friday was not a good day," I agreed ruefully. "Tell me, Holmes, what did you find Saturday morning to produce that exhibitionist display of omniscience you gave Lestrade? Some of it was obvious, the footprints and the hairs you found, and I take it the inferred cashmere scarf and camel-hair coat came from threads?"

"Where he laid his outer garments across a leg of the overturned kitchen table, which has a rough place on it where that monstrous puppy belonging to Old Will once attempted to eat the table. The dents in the floor came from a loose nail in the heel of the shoe, which does not occur with a quality piece of footwear. That they were both right-handed could be deduced from the pattern of how the objects fell when swept from the shelves, from the angle of the knife blades—two of them—in the soft furniture, from the location of the ladder, so that the right hand would have stretched for the last books, and from the foot that each man led with on climbing the ladder. There was an interesting smudge of mud on the alternate lower rungs, by the way, still damp when it was left there. It is not from around here, but must have been picked up earlier in the day. A light soil, with buff-coloured gravel in it."

"You'll do an analysis?"

"When the microscope is functioning, yes. However, the stuff is not immediately recognisable, so it will be of value only when we find its source."

"And the men? You said the leader had grey hair and stayed in the car?"

"Yes, that was most remarkable. I could not at first think why the two gentlemen kept going in and out, with much greater frequency than was required for the theft of our few belongings. Then I found the one grey hair, about three inches long, lodged in a sheaf of papers taken from your files. The pages had been dropped near the door, not next to your desk. It looked to me as though several armfuls of papers had been taken out of the room for examination and then brought back."

"Sounds pretty thin to me, Holmes. It could have belonged to anyone—you, Mrs Hudson, one of the cleaning women. Even one of my older tutors."

"The hair has a wave, and I think that a microscope will reveal an oval cross section. Mine is thin and straight, Mrs Hudson's considerably thicker and quite round."

"Which only leaves several dozen possibilities." I nearly laughed aloud at the expression on his normally sardonic features, which were caught between sheepishness and indignation.

"It is only a working hypothesis, Russell." With dignity, he held the garden gate open for me to pass through.

"It seems perilously close to a guess to me, Holmes."

"Russell!"

"It's all right, Holmes. I won't tell Lestrade the depths to which you stoop. Tell me about the knives."

"There is no 'guess' about those," he said with asperity. "Both were very sharp, and the one carried by the person with a loose nail in his shoe and an excess of hair oil was shaped to the suggestion of violence. The other was a more workmanlike blade, shorter and folding by means of a recently oiled hinge. It was wielded by the man in the round-toed boots and tweed suit."

"The flashy dresser carries a flashy knife. Not the sort one would wish Mrs Hudson to encounter." I lowered my voice, as we were nearing the house.

"No," he agreed dryly. "Mrs Hudson's talents are many and varied, but they do not include dealing with armed toughs."

"We won't hear from Mycroft today, or Lestrade?"

"Tomorrow, I should think. We cannot decide our actions until we have news from them, but I expect that we shall find ourselves moving our base of operations into London for a few days and incidentally giving Mrs Hudson a holiday. Sussex is a bit too distant from Colonel Edwards, Erica Rogers, and various mysterious Arabs."

"Meanwhile, the neighbours."

"And you, the lexicon."

"This case is wreaking havoc with my work," I muttered darkly. Holmes did not look in the least sympathetic, but was, on the contrary, humming some Italian aria as he left the house, walking stick in hand, cap on head, every inch the country squire paying visits on the lesser mortals. I opened my books and got to work.

Truth to tell, although I would not have admitted it to him, I regretted the interruption not at all. I thoroughly enjoyed that afternoon of immersing myself in Mary's letter, and I found it immensely exciting to see the lacunae fall before my pen, to turn the first choppy and tentative phrases into a smooth, lucid translation. This was original work in what appeared to be primary source material, a rarity for an academic, and I revelled in it. When Holmes walked in, I was astonished to find that I had worked nonstop for four hours. It felt like one.

"Russell, haven't your eyes fallen out yet? Shall I tell Mrs Hudson to leave our food in the oven while we have a swim?"

"Holmes, your genius continually astounds me. May I have another ten minutes?" There was no need to ask for the results of his interviews—it was in the look of dogged persistence he wore.

"Take fifteen. I don't mind climbing that cliff in the dark."

"Ten. You get together some towels and the bathing costumes."

Forty minutes later, we lay back in the shallow pool left by the receding tide, and I asked him what our neighbours had said.

"They saw nothing."

"That is very peculiar, in the countryside."

"Due entirely to a piece of bad luck. There was a "do" on at the Academy that evening, to welcome the new director, and the area was crawling with formal black automobiles, brought in from Brighton to ferry guests from the station. Several of them ended up in impassable lanes and farmyards before the night was through. Ours might have had another county's registration code on its number plates, but if so, nobody noticed."

"You should have—" I bit it back.

"Yes?"

"Hindsight. We should have had Old Will or Patrick come and keep watch that night."

"I had thought of that, but decided against it. Having enthusiastic amateurs involved is a terrible responsibility, and usually a liability. Neither of them would have been able to resist a confrontation with the intruders."

"You're probably right. Old Will certainly."

"I even considered, briefly, asking Constable Perkins to come out and sit in the bushes."

"My goodness. Desperate times indeed."

"I decided the measure was too desperate. Had I been absolutely certain they would come, I might have resorted to his involvement."

"He would have fallen asleep anyway, and we'd be no further along."

With which judgement we concluded our conversation, indulged in a vigorous sprint through the dusky waters, which I won, and climbed the cliffs for our late and well-earned supper.

After we had polished off Mrs Hudson's supper, down to scraping the bowls of the lemon custard, and after I had helped with the washing up,

Holmes lit a small fire to dry my hair, and I told him about the letter. I sat on the hearth rug with my back to the heat, the pages of my translation spread out on the floor, Holmes curled up before me in his frayed basket chair, with his face half-illuminated by the flames, and I read him my translation of Mary's letter. As I did so, I seemed to hear the woman's calm, melodious voice through the open French windows, a murmur beneath the distant rumour of the incoming waves on the rocky shore.

"I have to admit, Holmes, that Miss Ruskin was right. There is something profoundly moving about this document, and I am more than halfway to believing that it could indeed have been written by Mary the Magdalene, a lost apostle of Jesus of Nazareth.

"The letter begins in the traditional epistolary style, naming both the author and the intended receiver, then a greeting, followed by the message itself. It is in Greek, with a few Hebrew and Aramaic words, two of the latter written in the Greek alphabet, and includes a passage from Joel, in Hebrew:

"From Mariam, an apostle of Jesus the Messiah [That could be translated as 'Joshua the Anointed One,' but it seems awfully noncommittal, somehow] to my sister Judith in Magdala, may you be granted grace and peace.

I write to you in haste, with little hope for a reply to this, my last letter. Tomorrow we go down from this place, and I think we shall not return. I send this in the hand of my beloved Rachel, for I know you will care for her as her mother's mother can no longer do. Keep her in the way of God, and teach her well.

Jerusalem has fallen to the locusts, the Temple is defiled, the exile is upon us once again.

Let all the inhabitants of the land tremble,
for the day of the Lord is coming,
it comes near,
A day of dark and of gloom,
a day of clouds and heavy darkness.
Fire devours before them,
and behind them flame burns.
The land is like Eden before them,
but behind them a howling wilderness,
and nothing escapes.

My heart sickens when I look from my window, and the stink

of the soldiers fills my nostrils. I leave at dawn with my husband and his brothers, but Rachel the Romans will not have. Her future lies with you; I will think of the two of you among the pomegranates as I look out across my rocky desolation. I do not know how long the Romans will leave us there, but I think not long.

My sister Judith, many things lie between us. I do not know how I hurt you more, when I struck at you in my time of madness, or when I turned to the rabbi who healed me and followed him through the countryside. You heard madness in my words as I spoke of him, and I know you will hear only madness now. I will say only that in my deepest heart I know him to be the anointed of God, and I believe that somehow his life among us has transformed the world. Not overnight, as I once thought and some still look for, but nonetheless I believe in the sureness of it. I know that somehow beneath the turmoil and confusion of these times, his message is at work. I go tomorrow with a mind at peace and heart full of love for my family, my friends, and even some of my enemies. I try to love the Romans, as I was taught to do by the Teacher, but I find it hard to look past the blood on their hands. Perhaps if they did not stink so, it would be easier.

The night is late, and I have much to do before dawn. Say the prayer for the dead over me, when you receive this, and think no more of me. What lives of me is not on a rock overlooking a waste, but stands before you, in Rachel. Love her for me. My husband sends his greetings. Peace be with you."

The fire subsided into rustling embers, and Holmes sat curled up in his chair, sucking at an empty pipe and staring into the glow. I took up my hairbrush and began to plait my hair for the night while the voice of a woman whose bones had long since turned to dust echoed softly in the dim room.

# ELEVEN

*lambda*

$T$he following morning was spent waiting. A singularly frustrating experience, waiting, made more so by the feeling that the labours of others are neither as quick nor as thorough as one's own. I always envied Holmes his ability to switch off the frustrations of enforced inactivity and turn wholeheartedly to another project. He spent the morning pottering happily in the laboratory, while I turned resolutely to my books. I had intended to produce a first draft of my book (on the concept of wisdom in the Hebrew Bible) before the end of the year, but that was before Miss Ruskin's letter hit my desk. Something told me that hunting down her murderers was going to take large chunks of time from the coming days, if not weeks.

Through sheer determination, I managed to focus my mind on the words in front of me, though every time I came across a reference to *Sophia*, the Greek word meaning "wisdom," the figure of Mary would stir gently in the back of my mind. Eventually, I was surrounded by journals and books, as I followed a phrase from Proverbs through a recently published religious text from ancient Mesopotamia and tried to recall a similar theme from an Egyptian hieroglyphic inscription. When the telephone rang, my mind was far, far away, and I took up the receiver irritably.

"Russell. Yes, this is she." Where was that? I racked my brains. It was a reference to the goddess Ma'at, surely. Budge's book on— "Yes? Who? Oh, yes, certainly, I'll wait. Holmes!" I shouted, books forgotten. "Holmes, it's Mycroft." I listened hard for a minute over the sound of his descending footsteps, the earpiece glued to my ear. "He wants to see us, and could we get to London for dinner tonight? What's that?" I shouted into the telephone, then strained to hear across the distance and the numerous exchanges the call was coming though. "Oh. He says he has some grouse and a new port he'd like you to try," I told Holmes. "At least, I think that's what he said. Either that or he's in the house and has a few darts he'd like to let fly. In either case, perhaps we ought to go? Right." I drew a deep breath and re-addressed the mouthpiece. "We'll be there by seven o'clock. Seven! Right. Good-bye."

In the typically contrary nature of the beast, the telephone, which had sat obstinately silent all morning, rang again almost immediately. I picked it up and the operator informed me that it was another London call, would I please wait a moment, dear, so I did, until the line crackled into life. I bellowed my name into it, and that must have come near to rupturing Lestrade's eardrum, for his voice when it came was as clear as if he were standing in the room beside me.

"Miss Russell?" He sounded a bit tentative. I hastily lowered my own voice.

"Good day, Inspector. Sorry about that. I've just rung off from a very bad connexion, but this one is all right. Have you any news?"

"A few things have come in, and I'm expecting more this afternoon. Shall I give it to you over the telephone, or send it to you? I'm tied up here, unfortunately."

"Look, Inspector, we're coming into Town ourselves later today. Will you be at the Yard around, say, six o'clock?" Holmes, who had turned and come back downstairs at the second ring, gestured at me. "Just a moment, Inspector, Holmes is saying something."

"Invite him for dinner with Mycroft. There's sure to be enough grouse for a regiment," Holmes suggested.

"Inspector Lestrade? Are you free for dinner tonight? About eight o'clock, at Mycroft Holmes' rooms? Good. And you remember where he lives? That's right. You what? Oh yes, certainly, he would be flattered. Right. See you tonight, then."

I rang off, then got the operator back to place a call to Mycroft. While waiting, I spoke to Holmes.

"Lestrade would like a bottle of your honey wine to present to a lady friend of his on the occasion of her birthday."

"I am honoured."

"I thought you might be. He even promises not to tell her where it came from. He wants the substance for its own true self."

"Good heavens. Am I to become a rival to France? A honey wine to make you weep?"

"Weak, perhaps," I said under my breath, but I was saved from repetition by the call coming through. Mycroft was more audible this time, and when I told him he'd have to pluck another bird for Lestrade, he replied that he should be happy so to do, even if it meant performing the task with his own pale hands, which I doubted. I hung the earpiece back on its rest.

"I'll go pack," I volunteered. Leaving such a thing to Holmes could mean some interesting outfits. "Anything in particular you want?"

"Only the basic necessities, Russell. Anything undamaged is likely to be unclean, and we will be making purchases in London for our personae. I shall go tell Mrs Hudson of the change in plans—she had thought to leave tomorrow, but we can take her with us to the station."

"What about the box? Back in the beehive?"

"I think not. That was a temporary measure and would hardly stand against a concerted search. I recommend either putting it in a place they've already searched or else taking it with us."

"To Mycroft? Of course! If anyone could keep it safe, Mycroft could." I stood up and began to put away my papers and books, then paused. "Holmes, I should hate to have this mangled again; a good many hours have gone into it. What do you think of our chances of being invaded a second time?"

"Take anything precious with you. I don't think there's much risk, but there's always the chance. I did ask Old Will and his grandson to keep an eye on the place this time. The boy understands that he is to keep the old man out of trouble, even if it means sitting on him."

"They'll be thrilled." I grinned at the thought. Will was the gardener, but during the reign of Victoria he had also been an agent of what would now be called "Intelligence." Sessions in the herbaceous border or amongst the runner beans were invariably filled with anecdotes of spying behind the lines during "the War" (which was more likely to be the one on the North-West Frontier or the Crimea than the recent engagement in Europe). The boy, now sixteen, had been infected with his grandfather's enthusiasm, and he positively ached to be asked for such tasks by Sherlock Holmes himself. "Have you spoken to Mycroft yet about the lad?"

"I have. He was interested but agreed to wait until the lad has finished his schooling."

"Mycroft's people would pay for university, wouldn't they?" Whoever his "people" were, I added to myself.

"They would. They prefer gentlemen spies, or educated ones, at any rate. Look, you finish up here while I move up the arrangements with Mrs Hudson and Will. Don't take too many books, though. You may have to leave everything with Mycroft."

My brother-in-law, Mycroft, was much on my mind as I packed my papers and a few books and a toothbrush. I was very fond of that fat and phlegmatic version of his brother but had to admit that at times he made me nervous. He was possibly the most powerful individual in the British government by then, and power, even when wielded by such a moral and incorruptible person as Mycroft Holmes, is never an easy companion. I was never unaware of it, and always there lurked the knowledge that his power was without checks, that the government and the people lay nearly defenceless should he choose to do harm or, an appalling thought, should his successor prove neither moral nor incorruptible. I was fond of Mycroft, but I was also just a bit afraid of him.

His exact position in the governmental agency into whose offices he walked daily was that of a glorified accountant. It amused him to think of himself that way, though it was quite literally true: He kept accounts. The accounts he kept, however, seldom limited themselves to pounds, shillings, and pence. Rather, he accounted for political trends in Europe and military expenditures in Africa; he took into account religious leaders in India, technological developments in America, and border clashes in South America; he counted the price of sugar in Egypt and wool in Belgium and tea in China. He kept account of the ten thousand threads that went to make up the tapestry of world stability. He had a mind which even Holmes admitted to be his own superior, but unlike Holmes, Mycroft preferred to sit and have information brought to him rather than stir himself to gather it. He was, in a word, lazy.

I had heard him correctly, despite the telephone: He did have grouse and a superb port for us, although the heat and humidity of London took the edge off the appetites of at least three of us. By unspoken agreement, we ate without discussing the Ruskin case, and we took our port to his sitting room. The windows were opened wide in the hope of a breath of air, and the noise of the Mall at night poured in as if we were seated on the pavement. I put my wine to one side and brushed the damp hair from my forehead, wishing I could wear one of the skimpy new fashions without revealing parts of myself I did not care to reveal—automobile accidents and gunshot wounds leave scars.

"So," purred Mycroft, "you bring me another interesting little problem. Do you mind if we smoke, Mary?" The invariable question, followed by my customary permission. Mycroft offered cigars, and I settled myself into the chair that I calculated would be clearest of the drift of smoke. After the interminable fuss of clipping and lighting, Mycroft nodded at the Scotland Yard inspector, who was looking a bit stunned with the food and drink and, I think, with the august company.

"Chief Inspector Lestrade, if you would begin, please."

His small eyes started open, then blinked rapidly as he fumbled in an inner pocket for his notebook. As I watched him awkwardly holding the big cigar in one hand and trying to manipulate the pages with the other, I wondered how a man with such structurally unappealing features could manage to possess a certain degree of charm. His suit was ill-fitting, he needed a shave and a haircut, his collar was worn, his eyes were too small and his ears too large, but I warmed to him nonetheless. Suddenly, it occurred to me that my feelings towards the little man were distinctly maternal. Good God, I thought, how utterly revolting, and I turned my mind firmly to the problem at hand. Lestrade cleared his throat, looked doubtfully at the cigar, and began his report in official tones and a formal manner.

"In conversation with Mr Holmes on Saturday and Sunday, and subsequently confirmed by my superiors, we agreed to extend our investigations in three directions, each representing one area of known contact Miss Ruskin had in this country since she arrived. These areas are, first of all, Miss Ruskin herself, and any bank accounts, wills, et cetera, which she may have established while she was here. Second is her sister, Mrs Erica Rogers, and third is the gentleman she dined with just before she died, Colonel Dennis Edwards. We agreed that, for the moment, the possibility that people from outside the country were involved would be left in the hands of Mr Mycroft Holmes."

"I should like to say a few words when you have finished, Chief Inspector," said Mycroft.

"I'll be as brief as possible. Miss Ruskin herself creates something of a problem. She entered the country from France on Friday, reached Town just before noon, checked into her hotel at two-ten, and stayed there until the following morning, when she went up to Cambridgeshire to see her mother and sister. She remained with them until Monday evening, when she checked back into the same hotel. Tuesday morning, she went out and was not seen again until after ten o'clock in the evening. As yet we've no idea where she went."

"Two hours from Victoria Station to the hotel, you say?" murmured Holmes with a brief smile touching his lips, but did not elaborate.

"You've looked at the museums, for the missing Tuesday?" I asked.

"I have a man on it, working his way through a list of the more likely museums and libraries. I don't suppose she mentioned anything to you?" he asked without much hope, and I answered.

"No, she didn't, sorry. Did you try Oxford? She did say something in a very general way about being there."

"I haven't been able to spare a man for it yet, but I did direct the local force to begin enquiries. Nothing to date."

"If it would help, I could give you the names of some people in Oxford who might know if she'd been in town. There's an old man in the Bodleian Library who's been there forever and a day; he's sure to know her. It might save a few hours if you could reach them by telephone. Not that the old man would talk on the infernal machine."

"Couldn't hurt." Lestrade flipped to a blank page in his lined notebook, and I wrote down several names and where they might be found. He looked in satisfaction at my scrawl, then turned back to his place.

"Wednesday, she reached you at midday, which means she had very little time in the morning to see anyone, though the hotel was not certain just when she left. She came back to the hotel for a very short time Wednesday night, apparently to change bags, but not clothes, and met the colonel for dinner at nine o'clock."

"Tell us about the colonel," suggested Holmes, who looked deceptively near sleep in the depths of his armchair. Lestrade flipped pages, dropped ash onto his trouser leg, and cleared his throat again.

"Colonel Dennis Edwards, age fifty-one, retired after the war—a widower with one son, aged twenty-one. He was in and out of Egypt before the war, and in 1914 he was posted to Cairo. Went into Gallipoli in March of 1915, and stayed until the end, the following January. Given a fortnight's home leave and then was shifted to the Western Front. Decorated in 1916 when he pulled three of his men out of a collapsed trench under fire. Wounded in March of '17, spent six months in hospital, and returned to active service until the end of the war. There seems to have been some unpleasant business about his wife, though the exact story is hard to pin down. She died in York in July of 1918—he was in the thick of things at the Marne—though why York, nobody seems to know, as she had no family there. The boy, by the way, didn't go to her during the school holiday—he'd been sent off to an aunt up in Edinburgh."

"What did she die from?" I asked.

Lestrade rumpled his hair absently, thus adding another endearingly unattractive characteristic. "Funny thing, we haven't been able to find out. The hospital moved their offices three years back, and some of the records went missing. All they've been able to come up with is one of the older nurses, who remembers a woman by that name dying either, she says, of pneumonia or childbirth fever; she can't remember which. She thinks the woman was brought in by a handsome young man but couldn't swear to it. Don't know if I'd trust her if she could, anyone who can't even remember whether a patient was in the maternity ward or in with the respiratory diseases. However, it does seem that Mrs Edwards was brought in by a man, according to the one piece of paper the hospital found relating to her admission, but he signed his name as Colonel Edwards. The real colonel was, as I said, in France, had been for more than eight months, and the signature was not his."

"There are distinctly unpleasant overtones in all of this." Mycroft's distaste spoke for us all.

"Nothing conclusive yet, but I'd have to agree. Seems the colonel found the circumstances of his wife's death too much to take, too, on top of everything else. He was demobbed in February of 1919, and five months later he spent seven weeks in hospital, with a diagnosis of severe alcoholic toxaemia. They dried him out and sent him home, and after that he straightened out. He got himself involved with the local church and from there met this same group of retired Middle East hands who were about to provide the backing for Miss Ruskin's excavation—the Friends of Palestine."

"I've been wondering, Inspector," I interrupted, "how did the colonel miss the fact that it was a woman who was in charge of the project? Holmes said the man was surprised at that."

"Yes, that was odd, wasn't it? I spoke with two of his friends on the committee that recommended the project, and according to them, Miss Ruskin always signed herself as D. E. Ruskin and never corrected their form of address."

I had to smile. "Her articles were all published under that name," I admitted. "She was, after all, a realist and very anxious to get her dig. I doubt that it was deliberate to begin with, but she probably knew the sort of men she was dealing with and therefore allowed them to continue in their false assumption until they were in too far to back out."

"I imagine it appealed to her sense of humour, as well," commented Holmes.

"That, too. Can't you just hear her laugh?"

"Nothing else about Colonel Edwards?" asked Mycroft.

"We're still looking at bank accounts and family connexions. The son is still away, expected back this weekend."

"And the driver?"

"The colonel's man and the man's wife are the only permanent household servants. They've been with the family for thirty years, and the man's father served the colonel's father before him."

"Any change in their account of Wednesday night?" asked Holmes.

"No, we went over it again, and he says he left the restaurant around midnight, was driven home, and went to bed."

"Did you ask him about the telephone call he made from the restaurant?" Holmes asked.

"That I did. He says he was trying to reach the friend who arranged the meeting with Miss Ruskin, but he couldn't get into contact with him. We talked to the man—name of Lawson—and he agrees that he was not at home that night."

"No way of finding where the colonel phoned, then?"

"Afraid not. All the exchange can tell us is it wasn't a trunk call."

"A London number, then."

"Must've been. If, indeed, he actually made the call. Any road, there were no notable inconsistencies between his story and his servant's, not yet anyway. I'll question them both again tomorrow."

"Does he know yet that this is a murder investigation?"

"We left it as a death under suspicious circumstances, but he's not stupid. He may have guessed it's more than routine."

"Well, it cannot be helped. What about Mrs Erica Rogers?"

"I was up there again this morning, but I can't say we have too much on her yet. The neighbours say she was at home both Wednesday and Friday, as far as they can tell. However, Miss Russell will have told you that the house is peculiarly difficult to overlook—it is near the main road, but bordered by woods on one side and a high privet hedge between it and the nearest neighbour. Her lights did go off as usual around ten-thirty, both nights, and nobody noticed any car arrive after that. She lives alone with her mother; a day nurse comes in Monday, Wednesday, and Friday mornings. Doctor regularly, too."

"What's wrong with the old lady?"

"Just age, I think. Lots of small things, arthritis, bronchitis, heart— nothing quite big enough to carry her off. Must be a stubborn old thing. Totally useless trying to question her, by the way—hearing like a fence post and pretty near gaga to boot."

"It must be expensive, caring for an invalid. What income is there?"

"Investments by the father, for the most part—not big, but steady. He's been dead for twelve years. Two-thirds of the income goes to Mrs Rogers and her mother, one-third to Miss Ruskin."

"And the will?"

"Mrs Rogers directed us to the family solicitor, who showed me the will Miss Ruskin drew up ten years ago. It left everything to her mother and sister, aside from a few specific items, which she wanted sent to various individuals, some to the British Museum. A codicil added five years ago specified additional items, but that did not change the will itself."

"Any other family?"

"Now, that was an interesting thing. Mrs Rogers was most cooperative when it came to questioning the mother, and she came across with the solicitor's name, but as soon as we branched off onto the rest of the family, she seemed to lose interest in the conversation. She mentioned that she has two sons, and then it seemed we would have to leave, it was time for Mama's bath."

"Any idea what colour hair the sons have?" Holmes murmured.

Lestrade looked up at the question, then started to shake his head.

"There were two men among the photographs in Mrs Rogers's house," I remembered. "Nothing to give a reference for their height, but both of them had very dark hair."

"Ah. Lestrade, when you find them, if you can get a sample of their hair without being too obvious, it might be useful. Was there anything else?"

Lestrade had to admit that until such a time as the enquiries concerning wills and safe-deposit boxes began to come in, there was nothing else. However, I thought it was a tremendous amount to have pulled together in such a short time, and I said so. He blushed and looked pleased.

"I agree," said Holmes dutifully. "Well done. All right, I shall go over what I have learnt, though you've all heard parts of it already." He then touched his fingers together in front of his lips, closed his eyes, and reviewed the results of his work in the laboratory, the mud and the hairs left by the intruders, the examination of the papyrus. I brought out the box and allowed it to be handled and admired while I read my translation of the letter. I then gave box and manuscript to Mycroft for safekeeping. He took them off to the other room, then returned with four glasses and a bottle of brandy.

"It is becoming late, and I believe the good inspector has been short of sleep lately," Mycroft began. "I shall try to make this brief." He paused and turned his glass around in his massive hands, gathering our attention to himself—he was as much of a showman as his brother. He broke the tension by shooting Lestrade a hard look. "You understand that some of what I will tell you is not common knowledge and must under no circumstances make itself into any written record, Chief Inspector."

"Would you prefer that I leave?" Lestrade said stiffly.

"Not unless you prefer not to be put in the awkward position of having to withhold information from the official record. Your word is sufficient assurance of that for me."

"I have no real choice, have I?"

"I'm afraid not."

"Very well, I agree."

"Good. My information concerns Miss Ruskin herself. Like most of the English in the Near East, she was connected with Intelligence during the war, and in fact she worked for some months in an unofficial, but nonetheless vital, capacity for His Majesty in 1916 and 1917. It is mildly surprising that she and Colonel Edwards seem to have never crossed paths, but at the time he was in Cairo, she was a small and private cog, in addition to being for the most part, as they say, 'in the field.' A curiosity, perhaps, that they never met, but hardly sinister. Her work began with translation, first of documents and then in interviews and interrogations. She acted as a guide on a handful of on-the-quiet occasions, and several times as a courier. By late 1916, she had gained a certain level of independence in her activities and had befriended a number of leading Arabs. They were fascinated by her, as their brothers to the east were by Gertrude Bell, and gave her the freedom of movement and speech that normally only men are allowed in that society. Plus, of course, having access to the women's quarters.

"However, in 1917 a small thing happened. History is often made by small things, which is why it can be useful to maintain a person such as myself to take notice of them. The small thing that happened to Miss Ruskin was that her car broke down near one of the new Zionist settlements, and while she was waiting for the driver to return with a part, she ate a boiled egg that had sat too long in the heat. She became very ill. The Zionists took her in, their doctor cared for her, and she spent several days recuperating amongst the gardens they were calling into existence from out of the bare earth. She saw their commitment, the strength and pleasure they drew from the land and from their children, and by the time she drove away, she was a Zionist. A Christian still, perhaps even more of a Christian than she had been before, but a Zionist.

"She was a highly intelligent woman from all indications. I believe I should have enjoyed meeting her. It did not take her long to decide that Zionism and Arab self-rule were fundamentally incompatible. There are many people who would not agree with her, but Miss Ruskin became convinced that Jews and Mohammedan Arabs could not easily be neighbours in the same small country, and so she gradually withdrew herself from her former work and returned to archaeology. Her work for the Zionist movement has gone on, but quietly, so as, I think, not to oppose directly her Arab friends and not to burden the movement with an apparent turncoat.

"Inevitably, there were some members of the Arab faction who were angered by what they saw as her desertion of their cause, her betrayal. There was one family in particular with cause for bitterness. She had been supporting them in a land dispute before her, shall we say, 'conversion,' and afterwards she backed away. They lost their claim and were forced to move into town. Last year, the Zionists established a settlement on that piece of land."

"And equally inevitably, there are at least two young men in the family who are well educated, and they were in this country last Wednesday, and they naturally have black hair," I groaned. "Oh, why couldn't this be a simple case?"

"Don't complain, Russell," said my unsympathetic husband. "Just think how pretty it will look when you get around to writing your memoirs."

"I would settle for writing my Wisdom book, thank you."

"Well, you'll not have time for either just yet. There remains much to do. Lestrade, shall we meet tomorrow night to discuss tactics?"

"Here?"

"Mycroft?"

"Certainly. I cannot promise grouse again, but my housekeeper is always happy to oblige."

"Eight o'clock, then, Lestrade."

Good nights were given all around, glasses were cleared away, Mycroft excused himself, and I went off to our rooms to wash the late-night grit from my eyes. I came back, to find Holmes where I had left him, curled into a chair with his pipe, glowering fiercely at the scoured, empty tiles of the fireplace. I turned down the lights, but he did not move. The threads of smoke surrounding his head looked like the emissions of some hard-pressed engine, smoking with the fury of its labours. I turned at the doorway and watched him for a long minute, but he gave no sign of feeling my eyes on him.

Normally when Holmes was in this state, I would slip away and leave him to his thoughts, but that night something pulled me over to his chair. He started when I touched his shoulder, and then his face relaxed into a smile. He uncurled his legs, and I wedged myself next to him in the chair, which, being fitted to Mycroft, held the two of us with ease. We sat, silent, aware of the occasional clop of shod hooves, the growl of motors, the slight

shift of the building around us going to bed, once the call of a night ven-
dor wandered away from his home territory. The lace curtains moved
faintly and brought in a much-adulterated hint of a change in the weather.

Holmes and I had met when I was fifteen, and I became, in effect, his
apprentice. Under his guidance, I harnessed my angry intelligence, I found
a direction for my life, and I came to terms with my past. When I was eighteen, we worked together on a series of cases, which culminated with finding ourselves the target of one of the cleverest, most deadly criminals he
had ever faced. After that case, I was an apprentice no longer—I was, at
the age of nineteen, a full partner.

I was now twenty-three, though considerably older internally than the
calendar would suggest. However, for the last year and a half the partnership had been, in some ways, in abeyance. We had worked together on only
two serious cases since our marriage. Instead, I had immersed myself in the
rarefied air of Oxford, where I was beginning to make a name for myself in
the more abstruse divisions of academic theology. My only real contact with
the art of detection for some months had been in its theoretical aspects as
I helped Holmes with his magnum opus on that subject. Holmes had, I re-
alized now, been waiting, and now his world had come again to lay claim
upon me.

As if to underscore the point my thoughts had reached as I lay back in
the chair with my eyes closed, half-drowsing, I felt my left hand taken up.
In the silence of our breathing, he began to explore my hand with his, in
a slow, almost impersonal manner that left me unaware of anything else in
the universe. He ran his smooth, cool fingertips along each of my fingers,
exploring the swell of the knuckles and the shape of my nails, teasing the
tiny hairs, probing the soft webs between the fingers and the joint of the
thumb and the tendons and the large vein up to the wrist, arousing the skin
and the hand itself to a most extraordinary pitch of awareness. He ended,
at the point when the exquisite sensations threatened to become unbear-
able, by raising my hand almost formally to his lips, lingering there for an
instant, and then restoring it to me.

I sat for a long moment, eyes closed as before, but glowing now and no
longer in the least drowsy, and said what was foremost in my mind.

"What is troubling you, husband?"

I thought he would not answer me. Eventually, he disentangled himself
and reached forward to knock his pipe out with unnecessary violence into
the pristine fireplace.

"Data," he said, sounding like a man pleading for water in a desert place.
"I cannot form so much as an hypothesis without raw material."

I waited, but no more was forthcoming. He sucked at the empty pipe stem and squinted at the mantelpiece as if there were words to be deciphered in the grain of the wood. I finally broke the silence.

"Yes, we need more information. Neither Lestrade's information nor Mycroft's has changed that. Assuming that I followed your train of thought this evening, this means that you will have to go to Mrs Rogers, while I ingratiate myself to Colonel Edwards. I ask you again, why does this trouble you?"

"I don't—" He stopped, then continued more quietly. "I do not know why, and I realise it is unreasonable, but I find that the idea of your being in the colonel's house makes me profoundly uneasy. It brings to mind the day we returned from Palestine all those years ago, when I stood on the boat and watched you walk away, completely exposed, while I knew full well that the trap we were setting might catch you instead. It was, I think, the hardest thing I have ever done."

"Holmes," I said, startled into speech, "are you going all sentimental on me?"

"No, you're right, that would never do. What I am trying to say in my feeble male way is that I cannot think why the idea troubles me. I cannot see any signs of a trap, I could detect no threat in his manner when I met him, and I cannot put my finger on any one piece of data that makes me mistrust him. It is a totally irrational reaction on my part, but nonetheless, the thought of placing you within his reach disturbs me greatly."

I sat speechless. In a minute, he went on, his voice muffled by my hair. "My dear Russell. Many years ago, in my foolish youth, I thought I should never marry. I was quite convinced that strong emotion interfered with rational thought, like grit in a sensitive instrument. I believed the heart to be a treacherous organ which served only to cloud the mind, and now . . . now I find myself in the disturbing position of having my mind at odds with—with the rest of me. Once I would have automatically followed the dictates of the reasoning mind. However." I could feel his breath warm on my scalp. "I begin to suspect that—I shall say this quietly—that I was wrong, that there may be times when the heart sees something which the mind does not. Perhaps what we call the heart is simply a more efficient means of evaluating data. Perhaps I mistrust it because I cannot see the mechanism working. Perhaps it is time for me to retire once and for all. Do not worry," he said in response to my brief stir of protest, "I shall see this case to its end before I turn to learning Syriac and Aramaic and spending my days correcting your manuscripts. Until then, however, we must assume that the old man still possesses his full wits and that his nerviness is not unjustified. Take care in that house, please, Russ. For God's sake, don't be absentminded."

Holmes, although as energetic and scrupulously attentive to detail in the physical aspects of marriage as ever he was in an investigation or laboratory experiment, was not otherwise a man demonstrative of his affections (a statement which will come as no surprise to any of Dr Watson's readers). His proposal of marriage was less a proposal than a challenge flung, and expressions of affection tended towards the low-key and everyday rather than the dramatic and intermittent. I believe the reason for this was that I had become by that time too much a part of him to be the focus of the great alternating sweeps of manic passion and grey despair that had been characteristic of his earlier life. At any rate, I answered him lightly, but acknowledging his serious intent.

"You have succeeded in setting my nerves on edge, I assure you. At the slightest creak of a floorboard, I'll be out of there like a shot."

# PART THREE

## Tuesday, 28 August 1923– Saturday, 1 September 1923

*In a man's letters his soul lies naked.*

—Samuel Johnson

# TWELVE

*mu*

T

uesday was a day of preparation, a time of backstage hustle and the anticipatory discord of instruments tuning. I spent the better part of the morning in the shops, assembling a wardrobe appropriate to a salesgirl or a colonel's secretary, and most of the afternoon rendering my purchases down into a state of shabby gentility by the judicious use of too-hot water and an overheated iron, and by replacing the odd button with one that almost matched. Shoes were a problem, but in the end I settled on a good pair, for the strength of the heel and the relative comfort of the toe, and added a patina of age with grit and a poorly matched polish. The effect I was aiming for was someone who understood quality but couldn't quite afford it. Beyond this, my character's clothing needed to be innocently seductive, with the emphasis on innocence. Young, naïve, unprotected, determined, and a bit scared—that was the image I held in front of me as I tried on white lawn blouses, looked at embroidered collars, and studied the effects of different sleeves. I even bought six lacy handkerchiefs embroidered with the letter M.

Holmes came in at three o'clock. He had left immediately after breakfast, dressed in a singularly Lestradian brown suit (the sort that is obviously purchased with an eye to shoulder seams and the amount of wear the knees will take), a soft brown hat that looked as if it had shrunk in the rain, a new-school tie, and sturdy shoes, sporting a moustache that resembled a dead mouse and a tuft of whiskers in the hollow of his left jaw that the razor had missed. He returned smooth of chin and sleek of hair, gloriously resplendent in an utterly black City suit cut to perfection and a shirt like the sun on new snow, a tie whose pattern was unfamiliar to me but which evoked immense dignity and importance, cuff links of jet with a thread of mother-of-pearl, shoes like dancing pumps, a stick of ebony and silver, and a hat ever so slightly dashing about the brim but of the degree of self-assurance that guarantees there will be no label inside. Under his arm, he carried a bulky, roughly entwined brown paper parcel that reeked of mildew and the cleansing solution used in gaols and hospitals.

"Natty duds, Holmes," I commented deflatingly, and turned to hang another maltreated, over-ironed blouse from the door frame. Mycroft's rooms smelt like a bad laundry, all steam and scorched cotton, and now the added aromas from Holmes' bundle. "What is the tie from?"

He tossed his load down on a chair, where it burst open and began to leak garments that looked as unsavoury as they smelt. He fingered the scrap of silk on his breast.

"The Royal Order of Nigerian Blacksmiths," he said. "I am actually entitled to wear it, Russell. For services rendered." He eyed the dress I was systematically attacking, looked at it more closely in disbelief, and threaded his way past me and under my finished garments to our rooms. I heard the door of one of the phalanx of wardrobes click open, followed by the clatter of clothes hangers. I raised my voice a fraction.

"You know, Holmes, if Lestrade finds you've been impersonating a police detective, he'll be furious."

"One cannot impersonate what one is in fact, Russell," came his imperious and muffled reply. "Is anyone more a citizen of this *polis* than I? Is anyone more a detective? Where then lies the falsehood?" He reappeared, fastening the cuffs of a less dramatic shirt. "The pursuit of justice may be the trade of a few men, but is the business of all," he pronounced sententiously.

"Save it for the warders," I suggested, and bent down to rip out some threads from the back seam of a sleeve. "Did you find us rooms?"

"I found many things this day, including, yes, rooms. Two adjoining, ill-furnished and underlit rooms with a bath down the hall and back windows five feet above a shed roof. No bedbugs, though. I looked."

"Thank you. What else did you find?"

"An uninspired kitchen and mends in the curtains."

Very well, if he wanted to tantalise me, I would allow him to prolong the telling of what he had discovered while masquerading as a Yard detective.

"How did you find them? The rooms, I mean. Mycroft?"

"No, actually, the house belongs to a cousin of Billy's."

"Billy! I should have known. How is he?" Billy had come into Holmes' employ from the streets as a child and, as far as I could tell, remained willing to drop everything to serve his former master. A thought occurred to me, and I interrupted the description of Billy's ventures into the retail trade and his convoluted family life.

"Is he going to be keeping an eye on me?"

"Do you mind?"

With the morning's shopping successfully behind me and the knowledge of a husband who was no longer bored, I was willing to be benign.

"I don't want him following me about, no, but if he wants to loiter in the hallway listening for gurgled screams, he's quite welcome." I threaded a needle and started to mend the seam I had just picked out.

"He won't be following you, just available if you need auxiliary troops or messenger boys. He has turned into quite a sensible person." High praise indeed.

"That's fine, then. And you—you won't be coming back from Cambridgeshire every night, I take it?"

"I doubt it. It would look exceedingly odd for a member of the nation's great unwashed and unemployed to board the nightly five-nineteen for St Pancras. Too, I hope to worm myself into Mrs Rogers's affections to the extent of dossing down in her toolshed. I shall return Friday night. If you need to reach me before that, send Billy, or have Lestrade send a constable around to pick me up on a vagrancy charge."

"I assume Lestrade will have to agree to all this?"

"Oh yes. Unofficially, of course, but thanks to Mycroft, that will not pose a problem. Lestrade will take care that any police investigator who comes to one of the houses will either not know us or else be warned we're there and not to take any notice."

"Is there a telephone at the house of Billy's cousin?"

"You sound like a poor translation out of the French, Russell. But yes, there is a telephone at the house of the cousin of my friend. Utilize *chez*, feminine singular, masculine singular."

"And to his wife the unwashed tramp will telephone, is that not so?"

"But yes, with regularity the tramp his wife in the boarding house will telephone."

"*Merci, monsieur.*"

"*De rien, madame.*" He walked over to where I stood, took my free hand, and ceremoniously slipped off the gold band I wore. "*Mad'moiselle.*" He examined my fingers and tapped the pale shadow of the ring. "Put some dye on that," he ordered.

I dropped my stitching abruptly.

"All right, Holmes, what is it? What did you learn today?"

His eyes flared with gratified amusement, and he wandered over to the fireplace to fill his pipe from the tobacco cache Mycroft kept there.

"Your Miss Ruskin had something of value when she entered the country. Or at any rate, something she valued highly. It took her two hours to negotiate the distance between Victoria Station and her hotel, which could hardly have taken a full hour if she'd walked, dragging her suitcases behind her. Inspector Jack Rafferty, one of Lestrade's unrecognised Irregulars, discovered that the distinctive figure of Miss Dorothy Ruskin had deposited two leather valises with the left-luggage gentleman at Victoria, then reclaimed them nearly two hours later. He furthermore discovered, pursuant to his aforementioned investigation—do you know, Russell, I believe I shall write a monograph on the obfuscating peculiarities of constabulary vocabulary and syntax—that said Miss Ruskin had subsequently paid visits to no fewer than three banking establishments in the immediate vicinity—is it as difficult to listen to as it is to produce?"

"It is certainly tedious," I agreed, my head bent again over the seam.

"Good. Miss Ruskin was looking for a bank that would allow her access to its safety-deposit boxes outside of the normal bankers' hours. The first two seemed to consider her some sort of eccentric, I cannot think why, but the third bank was quite happy to oblige—it is owned by Americans, who are notoriously willing to cater to any behavioural oddity if the customer is willing to pay. She let a box for one week only, and into it she put a small parcel, wrapped in a checked cloth, and a thick manila envelope."

"They revealed all this to Inspector Jack Rafferty, the man with the dead mouse on his lip? I'd have thought even my fellow Americans would have some standards when it came to professional discretion, much less their employees."

"My dear child, what do you take me for? As soon as I realised what she was about, I nipped around the corner to change my persona." To one of his bolt-holes, I interpreted, those scattered and invisible hideaways that served as combined retreats and dressing rooms. I finished the seam and bit off the thread, admired the puckered stitching, and hung up the blouse.

"Holmes, I admit your infinite appeal in that gorgeous suit, but was that sufficient to crack the reserve of a senior bank official?"

"Ah, well, no. It happened that the bank manager is a sort of distant family connection. Second cousin twice removed sort of thing." I looked at him in surprise.

"Good Lord. I'm always forgetting that you have a family. You and Mycroft seem to have sprung full-formed from the brow of London."

"I haven't seen the man in twenty years and probably would not have recognised him had it not been for his nameplate. He certainly did not recognise me, but after a few of these gruesome cocktails everyone's tossing back these days, he became quite the old gossip. I fear I shall have to open an account there and demand the odd service at inconvenient hours to justify the curious slant of my questions."

I wondered if any blood tie had actually existed before that morning but decided not to press the matter.

"I take it that the cloth-wrapped parcel was the box. Was there any indication what the envelope contained?"

"No. But she returned to the bank twice: once early Tuesday, and again just before opening on Wednesday. At which time, unfortunately, she closed out her account and declared she had no further use for the deposit box."

"Oh dear."

"Yes. I had hopes in that box. It might have held documents, or treasure, or at the very least a will. But—nothing."

"So she only used it on Tuesday to fetch whatever was in the envelope and on Wednesday to remove the box and bring it to Sussex."

"So it would appear."

"Where, then, did she take the envelope on Tuesday?"

"Indeed. The other question being . . ."

I paused for a brief moment in my abuse of another defenceless frock in order to think.

"Did she wish to protect the envelope and the box in general, or did she envisage some specific threat to them during her trip to Cambridgeshire?"

"Excellent," he said.

"Elementary," I replied, and ripped off another button.


Lestrade rang up as we sat down to tea, to say that he had no further information and that he was being called off to Shropshire. Did we want him to send another inspector to take his place? he asked. Holmes settled himself next to the telephone with his cup and told Lestrade how we intended to obtain information concerning Colonel Edwards and Mrs Rogers. Their conversation took up an excessive amount of time, but there was never really any doubt about the outcome. Lestrade's objections were finally worn down against the grit of Holmes' determination and the hard fact of his authority, unofficial though it might be, and he submitted to Holmes' suggestion that we meet again on Friday. The field was cleared for our hunt.

\*   \*   \*

When I came into the dining room the next morning, following my lengthy toilette, Mycroft choked on his coffee and Holmes' face turned dark.

"I knew I should have left before you," he muttered. "Good Lord, Russell, is all that really necessary?"

"You told me what he was like, Holmes, so you have only yourself to blame."

He stood up abruptly and picked up the greasy rucksack that lay near the door. His unshaven cheeks and bleary eyes matched the clothes he wore, and I had absolutely no desire to embrace him with a demonstrative farewell. He paused at the door and looked me over, his expression unreadable even to me.

"I feel like father Abraham," he said, and my astonishment was such that it took nearly two seconds before the penny dropped. I began to laugh.

"If I am Sarah, I don't believe any Pharaoh on earth would mistake me for your sister. Good heavens, Holmes, shall I never get your limits? I didn't know you'd ever read the book."

"I was once snowed in with a group of missionaries near the Khyber Pass. It was either the Bible in my cubicle or their conversation in the common room. Good-bye, Russell. Take care of yourself."

"Until Friday, Holmes."

He left, and as I walked over to pour myself some coffee, the bemused expression on Mycroft's face caught my eye. I stirred the cup and said casually, "We said our fond good-byes earlier." He went blank for a moment, then flushed deeply, scarlet up into the reaches of his thinning hair, stood up, and bustled his way out the door, leaving the field to a thin young woman in a skimpy frock, laughing silently into her cup.

After breakfast, I went back and stood in front of the full-length mirror to study my reflection and to assume my rôle. The clothing, hair, and makeup went some long way towards the personality of Mary Small, but my normal stance and movements inside those clothes would create a glaring incongruity. The dress I wore was a light and frivolous summer frock, white cotton sprigged with blue flowers, a touch of lace at the Peter Pan collar and along the lower edge of the sleeves. The fabric and lace gave it an old-fashioned air, but the thin body-revealing drape and the length of the skirt (hemlines had dropped that year, and the shopkeeper had been irritated when I insisted that she raise mine to the extremes of the previous year) would have been considered inappropriate even for a child in Edwardian times. My arms looked thin and long beneath the short puffed sleeves, my legs even longer, and I reflected idly that my currently fashionable outline would no doubt have been someone's despair twenty years ago, when corsets and bustles filled in nature's wants. The heels on my shoes were higher than I was accustomed to and turned my stride into an indecisive wobble. I hoped I would not break an ankle. I bent around to examine the seams on my stockings. I had bought several pairs of sheer silk stockings, an extravagance for Mary Small, but if the colonel was a man who admired extremities, as I suspected he would be, the effect would be well worth it. My eyes told me that my ankles and several inches of calf were quite appealing, but then Holmes' reaction had already confirmed that.

I studied my reflection, starting at the top: cloche hat drawn to my eyebrows, hair beneath it in a prim bun which would soften as the day went on. I coaxed a few wisps to lie across my cheek and touch the neck of my frock. No earrings. I retrieved my makeup box, with which I had already lightened my brown skin, and added to the faint shadow under my cheekbones, to help me look slightly underfed. Taking off my spectacles, I rubbed a tiny smudge of purple into the skin under my eyes. The eyes were the hardest thing to disguise, always. One flash of intelligence at the wrong time could undo all my work. The horn-rimmed glasses with lightly tinted lenses I pulled on helped, and they made my face seem even more ethereal behind them. They would also serve to make me look naked when I removed them.

My chin was too strong. I practised dropping it, and my eyes. Shoulders drooping, as if the world was just a bit too heavy. Back and hips were already rearranged because of the shoes. I spent nearly an hour walking up and down in front of the mirror, refining the hang of my arms, the awkwardness of my hands in their demure white gloves, and the angle of my head. I sat in various chairs to practise until the seduction of my silken legs was completely unconscious. I lit a cigarette and coughed violently until I recalled the knack of diluting the smoke with air. Mary Small would definitely smoke, half-defiant, half-guilty. She also bit her nails—off came the gloves and I got to work with the nail scissors.

Finally, I could think of no other preparation—the rest of Mary Small would make herself known to me as the day went on. I stood in front of the mirror, and there she was, a young woman with my features but bearing almost no resemblance to Mary Russell in all the essentials. The doorman did not recognise me as he let me out of Mycroft's building. Cheap suitcase in hand, I went to stalk my prey.

I ran him to ground that evening, though I had known for some hours precisely where he was. At two in the afternoon, the omnibus had let me off at the bottom end of what had once been a village high street. I stood for a moment to survey the ground (without the suitcase, which lay in the wardrobe of the boardinghouse room Holmes had let) and was well pleased by what I saw.

It was ideal for my purposes, an area of London that yet preserved the social structures of the village it had been in the not-too-distant past, before London in one of its spasms of growth had surrounded it, found it impossible to incorporate due to a scrap of canal and the slightly inconvenient angle of its high street, and then, like an oyster with a piece of grit, had smoothed the foreign object's uncomfortable edges with a couple of thoroughfares and a bridge, and moved on, leaving the village, its two pubs and a post office, its church, shops, and teahouse, engulfed but more or less intact.

Some hours later, from my table in the front window of that same teahouse, I watched Col. Dennis Edwards walk through the doors of the Pig and Whistle public house. I had taken the table an hour before and had spent the time eating sandwiches and chatting with the waitress-owner. She now knew that I was new to the area and looking for work. I knew that she had corns, five children (one of whom was in trouble over a small matter of removing from a store an item of clothing for which she had neglected to pay), and a husband who drank when he was at home, that her mother had piles, her elderly Jack Russell terrier had become incontinent and she was afraid he would have to be put down, and that she had an appointment the following week to have the last of her teeth out. I also had somewhat less thorough but equally intimate biographies of half the inhabitants of the neighbourhood, including the occupant of "that great ugly house behind the wall up there," Col. Dennis Edwards. That gentleman, whom she seemed to think almost was but wasn't quite, had shown himself to be a parsimonious customer on the rare occasions that he ventured into Rosie's Tea Shoppe, had difficulties keeping female servants ("not that he's improper, mind, it's his temper, don't you know, specially when he's been at the bottle"), had a "real looker" of a son with roving hands, whose drinking habits were similar to those of the father, though he was happy rather than mean-tempered when in his cups. A fountain of information was our Rosie. She told me happily about the colonel's wife, who had died of pneumonia during the war, about his servants and his cars, his dogs and visitors, what he ate and how much he drank, where his clothes came from and her estimate of his net worth. I listened until she began to repeat herself, and I then commented on the young couple who walked past the window holding each other upright and listened with equal interest to ten minutes of their personal habits. Finally, I rose, thinking that the half hour he had been in the pub should have softened him and knowing that if I had to listen to Rosie's tumbling monotone for another minute, I should go mad. I left her a decent tip and took my sore feet off to the Pig and Whistle for something more fortifying than Rosie's tea.

I walked slowly, studying the contents of shop windows, until I stood looking in through the wall of small panes that formed the front of the pub, as if attracted by the warmth within. Two nights before, it would have been stifling inside, but the temperature had dropped at least twenty degrees in the past twenty-four hours, and most of the clientèle who would have been standing on the pavement were now inside. It did look warm and comforting, with its wooden walls, polished bar, and even a patch of orange-and-brown carpet on the floor. At the far right, I saw a boisterous party in a booth, the table littered with bottles and empty glasses. Two young women sat laughing uproariously at the antics of one of the men, who was hurling darts with exaggerated fury towards a frayed-looking target on an equally frayed wall. A man in a crisp black suit sat with his back to the window, watching the darts players. Two greying ladies whom I had seen earlier that day sat with a pair of strangely coloured drinks, vaguely green and unpleasant. Had I seen them in the knitting-wool shop? No, it had been the stationers, where I had purchased a lined notebook. A man and a woman stood behind the bar, the man pulling a pint for a second black-suited man and talking sideways to the woman in a way that spoke of a long, comfortable marriage. And there, halfway between me and the bar, was the object of my interest, a sturdy, moustachioed man nursing a glass of what I took to be whisky, watching the darts game.

I straightened my thin shoulders, summoned up a nest of mouselike thoughts, and walked in. The man in the dark suit stood with two glasses on the bar in front of him while he counted out a handful of coins. He slapped them down on the bar, made a remark to the owner, who laughed, and picked up the two brimming glasses. He ran his eyes across me, then, to my relief, he walked past the colonel's booth to join the similarly dressed man at the front window. I needed the colonel alone.

"Get you something, miss?" I turned to the publican, who smiled encouragingly to keep me from bolting out his door. I fiddled with the clasp on my handbag, then took a few steps towards him and opened my mouth to speak, but a great burst of laughter from the dartboard brought me to a stop. I glanced over at that side of the room, and on their way back, my eyes were caught by those of the colonel, who had turned around at the publican's question. I twitched him a shy smile, then looked back at the man waiting behind the bar.

"Yes, yes, please. May I have—oh, let me see, a sherry perhaps? Yes, a sherry. Oh, sweet, I think. Oh, yes, that would be fine, thank you." I counted the money from my little purse and picked up the glass, thanked the publican again, smiled at his wife, eyed the room indecisively, smiled again briefly at the man with the moustaches, and made my hesitant way past him to a chair at a table next to the window, a location that just happened to put me ten feet from him, at an angle that I could not see him without moving my chair, yet where he could hardly miss having me in full view at all times. I settled myself, and, since a goat tethered out in the jungle is of no use if it simply stands there quietly, I began my routine of helpless bleating, calling the tiger in to me.

I started by removing my gloves, shunning for the moment the obvious ruse of dropping one on the floor, and tucking my hair back into place. I sipped at my drink without gagging on the cloyingly sweet stuff, took a magazine from my handbag, and then let it fall shut after two minutes. I slipped my shoes off under the table and surreptitiously leant down to massage my feet, stared out the window at the receding tide of foot and vehicular traffic, froze in apprehension when the voices of the darts players erupted into anger, then gradually relaxed when the publican's wife put herself into the middle of it, turning it into a joke. After ten minutes, my glass was nearly empty, my eyes were smarting from the smoke and the fumes, and I was beginning to wonder how I could put myself any closer to Colonel Edwards without being obvious. I pulled off the heavy spectacles and folded them carefully on the table, then sat rubbing the bridge of my nose. There came a movement from behind me, male voices at the bar. I held my breath. If he decided to leave, I should have to play this all over again tomorrow. A dreary thought.

A large moving object came to a halt next to my left elbow. I took my face from my hands to look up, startled, at the man beside me, into a face ruddy with whisky and weather, a wide nose over a trimmed moustache, sand beginning to grey, that gave way to a full mouth and an ever so slightly weak chin. His expression was half-paternal, half-interested male. Ideal, I thought, if only he didn't look so much like Uncle John. Actually, it was the moustache that brought John Watson to mind, but I cautioned myself that I would have to beware of the affection I felt for Holmes' longtime partner and biographer. This man was not Uncle John.

He was holding out a glass, of the same sweet stuff I had been drinking. His smile broadened at my confusion, and I reached for my spectacles.

"I thought you might like a refill."

"Oh, well, yes, thank you. It's most kind of you, but I don't usually drink more than one."

"Well, you can't refuse a gift, can you? Besides, you looked all alone over here, and we can't have that, not at the Pig and Whistle."

"Oh no, I'm not all alone. I mean, I am alone, but not—oh dear, that's not coming out right, is it? Please sit down." I fumbled my shoes back on and straightened my back.

He placed his glass on the table and took possession of the chair across from me. He was a big man, not tall, but with broad shoulders and a bit of a belly to show for his intemperate habits. Erect bearing, still the military man.

"Colonel Dennis Edwards, at your service, miss." His hand sketched a humorous salute, and he grinned. Oh dear, I thought, what a very nice smile.

"Mary Small," I said, and held out my right hand to have the fingers shaken. Instead, he took my hand and raised it to his lips. I blushed. Yes, truly I did, although the wine helped. He was greatly amused.

"Miss Small—it is Miss, I trust?" I inclined my head. Direct lies were the most difficult, although Mary Small was not a married woman. "Miss Small, I don't believe I've seen you here before, have I?"

"No, I'm new to the area, Colonel Edwards."

"I thought as much. I didn't think I could overlook such a flower as yourself."

I did not know quite how to respond to this, and I decided that Mary Small did not know, either. I smiled awkwardly and sipped my sherry, grateful for the sandwiches I had eaten to absorb the alcohol. The colonel soon fetched yet another round, which left me feeling quite warm and seemed not to affect him, beyond stepping up his volubility. He talked about this neighbourhood as if it were his personal possession, told me about the process by which it was being swallowed by greedy London town, told me about his army career. He talked; I listened. Mary Small seemed very good at listening, first to Rosie, now to the colonel. In fact, people responded to her shyness with words, pouring out their life stories. By eight o'clock, two of the darts players had joined us, the publican's wife, and the publican himself occasionally, all apparently set on thrusting their personal histories on this tall, quiet, pale young woman in the tinted glasses. I have no great head for alcohol, and although I had managed quietly to rid myself of almost half of what was brought me, I had drunk more in the last couple of hours than I normally drank in a week. I felt flushed all over, my hair was coming down, the loud voices battered my senses, and a high and nagging voice spoke in my ear, warning me that I was going to make an awful mistake if I was not careful.

I rose abruptly, and five sets of eyes looked up at me uncertainly. I faced the wife and asked, with immense dignity, for the use of her facilities.

When I returned a few minutes later, considerably cooler and my hair under control, the party had broken up, but the colonel remained, and he stood when I entered.

"Miss Small, it occurs to me that neither of us have dined. Would you care to join me? Just a simple meal. There's a nice restaurant up the street."

This is really too easy, I thought happily.

"Oh, Colonel, it would be lovely, but I have to be up early tomorrow. I have an interview for a position at eight-thirty on the other side of town, and I really mustn't miss it, I'm getting—well, the situation is becoming a bit urgent. I must find work by the end of the week, or—well, I must, that's all. So I'd enjoy having dinner with you, but—"

"But of course you'll have dinner with me. Just a quick dinner, nothing fancy, and we'll have you in early. Where are you living?"

I told him where the boardinghouse was located and protested weakly, but of course he overrode my objections, and so we went to dinner. It was a pleasant-enough meal, and the wine was superb, causing me to regret the earlier alcoholic treacle that I had swallowed. The colonel drank my share, however, and seemed to enjoy it. I heard more of his story, his love for hunting, the book he was writing, his cars. Finally, over coffee, he fell silent, and as I looked down at my cup, I felt his eyes on me for a long minute.

"Don't go to that interview tomorrow," he said. I raised my eyes in surprise.

"Oh, but I must. I can't afford to miss the chance. I have to find work, I told you. If I don't, I shall be forced to go home." I made it sound most unpleasant.

"Where is home?"

"Oxfordshire. Outside Didcot." Not too far from the truth.

"And what do you do, that you interview for?" Here it came.

"Oh, anything, really. Except cooking," I had to add in all honesty. "I'm hopeless in the kitchen. But anything else. The interview tomorrow is for a personal secretary, which would be ideal. Correspondence, typing, a bit of research—she's a writer—driving. All things I can do, and it pays well. I can't let it go by," I repeated.

"Certainly you can. Come work for me."

The jackpot. O frabjous day! I thought, but I put on a face full of distress and embarrassment.

"Oh, Colonel, I couldn't do that. It's terribly nice of you to be concerned about me, and I do truly appreciate it, but I couldn't possibly take advantage of your kindness."

"It's not kindness; it's a job offer. My own secretary left several weeks ago," (slammed out of the house after the colonel had emptied a desk drawer over her head, according to Tea Shoppe Rosie) "and the work's been piling up ever since. And, as I said, I'm writing a book, and you say you can do research. I've never been much for libraries. Plus that, you drive. I don't. I get tired of taking taxis on my chauffeur's days off. What do you say?"

"Are you serious, Colonel Edwards?"

"Absolutely. What was the pay at the other job?"

I told him a figure, he increased it 10 percent, I protested that he didn't know my qualifications, said I refused to accept charity, so he lowered it to 5 percent, with the other 5 percent to come after review in a month. As I had no intention whatsoever of being with him in a month, I accepted, with the proper degree of gratitude and confusion. This pleased him greatly, and a bit later, after much brandy and talk, he accompanied me to Billy's cousin's boardinghouse with a proud, almost possessive set to his jaw and shoulders. As I closed the door and heard the taxi drive off, I couldn't help wondering if he thought he had bought me or won me, and further, if he would see a difference in the two.

I unbuckled the straps of my oppressive shoes and walked in stockinged feet through the still house, through the odours of tinned curry powder and stale cabbage and underwashed bodies, up the worn stair runners to my room. I turned up the gas with an irrational pang of hope that Holmes (with that customary disregard of his for agreed-to plans that made it impossible to depend on his whereabouts) might be revealed in a corner, but I saw only a slip of paper that someone had pushed under the door. It was from my landlady, to inform me that a gentleman had rung twice and would telephone again tomorrow night.

Tonight, really, I saw from my watch. So much for an early dinner. The realisation of the hour and the sudden contrast of stillness and solitude after the long, tense day made me feel dizzy, but I knew I could never sleep, not until my brain slowed down. I undressed mechanically, brushed out my hair at the leprous mirror, and thought.

I had to admit, grudgingly and to myself, that a part of me liked this man Edwards. The part of me that was closest to Mary Small responded to him and thought how very pleasant the evening had been. He was intelligent, if not particularly brilliant, and had an easy way of understanding how to make people relax and enjoy themselves. He had probably been a very good commander of men, with that ability. He had made me laugh several times, despite my (and my character's) anxiety.

Physically, he was the complete opposite of Holmes. Scarcely my height, he was heavily muscled and gave the impression of power. Even his expensive suit rode uneasily on his shoulders, but my mind skittered away from the thought that he would look most natural with few clothes on. His hair was still full and only beginning to show grey at the temples and ears. He seemed to be a hairy man, for in the restaurant the light had reflected from a dark copper fur on the backs of his broad hands and thick fingers, and his cheeks had shown stubble by midnight. Odd for a man with hair of that colour, I thought absently.

Yes, Mary Small had liked him, had, in fact, found him attractive. Sweet, protected virgin that she was, she found his attention and authority flattering. Russell, however—that was another matter. As Mary Small began to fade in the mirror and I continued to analyse the evening's currents, I found that I was, underneath, distinctly annoyed. What another woman might find appealingly masculine, I reflected, was also just plain boorish. From the first glass of sherry, unasked for and unwanted, to the dinner menu, ordered without consultation, the evening had been one of not-so-subtle manipulation and domination. It was, admittedly, the usual thing, but I did not like it one bit.

I studied my face and asked it why this was troubling me. Was it not precisely how I had planned it, down to my worn lace collars and crippling shoes? He had responded in exactly the way I had wanted. Why, then, was I not sitting here gloating? Part of the problem, I knew, was the sour feeling that comes with practising deceit on an innocent, and after all, he might be completely without blame in Miss Ruskin's death. That was compounded by the fact that I liked him as a person, but it was not all.

I sat enfolded by the boardinghouse, silent but for a rumbling snore from somewhere above me, and knew that I was apprehensive—no, to be truthful, I was almost frightened, by the man's strength. I had laughed at his jokes, even the ones I would normally find tasteless, and I had acquiesced to his decisions, completely, naturally. There was no doubt in my mind that this was a contest, but we were each playing a different game, by different rules, and I suddenly felt very unsure of myself, as inexperienced as Mary Small in the ways of dealing with men. I felt ill from the food and the drink and the smoke, and most especially from the words, the spate of words that had pushed and prodded and battered me all evening. I ached for Holmes, for the sureness of his hands and his quiet voice, and I wondered where he was sleeping that night.

The thought of Holmes steadied me. I looked grimly at my shadowed reflection and told myself, Enough of this, Mary Russell. You are here to track down the person who murdered a good woman, a friend. You are the former apprentice and now full partner of the best man in the business. You have a quick, trained mind that is second to few and certainly better than that of Col. Dennis Edwards. And you are the daughter of Judith Klein, who was by no means small in spirit. This rôle calls for caution and a sure touch, but it is nothing to be overwhelmed by, and you will not be intimidated by a large middle-aged man with overactive glands and hairy hands.

I went to bed then and listened to the night sounds of the city. With dim surprise, I realised that it was one week since Dorothy Ruskin had died, one week and a couple of hours and three miles from the site. I slept eventually, although I did not sleep well.

# THIRTEEN

## ν

*nu*

The rain started during the night, in its typical understated London fashion. The grumble of distant thunder grew imperceptibly from the dying roar of the traffic, and the eventual rustle of drops on stones and slate gradually came to underlie what passed in London for a quiet night. Nothing dramatic, just dull London wetness. I huddled under my black umbrella in the bus queue the next morning and thought, Here I cannot even turn to my neighbours and say how good it is for the crops—they'd look at me as if I were from another planet.

I escaped from the crowded omnibus and its smell of wet wool a full twenty minutes early, so I went into Rosie's for a cuppa to start the day. Rosie was busy, but she sloshed my tea with affection and asked what I was doin' out so early.

"I found a position! I start with Colonel Edwards this morning. I met him at the pub last night and he said he needed a secretary, and he hired me."

Rosie froze, and her face travelled through surprise and appraisal to suspicion and reappraisal, then ended up at a politely noncommittal "Good for you, dearie, so I guess we'll be seein' summat of you."

Ten minutes later, I splashed up the drive to my new job, berating myself. Fine detective you make, Russell, I thought. Can't even play a rôle without worrying about what a complete stranger thinks of you. I shook the water from my umbrella, squared my meek shoulders, and rang the bell.

The work of any decent detective is at least nine-tenths monotony, despite the invariably brisk pace of any detective novel, or even a police file, for that matter. Take, for example, the accounts written by Dr Watson of the earlier cases of Holmes: They give the overall impression of the detective leaping into the fray, grasping the single most vital clue in an instant, and wrestling energetically with the case until all is neatly solved. There is little indication of the countless hours spent in cold, cramped watch over a doorway, of days spent in dusty records rooms and libraries, of the tantalising trails that fade away into nothing—all are passed over with a laconic reference to the passage of time. Of course, Watson was often brought in only at the end of a case, and so he missed the tedium. I could not.

I will not recount the secretarial work I did for Colonel Edwards, because to do so would bore even the writer to tears. Suffice it to say that for the next few days I was a secretary: I filed and organised, I typed, and I took dictation. At the same time, of course, I had my ears fully cocked and my eyes into everything, at every moment. I listened in on telephone calls when I could, hearing long, dreary, manly conversations about dead birds and alcoholic beverages. I went systematically through each filing cabinet until my fingers and back cramped, and I dutifully chatted with the servants whenever I could manage to happen across them, receiving mostly monosyllabic grunts for my pains. No, if I wanted a life filled with nonstop excitement and challenge, I should not choose the life of a detective. High-wire acrobatics, perhaps, or teaching twelve-year-olds, or motherhood, but not detecting.

It is endurance that wins the case, not short bursts of flashy footwork (though those, too, have their place.) For the next days, I soaked up all possible information about Colonel Edwards and the people around him: his eating and drinking habits, what he read, how he slept, his likes, dislikes, passions, and hates—all the urges and habits that made the man.

The first day, Thursday, I spent all morning with the colonel in his upstairs study, sorting out correspondence and putting things to order. We ate lunch together in the study, and afterwards he showed me, almost shyly, the first pages of his book on Egypt in the years preceding the war. I promised to take it home and study it, which seemed to please him. We then sat down to dictation.

The first letters were to the managers of two manufacturing businesses, concerned with the upcoming yearly reports. The third was a short letter to a friend confirming a weekend bird-slaughtering party in September. ("Do much shooting, Miss Small?" "Why, no, Colonel." "Invigorating way to spend a holiday. Of course, it takes some strength to use a bird-gun." "Does it, Colonel? It sounds jolly fun.") The fourth was to a bank manager, with details for increasing the monthly allowance for the colonel's son, Gerald, when he returned to Cambridge. (Thank God it's Cambridge, I thought, and not Oxford. I'm not exactly unknown there.) The fifth was of considerable interest to me, addressed to a friend, concerning a comember of an organisation whose name set off bells. It read:

Dear Brooks,

I've been doing a lot of thinking about the little flap-up last week, and I have come to the conclusion that I shall have to resign from the Friends. It was a downright nasty trick Lawson played on me, keeping information from me until the last minute like that. I was the chair of that committee, after all, and it makes me look a damned ('I beg your pardon, Miss Small, change that to *confounded*, would you please?') fool not to know it was a woman I was meeting.

His supporters seem to have rallied round, and there's little chance he'll resign. If he apologises, I might reconsider, but not otherwise.

My best to the missus, and hope to see you both on the twenty-fourth.

Dennis Edwards

I did not think his resignation threat referred to the Society of Friends.

Two other letters followed, but I recorded them mechanically, taking little notice of their content other than seeing that they had nothing to do with my interests.

"That's it for today, Miss Small. Do you want to read them back to me before you type them?"

"If you like, but I think they're quite clear."

"Didn't go too fast for you, did I? Let me see."

"No, not at all. Oh, do you read shorthand?"

"I read a bit, but I don't recognise this. What is it?"

I couldn't very well tell him the truth, that it was my own system, a boustrophedonic code based on six languages, three alphabets, a variety of symbols mathematical and chemical, and a hieroglyphic, designed to keep up with even the fastest of lecturers and leave me time to record nonverbal data, as well. It was totally illegible to anyone but Holmes, and even he found it rough going.

"Oh, it's a system I learned in Oxford."

"Were you writing right to left?"

"On alternate lines. Makes it much smoother, not having to jump back to the beginning of the line each time."

"Well, live and learn." He handed me back my notebook. "Time for a little something. Sherry, I think, Miss Small?"

"Oh, Colonel Edwards, I don't think—"

"Now look, young lady." His mock sternness was meant to be amusing. "I never drink alone if I can help it—it's bad for the health. If you're going to be around here, you'll have to learn to be sociable. Here." He handed me a brimming wineglass, and I sighed to myself. Oh well, at least the quality was decent.

An hour later, he stood up. "I must go, though I'd dearly love to repeat last night's dinner. You go on home, take my manuscript, and finish the letters tomorrow. We'll go to dinner tomorrow night."

Not with Holmes due back, we wouldn't. "Oh, no, I couldn't—"

"Tomorrow or Saturday, one or the other, I won't take a no."

"We'll, er, we'll talk about it tomorrow," Mary Small said weakly.

"Or tomorrow and Saturday both, if you like. Here's the manuscript. Didn't you have a coat? Oh now, look at the rain out there. I'll have Alex run you home and come back for me; it'll take me that long to climb into my stiff shirt anyway." Protests were ignored as he stepped out and shouted orders to his man. "That's settled, then. I don't like to think of you getting wet. Here's your coat."

He held it for me, and his hands lingered on my shoulders. "Don't you think I should call you Mary?"

"Whatever you like, Colonel." I busied myself with my buttons.

"Would you call me—"

"No, sir," I interrupted firmly. "It wouldn't be right, Colonel. You are my employer."

"Perhaps you're right. But we will go to dinner."

"Good night, sir."

"Good night, Mary."


My portrait of Colonel Edwards was filling out. It now included his home, his investments, his relationships with servants and hired help, and the suggestive knowledge that he had been duped by colleagues over the gender of D. E. Ruskin, for some as-yet-unknown reason, and was very angry about it. In addition, I now had eighty-seven pages of material written by his hand and shaped by his mind, and nothing, absolutely nothing, is so revealing of a person's true self as a piece of his writing. I hurried through the substantial tea provided by Billy's cousin, a tiny, whip-hard little woman with the unlikely name of Isabella, and shut myself in with the manuscript.

At page seven, there came a knock at the door.

"Miss, er, Small? It's Billy. There's a, er, gentleman on the telephone for you."

"Oh, good. Thank you, Billy. You're looking well. Perhaps we can have a chat sometime, over a pint? Where's the 'phone? Ah, thank you."

It was very good to hear his voice.

"Good evening, Mary," he said, warning me unnecessarily of the need for discretion—he never called me Mary. "How does the new job go?"

"Billy told you, then. It's very interesting. I've learnt a great deal already. He's a nice man, though I've heard some talk about him. Hard to believe, though."

"Is it?"

"Yes, it is. And you? How are you getting on?"

"Well, as you know, the place is pretty run-down; there's a lot for someone like me to do. I spent yesterday morning weeding the rose beds and the afternoon digging in the potato patch."

"Poor thing, your back must be breaking. Don't pull anything." I more than half meant it—sustained physical labour was not his forte.

"I was inside today with a leaking joint in the kitchen, and she started me stripping wallpaper."

"Lucky you."

"Yes, well, that's why I'm calling, Mary. I won't finish the job tomorrow, so she wants me to stay on until Saturday."

I shoved away the rush of disappointment and said steadily, "Oh, that's all right. Disappointing, but I understand."

"I thought you might. And, would you tell those friends of yours that we'll meet them Saturday night instead?" Lestrade and Mycroft.

"Sunday morning?" I asked hopefully.

"Saturday."

"Very well. See you then. Sleep well."

"Not too likely, Mary. Good night."


I read the manuscript through quickly, then took myself off for a long, hot, mindless bath. The second time, I made notes for improving it, the secretarial and editorial review. The third time, I went very slowly, reading parts of it aloud, flipping back to compare passages, treating it like any other piece of textual analysis. At the end of it, I turned off the lights and sat passively, wishing vaguely that I smoked a pipe or played the violin or something, and then went to bed.

And in the night, I dreamt, a sly and insidious dream full of grey shapes and vague threats, a London fog of a dream that finally gave way to clarity. I dreamt I was lying in a place and manner that had once been very familiar: on my back, my hands folded across my stomach, looking up at the decorative plaster trim on the pale yellow ceiling of the psychiatrist's office. One of the twining roses that went to make up the border had been picked out in a pale pink, though whether it represented a moment of whimsey on Dr Ginzberg's part or her painstaking attention to the details of her profession, I could never decide. As it was directly in line with the gaze of any occupant of her analyst's couch, I suspected the latter, but I liked to think it was both, and so I never asked.

In the dream, I was suspended by the familiar languor of the hypnotic trance she had used as a therapeutic tool, like a vise that clamped me to the padded leather while she chipped delicately away at my mind, peeling off the obscuring layers of traumas old and new. They all felt very old, though most of them were recently acquired, and I had always felt raw and without defence when I left her office, like some newborn marsupial blindly mewling its way towards an unknown pocket of safety. I had been taken from her before I had a chance to reach it. I was fourteen years old.

My voice was droning on in answer to a question concerning my paternal grandmother, a woman about whom I had thought I knew little. Nonetheless, the words were spilling out, giving such detail of fact and impression as to sound almost clairvoyant, and I was aware of the onlooker within, who, when I came up from the trance, would be faintly surprised and amused at the wealth of information that had lain hidden. I do not remember what Dr Ginzberg's question was—there was a vague flavour of an adolescent's concept of Paris in the nineties, the cancan and sidewalk bistros and the Seine running at the foot of Notre Dame, so I suppose it must have been to do with the early years of my parents' marriage—but it hardly mattered. I was quite content to chunter on in any topic she might choose—almost any topic.

And then she laughed. Dr Ginzberg. During a session.

It is difficult to describe just how shocking this was, even doubly wrapped as I was in the dream and the dreamy world of trance, but my sense of rightness could not have been more offended had she suddenly squatted down and urinated on the Persian carpet. Her kind of psychotherapist simply did not react—outside of her rooms, yes, when she was another person, but Dr Ginzberg in the silent room with the yellow walls and the pink rose and the leather sofa? Impossible. Even more astounding had been the laugh itself. Dr Ginzberg's laugh (and outside the yellow room, she did laugh) was a quiet, throaty chuckle. This had been a sharp barking sound, a cough of humour from an older woman, and it cut off my flow of words like an axe blade.

I lay, paralysed by the wrongness of the laugh and the remnants of trance, and waited for her inevitable response to an unjustified pause, that encouraging "Yes?" with its echo of the Germanic *ja*. It did not come.

I became aware, with that logic of dreams, that I was younger than I had thought, that my feet were imprisoned in the heavy corrective buttoned shoes I had worn until I was six, and that the shoes came nowhere near the end of the couch. Dr Ginzberg waited, silent, in her chair behind me. I drew up my right foot and pushed with the heavy shoe against the leather, then twisted my body around to look at her.

Her hair had gone white, and instead of being gathered into its heavy chignon, it flared in an untidy bowl around her ears. She wore a pair of black, black glasses, like two round holes staring out from her face, hiding all expression. What bothered me most, though, was not her appearance—for she was still Dr Ginzberg, I knew that—but the fact that she held in her hands not her normal notepad but an object that looked like a small Torah scroll, spread across one knee while she made notes on it.

She stopped writing and tilted her head at me.

"Yes?" *Ja.*

I felt comforted, but gave a last glance at the scroll on her lap, and then I noticed her hands. They had wide, blunt fingers, and no ring, and a thick fuzz of dark copper hairs covered their backs. After a moment, the hands capped the pen, clipped it over the top of the scroll, and reached up for the black, black spectacles. I watched her hands rise slowly, slowly from her lap, past her ordinary shoulders, to her temples, and as they began to pull at the earpieces, I saw the shape of her head, the flat wrongness of it, and with a rush of childish terror I knew that I did not want to see the eyes behind those dark lenses, and I sat up with a moan strangling in my throat.

The boardinghouse seemed to throb with movement, but it was only the pounding in my ears. The shabby furnishings, grey in the light that seeped through the ungenerous curtains, were at once comforting and inordinately depressing. I sighed, considered and discarded the thought of finding the kitchen and making myself a hot drink, and squinted at the bedside clock. Ten minutes past four. I sighed again, put on my dressing gown, lit the gas lights, and reached for the colonel's manuscript.

It was not time wasted. By the time dawn overtook the streetlamp, I had confirmed a few hypotheses, drawn others into question, and given myself something to think about during the day.

# FOURTEEN

ξ

*xi*

The day proved to contain a surfeit of things to think about, even without the manuscript. The first was the figure who greeted me as I entered the study: The son had arrived home from Scotland. He looked up from his coffee and gifted me with what I'm sure he thought of as a captivating grin, which might have been had it reached his eyes.

" 'Allo, 'allo, 'allo, the pater's new secretary is certainly an improvement over the last one. I see he didn't tell you that the prodigal was coming home. Gerald Edwards, at your service." He was the quintessential 1923-model final-year Cambridge undergraduate, sprawled with studied negligence across the maroon leather armchair, dressed in the height of fashion in an amazing yellow shantung lounge suit. His dark hair was slicked back, and he wore a fashionable air of disdainful cynicism on his face, with a watchful awareness in his bloodshot eyes. He made no move to stand, merely watched my body move across to the desk and bend down to tuck my handbag into a drawer. I straightened to face him and answered smoothly.

"I'm Mary Small, and no, he didn't mention it. Is he here?"

"He'll be down in a tick. We were up until some very wee hours last night, and the old *sarx* doesn't recover as fast when you're Father William's age, does it?"

Looking back, I do not know what it was that raised my hackles at that point. His use of a Greek word to a marginally educated secretary could have been innocent, but somehow I knew, instantly, that it was not. The mind could not justify it, but the body had no doubts, and my heart began to pound with the certainty that this unlikely young man suspected that he was talking with no innocent secretary. Here was danger, totally unex-

153

pected, perceptible danger. I used bewilderment to cover my confusion.

"I'm sorry, I thought his name . . . What did you say about sharks?"

"*Sarx*, my dear Miss Small, *sarx*. *Corpus*, you know, this too, too solid and all that. But surely you know Greek, if this is yours." He held up yesterday's dictated notes and watched me calmly. "I mean, this isn't Greek, though it's Greek to me, but there are a goodly smattering of thetas and alphas."

"Oh, yes, *sarx*, sorry. Actually, I don't know an awful lot of Greek, or Hebrew, which is the other language there. Don't you use this system at Cambridge? Your father did tell me you were there, I think?"

"Aha, a secret Oxford hieroglyphic, is it? How did you learn it?"

"Well, actually, it was . . . I mean, well, there was this boy who taught it to me one summer."

"Taught you Oxford shorthand, eh, on a punt up the river? And did you learn a lot, moored beneath the overhanging branches?" He hooted most horribly, and I felt my face flush, though not, as he thought, with embarrassment. "Look at her blush! Oh, Pater, look at your secretary, blushing so prettily."

"Good morning, Mary. I didn't hear you come in. Is my son teasing you?"

"Good morning, Colonel. No, he only thinks he is. Pardon me, I'd like to get those letters typed." I retrieved my notebook, and the temptation to kick one long fashionably clad young limb as I passed was strong, but I resisted. Russell, I thought as I wound the paper into the machine, that young man is going to be a capital *P* Problem, even if you're wrong about his suspicious nature. Roving hands and a happy drinker, Rosie had said. Of the first, I had no doubt.

And so it proved during the day. While the colonel was off dressing, young Edwards perched on the desk where I was typing and undressed me with his eyes. I ignored him completely, and through tremendous effort, I made not a single typing error. After lunch, at which he drank four glasses of wine, he began to find excuses to brush past me.

In between episodes of avoiding the son, the father and I got on with our work. That afternoon, I reviewed the manuscript with him, made hesitant suggestions for expanding one chapter and reversing the positions of two others, and extended his outline for the remainder of the book. He sat back, well satisfied, and rang for tea. I accepted his offer of a cigarette and steadied the hand that held the gold lighter.

"So, Mary, what do you make of it?"

"I found it very informative, Colonel, though I haven't much background in the political history of Egypt."

"Of course you don't. I'm glad you find it interesting. What about going to Oxford the first part of the week and getting on with a bit of that research, eh? Think you could handle it?"

"Oh yes, I know my way around the Bodleian." I paused, wondering if I should ask one of the questions that had come to me in the night.

"Something else on your mind, Mary?"

"Well, yes, now that you mention it. It occurred to me, after I read it, that you make very little of the activities of women." That was putting it mildly: His two mentions of the female sex were both highly disparaging, one of them almost rabid in its misogyny. "Had you planned on—"

"Of course I haven't put women into it," he cut me off impatiently. "It's a book on politics, and that's a man's world. No, in Egypt the women have their own little world, and they don't worry themselves about the rest."

"Not like here, is it?" I deliberately kept my manner noncommittal, but he flared up with a totally unexpected and unwarranted violence, as if I had taunted him.

"No, by Jove, it isn't like here, all these ugly sluts running around screaming about emancipation and the rights of women. Overeducated and badly spoilt, the lot of them. Should be given some honest work to do." His face was pale with fury, and his narrowed eyes fixed on me with suspicion. "I hope to God you're not one of them, Miss Small."

"I'm sorry, Colonel Edwards, one of whom?"

"The insufferable suffragettes, of course! Frustrated, ugly old biddies like the Pankhursts, with nothing better to do than put ideas into the heads of decent women, making them think they should be unhappy with their lot."

"Their lot being laundry and babies?" He did not know me well enough, but Holmes could have told him he was walking on paper-thin ice. I become very quiet and polite when I am angry.

"It's a Godly calling, Miss Small, is motherhood, a blessed state."

"And the calling of being a secretary, Colonel?" I couldn't help it; I was as furious as he was, though where he looked ready to go for my throat, I had no doubt that I appeared calm and cool. I readied myself for an explosion, at the very least for the drawer to be emptied over my head, but to my astonishment, his face relaxed and the colour flooded back in. He suddenly sat back and began to laugh.

"Ah, Mary, you've got spirit. I like that in a young woman. Yes, you're a secretary now, but not forever, my dear, not forever."

I understood then, in a blinding flash of rage at his complacent, self-satisfied condescension, the deep revulsion a smiling slave feels for the master. It took every last iota of my control to smile wryly, take up my pen with

155

my trembling hands, and move across to my place at the typewriter. At the same time, singing through me alongside the rage and the remnants of a fear I could not justify, was the triumphant sureness that here, at last, as clearly as if he had dictated it, was a motive for the murder of one Dorothy Elizabeth Ruskin.

I excused myself from dinner with a headache and insisted that the following evening I had an unbreakable engagement with a cousin. Yes, perhaps Sunday, we should talk about it tomorrow. No, the headache was sure to be gone by morning, and I should be happy to come in tomorrow. No, it was a pleasant evening, the rain had let up, and no doubt the fresh air would help my head. No need for Alex to turn out. I bid good night to Colonel and Mr Edwards.

I walked the two miles to the boardinghouse through crowded streets, and though my toes hurt, my not entirely fictitious headache had cleared by the time I let myself in the front door. Twice during the walk, I felt the disturbing prickle of someone watching, but when I casually turned to browse in the windows, there were too many people on the streets to enable me to pick out one trailer. Nerves, no doubt, the same nerves that made me overreact to the colonel's temper tantrum.

After Isabella's hearty tea, which was geared more towards the labourer's appetite than that of an office worker, Billy and I went around the corner for a pint. The pub, considerably more working-class than the Pig and Whistle, was owned by a cousin-in-law of one of Billy's maternal aunts, and the bitter was brewed on the premises. I poured the dark yeasty liquid down my throat and with one long draught washed away the cloying tastes of sweet sherry, the Edwards household, and Mary Small. I put the glass down with a sigh, realising belatedly that I had broken character. Oh well, even Mary Small was allowed her quirks.

"So, Billy, what have you been doing with yourself?"

He answered me quietly, though in the noisy pub, it was hardly necessary.

"I'm taking up art, miss. Painting."

"Really?" I looked at his clean hands. "What medium?"

"Medium?"

"Yes, what do you paint with?"

"Tubes of stuff, oily paint. Makes an 'orrible stink, it does."

"What sorts of things are you painting?"

"Boards with cloth pulled over them, mostly."

"Canvases."

"That's right. Actually, we're neighbours during the day, as well, miss."

"Are we?"

"Yes, I have a studio place upstairs over the bookshop, down the street from where you're working."

"Ah. I see."

"Yes, so you see, if you ever needs something during the day, I'm quite often looking out the window."

"Of course. Do you have a patron?"

"A what?"

"Someone who supports you in your art?"

"Oh yes, I certainly does. Do. Another half?"

"Let me pay for this round. By the way, Billy, were you by any chance following me this evening, when you left your studio?"

"Not followin', exactly. It may have been I was walkin' the same way as you." He stopped, looking sheepish. "Didn't make a very good job of it, did I?"

"Oh, on the contrary, I didn't see you at all. I just felt someone watching me. Glad to know it was you. However, if you don't mind, I'd rather you didn't trail me about. It makes me jumpy."

"If you say so."

"Thanks. And Billy? Smear a bit of paint on your hands and clothes tomorrow, would you? Just for effect."

He looked down accusingly at his betraying hands, then shook his head. "And here I keep thinkin' I'm getting better at this kind of thing. Only good for fetchin' beer, I am."

"And following a person. A real artful dodger, you are."

He grinned at the compliment and pushed his way through the crowd to the bar, shouting jovially to every third person. A less likely artist it was hard to imagine, but with a palette and the smell of turpentine about him, he would pass a cursory examination. As for any paintings he might produce, well, almost anything passed as art these days. He seemed to be enjoying himself, at any rate.

Half an hour later, I put down my empty glass.

"I must be off, Billy, I'm expecting a telephone call."

"I'll go with you."

"Stay and have another, Billy. The night's young."

"No, I'll go."

He called good nights and shepherded me to my door.

That night's telephone call was again closely guarded. He was ringing from a noisy pub, and though I didn't exactly shout, I'm sure Isabella's top floor could hear my every word. We greeted each other, and he asked about my day.

"Much the same. The son was there today, a very sharp young man, too sharp for his own good. He'll cut himself one of these days. Wanted to talk about Greek, of all things."

"Greek? Why did he think you knew Greek?"

"That shorthand I learnt in Oxford."

"Interesting."

"Yes. And the colonel was a wee bit unhappy with me today. Seems he doesn't like uppity women. Truly doesn't like them, I mean."

"But you disabused him of the notion that you might be one of them?"

"That I did. He said he liked young women with spirit, but he seemed to think I should marry and have babies."

"Did he now?" Laughter bubbled underneath his nonchalance. "And what did you say?"

"Not a thing. I just went back to my typing."

"A ladylike response."

"What else could I do? And you, did you finish the wallpaper?"

"Started hanging it. Luckily, it's a dark room. She's a funny old bat, talks your ear off once she gets started."

"That's good. The work goes faster if you can carry on a good conversation. Is she nice?" "Nice" meant a probability of innocence.

"She seems nice, yes. Don't know about her sons yet."

"No. We'll talk about it tomorrow night, shall we?"

"I do hope so. Take care, and Mary? Watch out for those suffragettes."

"Ugly sluts, overeducated and badly spoilt. Need to be given some honest work."

Little spurts of laughter leaked out of the receiver, and the connexion went dead. A satisfactory conversation, all things considered. I had told him the colonel was violently misogynist, unless the *gyn* were in the kitchen or nursery (or, presumably, bedroom), and he let me know that Mrs Rogers appeared uninvolved, though the sons were an open question. On top of it all, I had given him something to laugh about, to soften the hard floor of Mrs Rogers's shed.

# FIFTEEN

# O

*omicron*

T here was no indication on Saturday morning that before the day ended I would be presented with three major additions to the case, all of them in the space of an hour: a rape attempt, a collection of esoteric publications, and a citation for speeding.

The morning was long and tedious, involving a systematic renovation of the business files and an equally systematic avoidance of young Mr Edwards's attentions. Lunch was heavy and alcoholic, and a cold drizzle prevented me from a temporary escape into the grounds. I went back to the study after an hour of male badinage, suffered with gritted teeth, anxious to get through the day so that I could hear what Holmes had found in Cambridgeshire.

Fortunately, the wine at lunch seemed to have slowed down the roving hands, for although Gerald followed me into his father's study and watched my every move, he didn't actually reach for me. The colonel went to his room to rest, and his son talked to me while I sorted files. His monologue dragged on, covering all the high points of cricket matches and rowing, and I occasionally nodded my head and watched for anything of interest in the files.

He did it cleverly, I'll give him that. I stood up to retrieve some files on the other end of the desk, and when I turned back, he was there, his arms clamped around me and his mouth seeking mine.

I do not know why I reacted so violently. I was in no real danger—I could have laid him out in three simple moves, or broken his neck in four, for that matter. I reacted in part because I was so immersed in the rôle of Miss Small, and even in 1923, few women would fail to react strongly to such an affront. Mostly, however, it was my sheer frustration and rage at the entire situation that erupted. I could feel the urge for his neck in my hands for one brief instant before sanity clamped down, and I considered what to do while dodging his reechy kisses.

The real danger was not to me and any honour I might possess, but to my rôle. If I were to overwhelm him physically, my time in the Edwards home would come to a sudden end. Mary Small would probably just scream, but aside from the fact that it was difficult to do with his mouth in the way, it would only delay the problem, not solve it. And, there was my pride. I wanted to hurt the slimy creature, but even a quick knee jerk would be out of character. Any injury must be bad enough to stop him, light enough to keep me from losing my position, and must appear completely accidental. All this reflection took about three seconds of grappling, and then my body assumed command.

I stumbled backwards half a step to put him off balance, with a twist, so he was forced to take a single step (my boy, your breath is foul!), and then leant away—all of them natural movements. I then rose slightly, twisted my head away from him, made certain of my balance and his full preoccupation, and finally swung one heel around hard to knock his feet out from under him while simultaneously giving a sudden stumbling lurch with all my weight behind me, my hip aimed at the sharp corner of the immovable oak desk just behind him. The high and satisfying scream that tore through the room did not come from my throat, and I stepped back to let him sink stiffly to the floor. He was not breathing. He looked quite green. I began to fluster about him before his knees hit the carpet.

The door burst open and Colonel Edwards was there, hair awry and pulling on his coat. I turned as he came in.

"Oh, sir, I'm so sorry. I don't know—"

"What in God's name is going on? Was that you I heard, or— Gerry? What the devil's wrong with him?"

As dear Gerry was somewhat preoccupied with curling into a tight knot and wheezing into a semiconscious state, I took it upon myself to answer, albeit quite incoherently.

"Oh, Colonel, I don't know. I just—he was—I fell, you see, and I must have hit his stomach or maybe the desk hit his back, and oh, shouldn't we call a doctor? He looks like he's having a fit; maybe he's dying." A tortured gasp followed by a deep groan told us that he had finally regained his breath. The colonel knelt beside him, saw no signs of blood, and stood up with narrowed eyes. He looked hard at me, took in the disarray of my hair and blouse, including a popped button, and started to smile grimly.

"I told him he'd get into trouble one of these days if he didn't keep his hands to himself. Wouldn't have thought it'd be you who gave it to him, but you never know."

"Gave it— But sir, I didn't mean to do anything. I just caught my heel on the carpet and tripped. Shouldn't we ring for a doctor?"

"Doctor couldn't help any. He'll get over it. It's nothing most men don't have happen sometime or another. Ice and a whisky should take care of it."

"But what—" I stopped. A complete innocence of male anatomical characteristics was surely not to be expected. "You mean I—oh dear. The poor boy." I knelt down, and Gerald, who had reached the sickly smile stage, smiled sickly up at me. "I'm so very sorry. I'm always so clumsy, and you did so surprise me."

"Yes, I imagine he did. Come, Mary, you'll not get much more accomplished today. Why don't you have a glass of sherry and then take your work home with you to finish up."

"But . . . we can't leave him here!"

"I'm certain he'd be much happier if we did, wouldn't you, Gerry?" A weak, uncontrolled flap of the hand signalled agreement and dismissal. "I'll send Alex in with ice and brandy. He'll help you up." We left the room, and the colonel began to chuckle. I stopped short and drew an audible breath.

"Colonel, do you mind if I use the small room for a few minutes? I'm rather . . . I would like a sherry after that, though."

"Certainly, my dear. I'll be downstairs."

I let myself into the large marble bath that lay between the colonel's study and his bedroom. His steps retreated down the hallway, and I heard him shout for Alex. Next door, the groans had given way to profuse, bitter, and unimaginative cursing. I grinned maliciously, locked the door, and turned on the tap in the basin.

I had three minutes, perhaps more. I moved swiftly to the other door, the one that opened into the colonel's private room, and pushed it open on noiseless hinges.

I did not know what I was looking for, but I was not about to pass up the opportunity. I ran my eyes over the room, inviting them to choose a target.

It was a large room, totally and unremittingly male: dark wood, undersized bow window, a thick, garish Persian carpet on the polished floor, cabinets—glazed on the top half, panelled below—covering one wall. There were two paintings: one of a man, which looked like a self-portrait by one of Rembrandt's third-rate students, all heavy moodiness and no technique, and the other a huge, gilt-framed, enthusiastically done nude of a remarkably well-endowed young blond woman who was cowering coyly before a thick, glossy, and lubricious snake. Not perhaps my image of Mother Eve, but the leering expression on the face of the snake was cleverly done, given the lack of facial characteristics to work with.

The cabinets were unrevealing, containing a variety of trophies and awards, family heirlooms (one assumed) and statuettes, predominantly of females in various stages of undress. One minute passed. The telephone rang, and I heard the colonel's voice. I pulled open a few of the wooden doors, to find clothing, no apparent hidden compartments, and enough dust to make it obvious that the housekeeper cut a few corners. I walked around the bed to the well-worn armchair that sat next to the window. It was oddly positioned, I thought, almost as if—ah! It was within arm's reach of a locked cabinet. I dropped next to the door and yanked a pin out of my hair, bent the end of it, and set to work. Two minutes gone. I heard voices downstairs, but not on the stairs yet.

After an agonising thirty seconds, the lock gave and I pulled the doors open, to find books. Pornography. Damn! I flipped through them quickly, but they were only books, mostly illustrated. I locked the doors again and heard the colonel bidding the caller good-bye. I made to rise, then froze. There, in front of my eyes, was a double row of cheap, well-thumbed pamphlets and paperback booklets. The title that jumped out at me was *Emancipation and the Enslavement of the Family.* There must have been nearly a hundred of the things, ranging from the inch-thick *Cover Their Heads* to a four-page *Suffragettes: The Devil's Hands.* I pulled out *Women's Suffrage: Against God's Plan,* noted the name and address of the publisher, and slid it back into its place as voices came shockingly loud directly outside the room. I plunged around the bed and closed the bathroom door behind me an instant before the knock came on the hallway door. I turned off the tap and hurried to pat my hair into order and correct the disarray to my person.

"Are you all right, Mary?"

"Oh yes, sir, I'll be down in just a moment."

"I have the files you were working on; you needn't go back into the study. I'll have Alex take you home; it's raining very heavily now."

"Thank you, sir. I won't be a minute."

Rapid repairs completed, I took several calming breaths and went downstairs to the loathsome and inevitable sherry.

"There you are, my dear, drink that. Look, Mary, I'm terribly sorry about the misunderstanding upstairs. Gerry's a bit impetuous sometimes."

Misunderstanding? Easier to misunderstand the intent of a gun barrel.

"It's fine, Colonel, really. Is he going to be all right?"

"Certainly. A bit sore for a day or two, but perhaps you've succeeded in teaching him discretion where I failed."

"But I didn't mean—"

"No, I realise you didn't intentionally hurt him. No one could have done that deliberately. Nonetheless . . . Look, Mary, I've just had a telephone call from a friend to invite me to a talk Monday afternoon. Would that be a good day for you to go to Oxford? I know it's not much warning, and if you would prefer to work on at the files before starting on another project, I'll understand."

And leave me alone with Lothario? No thank you.

"Monday's a good day. I'll take an early train. I'm quite looking forward to it."

"Good, good. I'm glad about that." He did look pleased, but something else, as well. Actually, I thought, he was acting oddly. Not remarkably so, just small things, such as the way he was fiddling with his glass, the way he looked at me, reserved, somehow, and appraising. Was it suspicion? No, I thought not. If anything, he seemed more confident and less attentive of me. Polite, but dismissive, as well. My speculations were interrupted by the arrival of Alex with my coat. The colonel held it for me, handed me the file of letters and manuscript, and said that he would see me Tuesday morning. No mention of dinner that night or Sunday. Interesting, very interesting. Just what was it that had changed the man's attitude towards me, and why?

Alex, uncommunicative as always, led the way to the garage. The roadster that Holmes had hypothesised was back now in its place, a very fast and slightly dented (along the sides) sleek, black Vauxhall. I exclaimed over it.

"Yes, miss, it belongs to young Mr Edwards."

"It is a beautiful thing. It looks fast, too."

"I believe he is in the habit of driving it in the high sixties, on the proper roads, of course." Cars were obviously Alex's weak point, as this one made him positively effusive.

"Cor, stone the crows, as my granfa' used to say," I said appreciatively. This pithy bit of vernacular struck home, and he actually broke down and smiled. I walked over to admire the gleaming enamel and the red leather upholstery more closely, and I thought that perhaps when this case was over, I, too— But then my acquisitive yearnings were stifled by the sight of a jumble of papers pushed into the front pocket, and my curiosity came to the fore. I circled the car under Alex's proud gaze, then, sighing like a love-struck adolescent, climbed reluctantly into the suddenly dowdy saloon car. I opened my bag as Alex went to his door, and I gave an exclamation of dismay.

"What is it, miss?"

"I don't seem to have my pen in here. I must have left it in the study. Would you mind awfully just waiting for a tick while I pop up and—oh dear. Mr Edwards will be there. Well, perhaps I'll just wait until Tuesday to retrieve it."

"Would you like me to fetch it, miss?"

"Oh, I couldn't ask you to do that."

"Not to worry. In the study, did you say?"

"Somewhere around the desk. It's where I was working when . . . It's gold," I finished weakly, to his well-hidden, butlerian amusement.

"Won't be a minute, miss."

I waited until his footsteps faded, then pushed open the door and leant into the front of the roadster. The corner of one piece of paper looked tantalisingly familiar. Several months before, I had been returning to an urgent appointment in Oxford, trying to coax a modicum of speed out of my amiable Morris, and had collected a summons for my pains. Here in my hand was an identical slip of paper. I turned it over, looked at the date unbelievingly, and felt a foolish grin take hold of my face. Gerald Andrew Edwards had not been in Scotland on the night our cottage had been ransacked, not unless he had spent the next twelve hours driving very fast. The following morning, he had been nabbed for speeding near Tavistock, about as far from Scotland as England went. I took my gold fountain pen from my bag, made a note of the details, and then, clutching the pen in my hand, followed Alex towards the house.

He was, of course, annoyed at his wild-goose chase after a pen that had fallen into the folds of a notebook, and he drove me in silence to Isabella's boardinghouse.

I climbed the stairs to my cheerless room and closed the door gratefully behind me. I shrugged off my damp coat and was arranging it over a chair and considering the effort of asking for a measure of coal to make a fire, when I heard a gentle knock. Billy stood there, holding out to me a wad of what looked like used butcher's paper that had been rolled, flattened, and folded.

"Letter for you, from a gentleman."

"A letter? Not a telegram?" I was astonished—I had received exactly five letters from Holmes in the eight years I had known him. (Holmes' chief method of distance communication was through brief telegrams, preferably so cryptic as to be unintelligible. One such had contained a deliberate misspelling that was corrected along the way by some conscientious telegraphist, thus rendering the message totally meaningless.)

"Not for you. A couple for me to send for him—one to Inspector Lestrade about a Jason Rogers, another for Mr Mycroft Holmes, something about sending a brown suit to be cleaned."

Which could mean, I realised, some prearranged code—All is known, must fly—or could mean merely that the brown suit wanted cleaning. I took the wad of paper apprehensively. "I'm glad he finally surfaced, if briefly. You saw him, then?"

"I did, for two minutes as he changed trains. He told me to say he was sorry he couldn't come tonight but that he'd see you tomorrow night."

"I'll believe that when I see him. How did he look?"

Billy hesitated, his worn face searching for words. He had begun life on the hardest of London streets, employed and fostered by Holmes, and though he was quick, he was not an educated man. He finally settled for: "Not himself, if you know what I mean. Of course, he was wearin' them old things and hadn't shaved, but he looked tired, too, and stiff. Not all an act."

"Hardly surprising. I hope he gets a proper bed tonight. Thank you for this." I held up the flattened scroll.

"He said you might want me to take it to someone else later. If you do, I'll be home." He jerked his thumb to indicate the room across the hall. I thanked him again and closed the door, put hat and gloves and shoes in their places, and poured myself a small brandy, which I took with the letter to the chair next to the window. I raised my eyebrows at his first paragraph.

My dear Russell,

I write this hurriedly on, as you will no doubt have noted, a train car whose underpinnings have seen better days. The information it contains may be of use to you, but the presentation of that information is of value to me: I find myself in the singularly vexing position of possessing a series of facts which, as you know, I habitually review aloud and put into order, even if my audience is no more responsive than Watson often was. However, you are off on your own track, Watson is in America somewhere, and I haven't time to wait about for Mycroft or Lestrade. Hence the letter. I should prefer to have the patterns reflected either by your perception or Watson's lack thereof; however, a stub of lead pencil and this unsavoury length of butcher's paper will have to suffice. (From the expressions on the faces of my compartment mates, none of them has ever before witnessed the miraculous generation of the written word. I shall attempt not to be distracted.)

First to the information: I successfully ingratiated myself

into the employ of Mrs Rogers by the approach we had agreed upon—that is, I am an unemployed sailor who knew her husband, and I am as offensive as possible without quite coming to blows. She positively melts in my unshaven presence.

I was up on a ladder in Mrs Rogers's guest room, cursing the general intractability of inexpensive wallpaper, when I heard a car drive in, and shortly thereafter, without a knock, came the sound of heavy feet in the kitchen below. Murmured conversation followed, and I cursed further the unsuitability of my position for overhearing what was happening downstairs. In a few minutes, however, the feet came up the stairs and a head of thick black hair appeared in the door, then stared curiously at me and my work.

The owner of the hair, as you can imagine, interested me greatly. I gave him an abrupt greeting, typical of my character, and narrowly avoided dropping a length of paste-sodden paper on him. He commented on the quality of my work. I told him that she was getting what she paid for, that I never claimed to be a paperhanger.

"What are you, then?" he asked.

"Jack of all trades, master of none," I replied.

He reacted to this bit of originality with a sneer.

"I'd believe that you've mastered none, by the looks of these walls. What are you good at?"

"Ships. Machinery. Automobiles." This last was after I had seen the grease stains under his nails and the condition of his shoes and trousers.

"Hah. Probably can't even so much as change a tyre."

"I've changed a few," I said mildly, and deposited a globule of paste on his shoe.

"Well, you can do another if you like. There's a slow puncture in the car in the drive outside, and I'm in a hurry. You go take it off and see if you can find the hole."

I obediently laid down my brush and knife and took up the wrenches from the car's toolbox. It was not his automobile, of that I was certain. Too staid, too expensive, too well kept up. I would have given much to hear what was said during the next fifteen minutes, but short of climbing the wall—in broad daylight, without ivy or a convenient rope—and putting my ear to a window, I could not. I found the hole, patched it, and was putting the wheel back in place when he came out again.

"Here, don't tell me you've just started?"

"Oh no, it's all ready to go. Sir, if you'll hand me that pump, I'll finish it."

As the tyre filled with air, I admired "his" automobile.

"Is it yours, then?" I asked casually.

"Nah, it's borrowed."

"I thought it might be. I'd see you in something a touch flashier, somehow, and faster."

"Oh, this one's pretty fast."

"Don't look it," I announced sceptically, so he proceeded to tell me precisely how long it took him to drive from Bath, despite the hay wagons. I whistled appreciatively.

"You must've had to push it hard on the straight patches. A good friend, to let you treat his machine like that."

"Ah, he'll never know. Some of these old [censored] own these [censored] great hogs and never use them properly. Does a machine good to be stretched a bit."

"You ought to charge him extra for it," I jested, and he took the bait.

"Too right, add it to his bill."

Much laughter and joviality followed and an exchange of opinions regarding pistons, body frames, and the like. (Many blessings, incidentally, were called upon Old Will's grandson for his tutorials in automotive arcana.) He climbed into the luxurious transport that was not his own, and I stuck my head over the passenger side.

"Enjoy your drive back, Mr—"

"Rogers, Jason Rogers."

"Enjoy the road, Mr Rogers. I hear tell there's a very watchful constabulary round Swindon side, so if you're going through there, you better keep a light foot on it."

"Thanks for the warning, Basil. Give me a start, my man."

I obliged, and he slapped the car cruelly into gear and roared off down the way.

So, as you can see, Russell, I am off to Bath, on a somewhat slower but considerably safer means of transport, to look into the possibility of a motorcar-repair establishment run by a Mr Jason Rogers, grandson of Mrs Erica Rogers, a right-handed, black-haired man of about five feet ten inches, thirteen stone, with rounded shoes, who looks the sort to own a brown tweed suit and a workmanlike folding knife. I hope to have some interesting contributions to add to the discussion tomorrow evening.

Now as to the pattern into which this information may fit: As I mentioned, Mrs Rogers is a talkative woman, easily steered into one topic and another, with certain very definite exceptions, when a thick window shade is pulled down behind her eyes and she discovers that it is time to make a pot of tea or check on her aged mother. She is not wildly intelligent, but she is very, very canny, and her suspicions bristle whenever the topics of money (particularly inheritance), grandsons, the education of women, childbearing outside of matrimony, and dogs come up. Which of these areas might concern us, and which are merely extraneous remnants of personal history, is as yet difficult to discern, although some of the subjects are highly suggestive.

Certain oblique statements, gestures, and expressions have caught my interest, buried as they were in the flow of gossip, childhood reminiscences, and explanations of the proper technique by which a job is to be done. I shall not burden you at this point with the details of those conversations, which would exhaust my supplies of paper, lead, and time; however, the following points should be noted:

First and foremost, Mrs Rogers is possessed of a deep mistrust of close family relationships. Her asides about ungrateful siblings and faithless children do not, however, appear to extend to mothers or male grandchildren. Hence my rapid departure by rail.

Second, you noted that she seemed fond of that drivel perpetrated by Watson on the unsuspecting public, yet when I walked into the house, there was not a single thing more demanding of thought than an old copy of Mrs Beeton's cookery book. A spot of gossip with the neighbour's lad (never underestimate the observational powers of an intelligent child, Russell!) revealed that a load of things were carted off a few days ago, including several tea chests filled with books. Which goes to explain ten linear feet of sparsely occupied and recently scrubbed shelves upstairs. Canny, very canny.

Third, you were quite correct about the recent departure of household help. This was in the person of a rather dim child of seventeen years who was perfunctorily dismissed on the day Miss Ruskin left Cambridgeshire, sent home to her family with two weeks' pay and no explanation.

As Pascal says, I have made this letter long because I lacked the time to make it short, but time and paper both are drawing to a rapid close, and I shall have to sprint across town to make the Bath connexion. You might have Billy take this to Mycroft and Lestrade, if he's available.

Take care, wife.

Holmes

Postscript—I had thought to keep the following with me, but perhaps that is not a good idea. If it were found in my possession by the gentlemen I intend to visit, it could be difficult to explain. I do not need to warn you to guard it closely. I found it in a desk drawer in Mrs Rogers's room, inside an envelope which, as can be discerned from the letter itself, was stabbed and gouged repeatedly with an ink pen, leaving pieces of the nib embedded in the paper. The letter was in a prominent spot in the drawer, but it had been returned to its envelope before it was attacked and not removed from the envelope since then. I left the empty envelope behind, lest Mrs Rogers notice its absence. I am quite aware this is not an entirely appropriate means of obtaining police evidence, but really, I could not leave it there. If I have not returned by to-morrow evening, take it with you to Mycroft's and give it to Lestrade.

H.

The letter, in the distinctive strong hand of Dorothy Ruskin, read as follows:

22 November 1920
Jerusalem

Dear Erica,

I hope this letter finds you and Mother well and your son's wife recovering after her fall. My return voyage was as uneventful as possible in this day, and I have returned safely, which is all one can ask for.

Erica, I have given much thought to what I am about to say, and I pray that it will be read in as charitable a mood as it was written. I cannot leave that topic we touched on during my last week with you. I told you that I was worried about your health, but I may not have expressed myself clearly. Erica, there is no longer any reason to feel that mental imbalances are any less deserving of straightforward medical treatment than are physical weaknesses. Even more, perhaps, for the former can easily lead to the latter. Please believe me when I say that I wish the very best for you. You are my sister, my only family, and (to speak honestly) I do not believe that you are yourself.

I know that you feel quite normal, but I could see clearly that you are not. Mental illness is a beast who wanders about inside one, seeking which part he may devour, and that beast is loose inside you now. Please, dear sister, do not let him remain uncaged. I am willing—indeed, I should be happy—to pay for the cost of psychoanalytic treatment and for the cost of care for Mama if necessary during that time.

I will ask a friend to be in touch with you with some names of good doctors. I hope you will at least go to see one, for my sake, if only to obtain a clean bill of health and prove me wrong.

Speaking of health, we are in the midst of an outbreak of dysentery here, as it seems that in my absence no one bothered to educate the new cook on basic sanitation issues. I am writing this in Jerusalem, where I have come to buy the necessary medications.

Please know that I write this letter out of affection and concern for you and that I remain, as always,

Your loving sister,
Dorothy

# SIXTEEN

## π

*pi*

I did not go down to supper that night, though Billy later brought me up a piece of apple tart and some cheese and coffee. I stood at the window and watched the London night fall. The rain stopped abruptly just before dusk, and I thought of Patrick on the farm, praying for some dry days to finish the late harvest.

For a few hours this afternoon, I was so sure of myself, I thought. Where there were clear motive and opportunity, could firm evidence be far behind? And now Holmes tells me the trail lies elsewhere. My efforts since Tuesday have been in vain. Thank God I don't have to go there tomorrow—I don't know how long I can keep it up, knowing there is a good chance that it is futile. But, why the sister and the sister's grandson? The murder was calculated, not merely an act of insane rage. Money, then, that most ubiquitous of motives?

I stood unseeing and rubbed at the dull ache in my right shoulder, my mind an undisciplined welter of unconnected images and phrases. A thin memory wafted up, evoked no doubt by the reference to wall climbing in the letter I had just received. A memory of salt air, and a strong, young body, and the wonder of life opening up. A memory of a girl, not yet a young woman, sitting at the edge of a cliff, tossing pebbles at the rocky beach far below. Her blond hair is tugged out of the long plaits by the wind, and wisps blow into her mouth and across her steel-rimmed glasses. The lean grey-haired man next to her sits quietly, one knee up under his chin, the other dangling carelessly into space.

"Holmes?"

"Yes, Russell."

"What do you think makes a person kill?"

"Self-defence."

"No, I mean murder, not just defending oneself."

"I know what you meant. My answer is, self-defence, always."

The young face squints out across the Channel haze.

"You are saying that all murders are committed because the killer feels that he is being threatened by the other person."

"I should qualify that, I suppose, to admit the occasional unhuman who kills for pleasure or payment, but for the rest, yes. The injunction against the taking of human life is so strong, the only way most people can break it is to convince themselves that their life, their welfare, or the life of their family is menaced by their enemy and that, therefore, the enemy must be removed."

"But, revenge? And money?"

"Subdivisions of self-defence. Revenge returns the killer to a position of self-respect and reestablishes his sense of worth and power in his own eyes. The cousin of revenge is jealousy, anticipating the need for revenge. The other subdivisions are all forms of power—money being the most obvious and the most common." And, his voice added, the least interesting.

"What about the fear of being caught?"

"It acts as a balance to the urge for self-defence. Most people know at least one person whom they could be tempted to do away with, were it not too unpleasantly messy, but for the fear of being caught and having freedom, honour, and perhaps even life itself taken away by the judicial system. Be honest, Russell. If you found yourself in a position where you could rid yourself of another person, and you were absolutely certain that no one would ever even suspect you, would you not be sorely tempted?"

"Oh yes," I said with feeling.

Holmes laughed dryly. "I am glad your aunt could not see your face just then, Russell. I promise you that I won't mention this conversation to the local constable if her body is found one of these days." Holmes, who had never been formally introduced to my aunt, was no fonder of her manipulative ways than I, her orphaned ward.

"I'll remember that. But, Holmes, if all murderers—most murderers— are only acting in self-defence, then how can you condemn them? Any animal has the right to defend itself, doesn't it?"

His response was as unexpected as it was electrifying. My friend, my mentor, turned on me, with a look of such absolute disgust and loathing that I could not breathe, and had I not been frozen to the spot, my body would probably have fallen forward off the cliff just to be free of that awful gaze.

His voice was tight with scorn, and it shattered my fragile adolescent attempts at self-assurance.

"For God's sake, Russell, human beings are not animals. For thousands of years, we've fought our way up from being animals, and the veneer is a fragile one at best. Some people forget this, but don't you, Russell, you of all people. Never forget it."

He stood up swiftly and stalked away, and I began to breathe again. After a while, I took myself home, shaken, confused, angry, and feeling about four inches tall.

That night after dinner, I went upstairs early to avoid my aunt's eyes and to think. My room was small, had no view to speak of, and was located on the cold north side of the house, but it had one invaluable feature: The stones of the main chimney stepped up along the outside wall just under my window, so that with the aid of a fine, nearly invisible rope, I could leave the house unseen. I used the escape route rarely, but knowing it was available transformed the room from a prison into a safe haven. I had even mounted a bolt on the door, which I threw now, and I stood with my forehead against the cool painted wood as the confusion and the emptiness welled up in me. Holmes was my only friend, all the family I possessed, and the thought of his disapproval devastated me.

A slight noise came from behind me. I whirled around, my heart in my throat, to see the man himself in the armchair next to the window, leaning forward to replace a book on the bookshelf, his unlit pipe between his teeth. I stared at him. He took the pipe out of his mouth, smiled at me, and spoke in a low voice.

"Good evening, Russell. If you do not wish to have uninvited visitors, you ought to pull the cord up after you."

I found my voice.

"Most people use the front door, for some reason."

"How odd. Would you prefer I went around . . ."

"It would seem somewhat anticlimactic. What are you doing here? I'm afraid I can't offer you any refreshment, if you are here because Mrs Hudson has decided to go out on strike."

"What a terrifying thought. No, I am not in need of refreshment. I came to apologise, Russell. My words this afternoon were unnecessarily harsh, and I did not wish you to be disturbed by them."

I turned to tidy an already-neat stack of papers on my desk.

"It is not necessary to apologise," I said. "It was a stupid thing to say, and I deserved your response. I am relieved that you aren't angry with me," I added.

"My dear child, it was not stupid. The question of human responsibility is one that every adolescent must ask, or grow up never knowing the answer. The problem is that I forgot you are only sixteen. I often do, you know. It was a valid question, and I treated it as if it were a moral flaw. Please forgive me, and I beg you, do not let it stop you from asking questions in the future. You say what you like, and I shall attempt to avoid acting like an old lion with a toothache. Agreed?"

Embarrassed and relieved, I grinned and stuck out my hand. He stood up and took it.

"Agreed."

"I'll be off, then, before Mrs Hudson sends out the hounds for me. There may be something in your macabre joke after all—this will be the third time in a week I have made her serve me a cold supper. Ah well. Until tomorrow, Russell."

He reached down and pulled up the noiseless window, then threaded his long body out into the darkness.

"Holmes," I called. His head reappeared.

"Yes, Russell."

"Don't come here again," I said, then realised how it must sound. "I mean, while my aunt lives here, I can't—I don't—" I stopped, confused.

He studied me for a moment, and then his hard face was transformed by a smile of such unexpected gentleness that I clamped my jaws hard to block the prickle in my eyes.

"I understand," was all he said, and was gone.

But I never forgot his words on the cliff.


What had Miss Ruskin possessed that could turn two, perhaps three, human beings into killers? What of hers, what piece of paper or small, flat item could have driven someone to the extremity of running her down with an automobile? If I knew what it was, I would know who. If I knew who, I could deduce what it was. I knew neither.

So I went to bed.

# PART FOUR

## Sunday, 2 September 1923

*[In Nature there are] no arts, no letters, no society, and worst of all continual fear and danger of violent death.*
—Thomas Hobbes

# SEVENTEEN

ρ

*rho*

Sunday morning began with the richly evocative sound of changes being rung on the bells and the sun streaming through a gap in the curtains, and deteriorated rapidly. For ten whole minutes, I lay happily contemplating the floating dust motes and deciding how best to use a beautiful, warm, free, late-summer Sunday in London. I luxuriously considered the riches available to me. Were I in Oxford there would be no doubt but that I should take to the river with boat, book, and sandwich, but where in London might I find a combination of strenuous work and pointlessness? Perhaps I could take a boat downriver to—

My blissful self-indulgence was broken by a sharp rap on the door, followed by Isabella's equally sharp voice.

"Miss Small? Gennleman downstairs to see you."

"A gentleman? But—" No, surely not Holmes. Who, then? Lestrade? Could something have happened to— Oh God. "Did he give his name?"

"A Colonel something, miss. Come to take you to church."

"To church!" I was absolutely flabbergasted.

"Yes, miss, it bein' Sunday and you new to the area and all, he says. What do you want me to tell him?"

"Tell him—" Dear God, of all the things I did not want to spend the morning doing, sitting in a stuffy building and singing muscular Christian hymns was fairly high up on the list. "Tell him I'll be down in ten minutes, would you please? No, better make it fifteen."

Make no mistake—I have nothing against Christian worship. Although I am a Jew, I am hardly a fanatically observant one, and at university I regularly attended church for the sheer beauty of the liturgy and the aesthetic pleasure of a lovely building being used for its intended purpose. However,

I had a fairly good idea of where and how the colonel worshipped his God, and it was bound to be worlds removed from evensong at Christ Church. Nonetheless, a job was a job. And, I could always develop a headache or the vapours and return here.

The flowery cotton frock, white gloves, and wide-brimmed straw hat I appeared in seemed to meet with Colonel Edwards's approval, and he rose from his chair in what Isabella called her parlour and greeted me with an oddly formal half bow. He positively sparkled with his Sunday-morning polish, looking jovial and avuncular and nothing at all like the man whose pale rage had actually frightened me two days before.

"It occurred to me this morning, Mary, that I was being remiss in my duty as a neighbour to abandon you to your own resources on Sunday morning. If you've already made your plans, I should be most happy to take you to your own church, but if not . . ." His voice trailed off in a question. I did not allow my baser self to take the offered escape.

"I should be delighted to join you, Colonel. I had no plans."

"Good, very good. Come then. We'll be late."

It was precisely as I had envisioned it, a nominally Anglican service conducted in an ugly Victorian monstrosity with no open windows, packed with overdressed enthusiasts, and complete with a sweating, roaring sermon based on an unspecified text but touching on topics ranging from employment problems to women's suffrage to the duties of an imperial power. The sermon was one of the longest I have ever had the misfortune to be subjected to, and as the man could not even manage to cite his biblical references properly, I did not feel it incumbent upon me to listen properly. I let myself sink into a light hypnotic trance, fixed an attentive look on my face, and reviewed irregular verbs. I worked my way through Greek, Hebrew, Latin, German, French, and Italian, and had begun on Spanish when the sermon thundered to its foregone conclusion. We paid our silver, sang a few more thumping hymns, and were given a blessed release.

But not to freedom. The ordeal moved to the next stage, which consisted of the stewed tea and watery coffee prepared by the Mother's Union to accompany their pink- and green-iced biscuits. Everyone knew the colonel, everyone came over to talk with him, and everyone glanced sideways at me before being introduced. I was certain that at any minute some acquaintance would recognise me and all would be lost, but I was spared that. I suppose the circle Holmes and I moved in, if it can be described by that term, had little overlap with that particular church population.

I was positively quivering by the time the colonel bade his farewells to the few remaining parishioners in the church hall, though whether my reaction was one of suppressed hysterical laughter or the urge to commit mass ecclesiasticide, I am still unsure. The colonel, however, was rarely unsure of anything, and he interpreted my withdrawn expression and trembling hands in a way that suited him.

"My dear Mary, how thoughtless of me to make you stand about sipping tea and chattering; you're obviously ready to break your fast. Come, I've made reservations at Simpson's. Now, where is Alex?"

Simpson's! Where even the busboy knew me as Mrs Holmes? That would never do.

"Colonel, I'd really rather not go to a restaurant just now. Do you mind?"

"Oh, well, certainly, my dear." My contradiction took him aback. "What would you like to do?"

"I had thought this morning of going to Kew. I know that half of London will be there, but I should greatly enjoy a walk." And hope that anyone who might normally know me would be put off by my change in dress, manner, and posture. I could always hide behind my hat.

The colonel puzzled at my rebellion for a moment, and then his face cleared with inspiration.

"I have just the thing, my dear girl. Just the thing. Here's the car. Only a bit of a drive is all. Alex, we want Westbury's."

"Very good, sir. We shall need some petrol before the day is through."

"They'll have it there for us."

"Colonel," I inserted, "I must be back by six o'clock. I told a cousin of my mother's that I'd take dinner with him."

"Six, you say? Oh, that's too bad. They do a very pleasant dinner at Westbury's. Perhaps they'll give us a good tea, though. Make yourself comfortable, Mary. We'll be about three-quarters of an hour."

"What, or who, is Westbury's?" I asked.

"Who, definitely. Though I suppose 'what' would not be too far off the mark. Westbury is a friend of mine, with the most magnificent house set into grounds by Capability Brown himself. Westbury has a large number of friends, and he and his wife love to entertain and do it very well, too. Unfortunately, Westbury is embarrassingly short of the old folding stuff— the dratted new tax laws, don't you know? So rather than confine themselves to the occasional small party, they hold one every weekend, Friday night to Monday morning."

He nodded to himself as if to admire a clever solution. I had obviously missed a key word somewhere.

"I'm sorry, Colonel, I fail to see how this avoids the expense."

"Oh, well, you see, the servants present each guest with a bill for services, be it afternoon tea or the full weekend with Saturday-night dance.”

“Ah, I see. Westbury’s is a weekend resort hotel.”

“Oh, no!” The colonel was shocked. “The Westburys have guests, all friends. The servants handle the financial side of it, and it’s all quite fair, a reasonable bill—they have a superb kitchen, a cook who is totally loyal since Westbury saved his life in the trenches—plus ten percent, of course. I occasionally do wonder if Westbury isn’t given some part of it, by some means or another, but they aren’t in business, oh my, no. It’s just that their friends want to help out, and it’s really such a pleasant place, it would be such a pity to open it up to the Americans and have charabancs full of day-trippers pocketing the silver and treading down the flowers, and one doesn’t mind doing one’s bit to cover costs, don’t you know? They’re such very nice people. Unfortunate about the money, though. Hmm.”

I opened my mouth, shut it, and sat back in the leather and laughed until the tears came into my eyes, in a manner of total abandonment most un-suited to Mary Small. I laughed at the startled eyes of Alex in the mirror and at the Westburys’ friends and the tax laws and the total madness of it, and the colonel eyed me uncertainly and then began to chuckle politely, as well. I very nearly told him then who I was, to put an end to the farce, but something stopped the words on my tongue, and I changed what I was going to say.

“Colonel, I—the whole thing sounds most delightful. Considerably bet-ter than Kew. I only might wish I had worn more practical shoes, so that I might take advantage of the grounds.”

That distracted him, and we both peered down at my fashionable and therefore impractical heels, topped by the sleek sheen of my silk stockings. He cleared his throat and glanced out the window.

“Perhaps Mrs Westbury could help you. I say, do you ride?”

“I do, but not in these clothes.”

“Oh, that would not be a problem. Westbury’s is always prepared for that kind of thing. Course, the riding’s nothing like before the war, but the few nags they manage to scrape together are usually sound. Wrong time of year for a hunt, sorry to say.”

“That’s just as well. My sympathy would be entirely with the fox.”

He chuckled patronisingly, as if he had expected my reaction, then changed the subject. Actually, I am not against the killing of foxes, being a farmer myself and having lost numerous poultry to them over the years. What I dislike is the unnecessary glorification of bloodthirstiness. We no longer execute our criminals with the prolonged agony of stoning or tor-ture, and I cannot see why we should grant a wild creature any less dignity.

When we have a fox, Patrick and I take turns sitting up with a gun until it shows up, and we kill it cleanly. We do not run it to ground in terror and turn the dogs loose to tear it to pieces. Such a process demeans both hunted and hunter. But I digress.

It was indeed a magnificent house, and circling past the playing fountain to the portico, I could well imagine that it would be an appallingly expensive establishment to maintain. Two acres of roof? Three? I said a short prayer of thanksgiving that my own inheritance was too nouveau to have been bogged down in stone, glass, marble, and lead. Oak, plaster, and tile were more to my taste. Besides, a house like this means a plethora of servants, and I prefer freedom.

We were greeted by music and a gentleman who could have been a butler of long service or an hotel manager, a figure both subservient and authoritative.

"Good day, Colonel Edwards, it's good to see you again. I'm sorry I was not informed that you were coming, or I should have arranged something for you." There was just the slightest hint of reproach in his voice.

"No, Southern, I didn't know myself until we got into the car an hour ago. We're not here for dinner, just the afternoon, if there are a couple of spare mounts. However, I think Miss Small here would appreciate a crust of bread first and a change of clothing. Do you think the missus could help us?"

"Certainly, sir. I'll take her in now, if you like, and then bring her around to the terrace buffet."

"That's grand. You go with Southern, Mary; his good wife will fix you up with something to ride in."

The riding jacket I ended up wearing had been designed for a woman with less in the way of shoulders and height and considerably more in the way of breast and hip, but the breeches were long enough and the boots fit. Mrs Southern assured me that I need not dress for the terrace luncheon, and when I saw the gathering, I understood why. The guests wore everything from dazzling white linen and twenty-guinea sandals to egg-encrusted waistcoats and boots that Patrick would have scorned for mucking out the cow barn. I stood in the dark shadow of a portico and enjoyed the multicoloured crowd of perhaps sixty people, equally matched between men and women, eating and drinking and talking in the glorious sunshine all along the magnificent flower-blazoned terrace. Halfway down the terrace, stones cast out a triangular shelf into the formal flower beds, and on this platform a string quartet was playing gamely.

The colonel was standing with a group of three other men, a stemmed glass small in one hand and a delicate sandwich in the other. I made to step out into the light, then stopped dead as my eyes lit on the group coming up the terrace behind him. Damnation, just what I had feared all morning, someone who knew me well enough to see through the façade: the sister and cousin of a housemate from my undergraduate days, with whom I had gone to a rather poor ballet and spent a dreary weekend in Surrey. They moved up to the colonel's party and rooted themselves there.

The quartet swirled to an end, which reminded people of its presence, so that everyone turned and applauded politely. The cellist wiped her brow prettily and went to greet the colonel. Mrs Westbury, I decided, and pressed back into the building as the colonel looked vaguely towards the house. I should just have to wait until he came to find me and then insist I was not hungry, though I did not care much for the idea of a long ride on nothing more filling than two pink biscuits. There was no choice, however; I couldn't go out there now. I ducked back into the house, wondering hope-fully if I might come across an untended pantry.

My path took me by the drawing room, which I had glimpsed on my pre-vious journey down the hallway, and as I passed, there came a sweet, sharp burst of notes from a clavier. The scales tripped up and down the keyboard for a minute or two before settling competently down into a Scarlatti sonata I'd heard before. I edged my head around the door and saw an un-mistakably familiar elegant back, all alone in a vast, ornate hall of mirrors and gilt, seated before a double-keyboard instrument whose rococo intri-cacy set off the performer's exquisitely simple grey suit and sleek towhead with startling perfection. I sank into a knobbly chair that might have come from the same workshop as the clavier, watching him with the pleasure that comes from witnessing one of nature's rare creatures in its own habitat.

The sonata came to what I remembered as its end, but before I could make up my mind either to slip out silently or to shuffle my chair noisily, the trailing notes gathered themselves again and launched into an extra-ordinary piece of music that sounded like a three-way hybrid of Schubert's "March Militaire" performed as a Goldberg Variation by Bach with Scott Joplin occasionally elbowing in. Nearly two minutes went by before I could sort out the central theme: He was improvising a musical jest on "Yes, We Have No Bananas." I snorted in laughter.

The clever hands jerked in discord, and he whirled around and off the bench to face me, but before I could feel remorse, the tense control in his shoulders and the taut line of his jaw had relaxed into pleased recognition.

"Good Lord, it's Mrs Sherlock!" The foolish, slightly lopsided face with the too-bland eyes registered amazement at seeing me in this setting.

"No, it is not," I corrected him severely. "It's Miss Mary Small, whom you've never set eyes on in your life."

His grey eyes flared with interest and amusement even as his face and posture lapsed instantaneously into the silly-ass act he did so well. "Miss Small, of course, so pleased to make your 'quaintance. Reminded me for a tick of someone I know—don't know her well, of course, only met her— a party somewhere, I s'pose. Come to think of it, you don't look the least like her. Maybe something around the eyes? No, must be the shape of the spectacles, and as I remember, she had brown hair. A short little thing, too. Nothing like you. Mary Small, you say? How d'you do, Miss Small?"

His high voice burbled to a close, and he held out a deprecating hand, which I took with pleasure and a laugh. "How are you, Peter? You're looking well." Despite his violent reaction to being startled, he did appear less strained and not so thin as when I had last seen him, some months before. He had had a bad war indeed, and he was only now beginning to crawl out of the trenches.

"Not so bad," he said, and then, probing politely, asked, "Is there anything I might do to assist, Miss Small?"

"Thank you, Peter, but . . ." I paused, struck by a thought. "I might, actually, ask a small favour."

"But of course—gallant is one of my overabundant middle names. What dragon does milady wish slain, what chasm spanned? A star pluck't from the heavens, a cherry that hath no stone? Some shag for your pipe, perhaps?"

"Nothing so simple as dragons or bridges, I fear. I need two young ladies removed so that I might get at the groaning board, where they stand waiting to recognise me for whom I am not and address me loudly by a name I had rather not have heard."

"You wish me to murder two women so you can eat lunch?" he asked with one politely raised eyebrow. "It seems just a bit excessive when there are servants willin' and able to bring you a tray, but I dare say, any friend of Sherlock Holmes—"

"No, you idiot," I said over the giggles he always managed to draw from me. "Just remove them for twenty minutes. Take them to view the peacocks, or see the etchings, or bring them in to hear you play something horrid and dissonant on this machine."

"Please, don't insult the poor thing. It can't help how it looks, and its inner parts deserve better than the twentieth century." He patted the encrusted inlay of the top reassuringly.

"Play them Bach or Satie, I don't care, just so I have time to eat and escape into the grounds. In those dresses, they can't plan to venture far from the house."

"Deep waters, Holmes, and no small danger, from the peacocks if nothin' else. But your faithful Watson is ready as always to plunge into the fray, all enthusiasm and no wits. Who are these two delectable creatures awaitin' my seductive wiles, and if I may be so bold, on whose ears is not to fall the name of Holmes?" He held the door for me, and we entered the dark corridor.

"The ladies are silly but sweet, and you won't have to think of topics of conversation. The ears belong to a Colonel Dennis Edwards, who currently employs Miss Mary Small as his secretary."

"Edwards, you say? You do move with strange fish, my dear. I will demand payment for this onerous deed, you know. Which are my victims?" he added, peering alertly through the open door. I pointed them out to him, and he sighed. "Yes, we have met. A policeman's lot is not an 'appy one. Adieu, my lady, and if I do not survive this day, tell my mother that I loved her."

He screwed his monocle into place with a gesture of buckling on armour, then glided smoothly out into the crowd. I watched with amusement as he greeted his hostess, kissed the fingers of a matched brace of dowagers, shook various hands, greeted the colonel and said something that made him laugh, scooped up three glasses of champagne from a passing tray, and finally, with the ease of a champion sheepdog, cut out his two victims from the flock. Within four minutes from leaving my side, he was strolling down the terrace stones, one fluttering female on each arm, and I stepped out to take a plate. Rule, Britannia, with an aristocracy like that.

I applied myself industriously to a plate of assorted foodstuffs, drank thirstily several glasses of the excellent champagne, nodded politely to the bits of conversation that came my way, and watched warily for other familiar faces. The colonel seemed taken aback by my brusque manners, so after slapping my empty plate down onto a nearby tray, I made an effort to smile ingratiatingly at him before urging him to lead me to the stables.

Inside that dim and fragrant environment, I managed to avoid both the sidesaddle and the placid mare the colonel would have chosen for me, settling instead on a rangy gelding with a gleam of equine intelligence in his eye and airily brushing off the colonel's worried fussing that it was too much horse for me. Mary Small was slipping away fast, and I was fortunate that the horse had already been out that morning and was therefore less interested in bolting or scraping me off under a branch, situations that our Miss Small might have found trying.

Once away from the house, I began to breathe more easily, and I settled down to the business of enjoying myself. During the shakedown canter through the shady lane, the horse and I had a discussion about our partnership's chain of command, and when that had been settled to my satisfaction, I gave him some rein and aimed him at a fence. Despite his looks, his legs had springs like a Daimler, and when he recognised that he had a rider who appreciated his skills, he settled his ears with a nod of prim satisfaction and happily set about proving his worth.

A couple of miles later, I belatedly became aware of my escort and employer on my heels, and half-turning, I shot him a grin of pure enjoyment. He came alongside with a grin of his own, and we rode under the hot Kentish sky in something very like companionship. He was different mounted on the horse in his borrowed coat, more sure of himself, yet paradoxically less assertive. I thought he would be the same when engaged in any physical activity, hunting or rugby, closer to his essential nature than when in his too-large house in the city. He sat the horse well and took the hedges and walls smoothly, and he politely allowed me to win the race to the far edge of Capability Brown's compulsory lake. We dismounted and I unpinned my hat, unbuttoned my gloves, and rinsed out a handkerchief in the rather muddy water to cool my face. I spread my borrowed jacket out on the grass and lay back on it to let the sun work at increasing my freckles, listening to far-distant voices and birdcalls and the occasional slight jingles of the grazing horses.

"You ride well, Mary. Where did you learn?"

"I am a farmer." I came to myself with a start. "That is, I grew up on a farm in Oxfordshire."

"What does your family grow?"

"A bit of everything, really. Hay, market vegetables, a few horses, cows."

"That's where the calluses on your hands come from?"

I held them up against the sky and studied them.

"Not a city girl's hands, are they? Too many cows to milk." The musculature was much too generalised for that, but I doubted that he would notice my lack of the milkmaid's characteristic bulging carpal muscle. I flexed my fingers, then dropped my arms down at my sides and closed my eyes.

Moments of pure relaxation were rare for me. There was always the nagging of books unread, work undone, time a-wasting. For this brief slice of an afternoon, though, the choice was taken from me; the only alternative to relaxation was fretting. But the sun was too warm and my muscles too pleasantly loosened to fret, so I stretched out my long legs, crossed them at the boots, folded my glasses onto my stomach, and gave myself over to the sheer debauchery of simply lying in the sun. I was vaguely aware that I was presenting a sight shocking to the eyes of an Edwardian gentleman, long jodhpur-clad limbs and thin blouse, bare head and naked face and hair awry, giving herself over to a shameless and unafraid snooze. I smiled at the thought.

In the arms of Nature's soft nurse, I half-dozed, aware of the sun on my eyelids and a fitful breeze across my cheeks, the food in my stomach and the good air in my lungs and the faint remnant of wine in my blood, the odours of cleaning fluid and cedar from the coat under my head and the clean smell of horse moving off and the aroma of a warm male human nearby. I held the awareness of all these things of the day and the birdsong in a compartment, a light place into which I could reach at any instant, and allowed the rest of myself to sink away into the silent, warm, dark place that lies within.

Mary Magdalene. I had not thought of her in days, and yet a week ago, reading her letter aloud to Holmes, I should have said she would remain before my eyes for the rest of my days. Mary of Magdala, one vital link between the ministry of Jesus the Nazarene carpenter, the crucifixion of Jesus the political criminal, and the resurrection of Jesus the Son of God—a link who, having brought the news of the resurrection to the male disciples, vanishes utterly on Easter afternoon. I reflected, not for the first time, on the irony that this woman, later called a harlot, traditionally identified with John's "woman taken in adultery," this mere woman and her vision of the empty tomb was the foundation stone on which two thousand years of Christian faith was laid, and at that moment, lying there in the sun, I knew in my heart that, despite the difficulties, I accepted her authorship of my papyrus. I was filled with admiration for the pure, distilled strength of the woman with her simple, deadly decisions—and for the first time I wondered what had become of the granddaughter, Rachel, how old she had been, if she made it safely to Magdala. "I look out across my rocky desolation," the woman had written, in that flowing and spiky hand that gave the impression of hurried calm even before I knew her words, a rocky desolation and fleeing the coming wrath of the conqueror that would turn the holy place that was the heart of Judaism into a ruin where jackals would howl and soldiers empty their bladders, the same soldiers who carried pikes and swords and who stank of garlic and stale sweat in that land of sun and little water, a smell very unlike the cedar and the tobacco and the fresh male smell that was in my own nostrils now, which combination was evocative of Holmes. I lay limp, part of me drifting on a hillside in a long-off age under a different sun, and a bit of me aware of Mr Brown's cultivated natural landscape, and gradually a third part of me becoming aware of a series of distinctly arresting sensations that slowly transformed my state of torpid dreaminess into hypnotic attention, a third point of awareness that kept me frozen and divided, the awareness of lips exploring the exquisitely sensitive tracery of veins that ran up the inside of my wrist.

It was overwhelmingly erotic, the feather touch and dreamlike movement of his breath and mouth and moustache in my palm, on the swell and hollow of my thumb, up the line of my tendons, the amazing, unexpected, electrifying gentleness and sensitivity of his mouth taking possession of my right hand, and I arched my fingers to him and took one deep, shuddering breath, and an instant later I was on my feet, stumbling away from him, seeking the safety of my horse.

I scrubbed my palm and the inside of my wrist hard across the bristle of the animal's coarse hip, and as I yanked at the girth with unnecessary violence, I cursed my stupidity, my carelessness, my—yes, damn it, my absentmindedness—and I cursed as well my overreaction, for the second time in twenty-four hours, to an Edwards male. He came up behind me and held out glasses, gloves, hat, and jacket, and I clothed myself and mounted the horse without looking at him or taking his offer of a hand up.

"Mary, I—"

"No, Colonel. No." My rough voice was pure Russell. "I am sorry, but no. It's time to be getting back." I drove the hat pins roughly home, buttoned the gloves, and then forced myself to look down at him, but he only looked puzzled and a bit hurt, then slightly amused.

"Very well, Mary, if that's how you want it." He turned away to catch his own horse, but I couldn't leave it at that.

"Colonel? Look, I am sorry. It has nothing to do with how I want it, but it's how it has to be. I can't explain, not just now. I am sorry." And for a moment, with the tingle still warm on my wrist, I was truly sorry, and he saw it, and he smiled crookedly.

"I understand, Mary. It was foolish of me to think that you could be interested in an old man like me. I do understand."

I swallowed hard the protest that rose up, a bitter mouthful indeed. We both left the topic as it stood, and after he had mounted, we turned and rode back in a silence that was, oddly enough, not unfriendly. When the stable lads had received back their charges, I excused myself to go and reclaim my own clothes. Walking warily through the corridors, I made the upstairs room without challenge. Once there, I dismissed the maid as firmly as I had before, took my clothes from the wardrobe, and dressed quickly. I had just begun to pin my hair back together when a light tap at the door startled me.

"Yes?"

"Saint George here, slayer of dragons, at your service," drawled a light male voice.

I opened it, and my rescuer slipped in.

"I thought I'd check to see if my services were still needed, though short of a bigamous elopement, I cannot see how I might keep those two from the dinner party."

"Heaven forbid. No, we're going, as soon as I've taken my leave of the Westburys. Do you think you could—"

"A glass of bubbly under the rose bower is the most I can manage, I'm afraid."

"That would be perfect. Thank you, you dear man, you've saved me from a potentially difficult situation."

"The salvation of fair ladies is the entire purpose of my class, in case you had not realised. When ladies stop being in need of rescue, all like me will fade away."

"Like King Arthur, waiting to come again when England has need of him?"

"Good Lord, what a dreadful thought. Give me an honest retirement anytime. Speakin' of which, kindly present my greetings and regards to the gentleman with the pipe."

"I will. Come down for a weekend when this is all over, and I'll tell you all the sordid details. There's even an immensely early manuscript for you to admire."

"A first edition?"

"Without a doubt."

"Interestin'. I shall hold you to the offer. Well, it's been loverly, ducks, but two other ladies await my escort services. Give me five minutes to remove the dragons from downstairs, and the coast, as the fogbound lighthouse keeper said to his wife, will be clear."

"Thank you," I said again, and impulsively leant forward and kissed his cheek. He very nearly blushed, then busied himself with cleaning his monocle with his silk handkerchief and screwing it energetically over his eye.

"Yes, well, ta and all that. Cheerio."

I turned back to the mirror, smiling, and was surprised to see his fair head reappear at the door, the silly-ass attitude temporarily suspended from face and voice.

"By the by, Mary, a word in your ear. Doubtless you know already that your colonel has a potential for nasty behaviour, but you may not have met his son yet. If you do, watch yourself: He's a felony waiting to happen, and in him, the nasty streak goes clear across.

"We've met."

"Yes?"

"Indeed. He may walk carefully around sweet young things for a while."

"Hello, hello, do I see a gleam in your eyes? Heaven protect me from an emancipated woman who can throw men over her shoulder."

"I should think you know me better than to accuse me of something as unsubtle as that."

"But no less painful, perhaps?"

"Well . . ."

"Take care, Mary." He laughed, then went down the hall whistling something complicated and Mozartian.

# EIGHTEEN

## σ

*sigma*

I expected the drive back to London to be something of an ordeal, but it was not. The colonel was, if anything, more relaxed and friendly, almost as if he were relieved to have some bothersome question out of the way. The clouds, actual rather than metaphorical, gathered again as we neared London, and it was raining lightly when Alex pulled up in front of Isabella's boardinghouse. The colonel moved to open his door, but I put out a hand to stop him.

"Colonel, I just would like to say thank you for such a nice day. It was perfect. All of it." I looked into his eyes for a moment, then leant forward to plant a daughterly kiss on his rough cheek. He seemed very pleased, so I let it go at that and got out when Alex opened my door.

Holmes was not there. Drat the man. I bathed, dressed, fidgeted, and at seven o'clock put a call through to Mycroft.

"Good evening, Michael," I said. "I was calling to see if by any chance you had news of a friend of mine? I was halfway expecting him to appear before this."

"No, I haven't heard from him." His voice was surprised but untroubled. "If he hasn't shown up by now, he will probably come directly here. There's no reason to let his absence spoil your dinner."

"I suppose you're right. I'll give him a few more minutes, then come on over."

I fidgeted for another eight minutes, then threw up my hands and went down to find a cab. I stood in the protected doorway and looked in disgust at the unceasing rain, wondering how long it was going to take me to find an unoccupied taxi on a wet Sunday night. Fortunately, my luck was in, for a shiny black taxi cab, empty but for the driver, came cruising down the street. I waved for it to stop, bent down under my umbrella, and climbed in without waiting for the driver to open the door for me. As I sat back in the seat, he clashed the gears irritably and growled at me through the speaking window.

"Damn it all, Russell, you had more sense when you were fifteen than you exhibit now. How many times have I told you—what are you laughing at, woman?" I was laughing, suddenly intoxicated with the sheer pleasure of being back in the presence of this ageing, supercilious, impossible man who was often the only thing in my life that made any sense.

"Oh, Holmes, I knew it was you the instant I saw the taxi start up. You know, if you wanted to make a truly dramatic entrance instead of something predictably unusual, you could astonish everyone by merely walking up the stairs, where and when you were expected. Oh, don't look so crestfallen. I'm glad to see you're having a good time." I caught his eye in the mirror and watched as he began reluctantly to match my grin. "Now tell me what you're doing in this cab. The last I heard, you were going to Bath. Did you finish with Mrs Rogers, then?"

He held up his left hand silently, and by the light of the streetlamps I could see the fading wounds of a lengthy battle with thorns and the extreme dryness of skin that comes from long hours of chafing and immersion in wet glue.

"Yes, I see. Did you do the entire house?"

"Two rooms. I told the good lady I would return Tuesday morning."

"And is she a good lady?"

A long pause followed, only in part due to a surge of traffic around a cinema house. When we had negotiated the tangle, Holmes spoke again, musingly.

"I do not know, Russell. There are a number of oddities about this case, and not the least of them is Mrs Erica Rogers."

When we arrived at Mycroft's, Holmes parked the car with neither incident not illegality and turned to look at me through the glass partition.

"No one on our tail?"

"None I could see, and I was watching carefully."

"So I observed. Do you know, Russell, it is a distinct pleasure to look upon your features again. The floor of Mrs Rogers's shed was both hard and cold. Now," he went on before I could answer, "I just need to get something from the back."

The something from the back was a wooden crate that rattled metallically. He volunteered no information, and I did not spoil the surprise by asking. The doorkeeper eyed us closely before admitting us, and Lestrade opened the door with a glass in his hand.

It was, as always under Mycroft's roof, a superb dinner with agreeable conversation. Holmes, more formally clad now in clothing he kept in his brother's guest room, entertained us with stories about a one-armed tattooist in the West End, a woman who had a counting horse up in Yorkshire, the craft of stained glass, and the distinctive familial patterns of Kashmiri rug makers. Mycroft, more phlegmatic but with a nice line in what the Americans call "deadpan humour," contributed a long and absurd story concerning a royal personage, a hen, and a ball of twine, which may even have been true. Even Lestrade kept up his end, laying out for us the latest escapade of his nephew—an episode which had convulsed the lad's boarding school for a week and left the headmaster with a red face even longer. His tale ended with him saying, "Butter wouldn't melt in his mouth. That lad'll make a fine detective." When the laughter had subsided, Mycroft stood up.

"Shall we take our coffee and brandy in the next room? Mary, would you—"

"No, I do not mind if you smoke."

"Thank you, but I was going to ask if you preferred something other than brandy. A glass of sherry, perhaps?"

"God no!" All three men looked at me in varying states of astonishment at my vehemence. "I'm sorry, it's just that sherry seems to have played a somewhat excessive part in my life the last few days. I don't think I'll drink a glass of the stuff by choice for several weeks. Just the coffee, thanks."

"I do understand," said Mycroft. "I'll just see to it. Sherlock, perhaps you would stir up the fire." Lestrade followed him, leaving Holmes and me to choose chairs in front of the fireplace. Holmes threw some coal on the glowing remnants, then lowered himself into his armchair. With great deliberation, he stretched out first one long leg and then the other, and sighed deeply.

"Are you well?" I asked. His reply was to open one eye and look at me. "You drank rather more wine at dinner than is your custom, and you seem in some discomfort."

"I am getting old, Russell. Gone are the days when I could scramble about on the moors all day and curl up happily at night with a thin blanket and a stone for a pillow. Three nights on floorboards and one night without sleep following three days at strenuous labour make me aware that I am no longer a callow youth."

"Have the results matched the effort?"

"I think so, Russell. I believe they have. But it is a fine thing to stretch to one's full height in a soft chair. As you would no doubt agree," he added. My normal five feet eleven inches was intimidating for many people, so Mary Small stood a full two inches shorter. My back, too, had ached since Wednesday.

Brandy and coffee arrived, and with them a certain reticence, a hesitancy to cut into the festive mood with the hard edges of information and analysis. We each sipped our coffee with undue attention, then gathered ourselves, until finally I put down my cup with a shade more clatter than necessary and cleared my throat.

"Ladies first, I suppose, particularly as I was so remiss over the dinner table. Also, it will allow me to go through my material before my brain gets too fuzzy. Very well, then: Wednesday. You know where the colonel lives, and as you all know London better than I, you also no doubt are aware that it is one of those backwaters that remains a village within the city, complete with shops on the high street and small-town gossipmongers. Mycroft, you may not know that the colonel lives in a large turn-of-the-century—the last turn, that is—house slightly removed from the village centre, in the remnants of what were once lovely grounds. Although he seems to be unpopular with some of the chattier, and therefore more inquisitive, shopkeepers, he is very much the village squire, in his own mind at any rate. He drinks in the local pub with the workers and the shopkeepers, and that is where I arranged to meet him. Quite by accident, of course, but it just so happened that I possessed the qualifications for a personal secretary and knew he needed one."

"A bit chancy, that, wasn't it," Lestrade asked, "depending on his needing a secretary?"

"With a big house and only two permanent staff, and considering the problem of hiring servants these days, I knew he'd be sure to need somebody. And Mary Small is versatile. If he had needed kitchen help or someone to scrub the floors, I would simply have lowered my accent a few notches and rubbed some dirt under my fingernails. I might have had some problem if he'd needed a valet, though," I admitted.

"You'd have managed somehow," Holmes commented dryly.

I continued with my narrative and told of the dinner, the work, the colonel, and his son. I found myself curiously hesitant to give specifics of the colonel's attitude towards me, and I gave the barest account of the son's attack (Holmes laughed when I described how I had retaliated; Lestrade and Mycroft winced), but I could see that Holmes read between the lines.

I promised him wordlessly that I would go into greater detail when we were away from the others, and I could see that he received the message. The colonel's bedroom and its contents spurred considerable discussion, and by the time I finished with Gerald's traffic summons, it was after eleven o'-clock. I dismissed the current day's events with two flat sentences, ignored a curious look from Holmes, and closed my mouth. After a moment, Lestrade looked up from his notes and broke the silence.

"You're saying, then, that you could see Colonel Edwards behind this?"

"I could, yes. I will admit that I rather like the man, though I detest a number of things about him, not the least his attitude towards women. He's appealing, somehow, and I can easily see him in charge of men who will do anything for him. Authoritative, yet slightly bumbling. Of course, it has to be at least in part an act—he was, after all, a soldier who spent the war years efficiently going about the business of getting his men to kill. In any case, yes, I can visualise him as the murderer of Dorothy Ruskin. Not just any woman, but that particular one, under those particular circumstances, yes.

"There is, I must say straight off, no evidence concrete enough to be called by the name. One might analyse the man's writing to the point of knowing what colour his necktie will be on a given day, but it counts for nothing before a jury. Here, in this room, however, I can say that there is a faint odour of brutality in his writing, a clear delineation of 'us' and 'them' and a subsequent disregard for 'their' rights and indeed 'their' very humanity. Particularly when 'they' are women. In more specific terms, though, points witnessed." I ticked them off on my finger. "First, there's his temper. He was not far from real violence with me, over a chance remark, and with Miss Ruskin he was faced not only with—point two—a woman who embodied everything he hates—independent, successful, intellectual, and with a sharp tongue she was willing to use—but, worse—point three—the knowledge that he had been tricked by a colleague, another man, who had deliberately put him in the humiliating position of being suddenly confronted by the fact of her gender, and knowing that there wasn't a thing he could do about it, that it was too late to deny her the funding for her project. I suspect, and he probably did, too, that his colleague and the man's friends within the organisation did it to laugh at him."

"I should have thought a military man would have more self-control than that," Mycroft objected. "Surely he must be driven to the brink of murder every day in this town, if he's so infuriated by women of that sort."

"He probably wouldn't have done anything other than storm furiously out of the restaurant and send off his resignation to the Friends, but for one thing: point four. I believe Miss Ruskin told him about the manuscript. You've heard it; it is very powerful. How would it have affected him? That document, even if its authenticity were never finally proven, would still turn the Christian world on its head. Mary Magdalene, an apostle of Jesus? To many people, the only thing more shocking would be if someone produced evidence that Peter was a woman, or Jesus himself. The colonel couldn't help seeing that, couldn't help being driven nearly insane by this woman, casually producing a document that would turn everything he stands for into a farce.

"I can see you have something you want to put in here, Inspector, but I'm nearly through. Can it wait? Good. Finally, there's the son. A current and, I think, valid, psychological theory says that a child reflects the subconscious, or unconscious, attitudes of the parent and that repressed hostilities and drives of the adult are often acted out openly by the offspring. Stripped of the jargon, it is simply that children absorb what their parents actually feel about someone or something, not just how the adult acts on the surface. Holmes, I think you used a version of this theory thirty years ago with the Rucastle case, didn't you? Obviously, the older a child becomes, the more tenuous the link becomes, and at twenty-one, Gerald Edwards can hardly be thought of as a child. However, his attitude towards Mary Small, a sweet young thing if ever there was, is positively predatory. Or, I should say, it was until yesterday afternoon. Even more revealing was the attitude Edwards took concerning his son's actions: slightly amused, somewhat proud parent looking on, exasperated, but not taking it any more seriously, and seeing no more need to apologise, than if his dog had anointed a neighbour's tree."

I had kept my voice to a dry recitation of the surface events, pushing away the uneasiness I felt remembering the actions, not of the son, but of the father. I told myself that it was merely the unexpectedness of the man's sudden fury that had taken me aback, and I decided not to mention it. Holmes would not need much of an excuse to pull me out of the Edwards house, and although a part of me would appreciate the gesture, I knew I had to remain there until my job was done.

My distraction functioned admirably, and I found myself faced by three variously affronted and indignant males. Their chivalrous attitude was nearly funny, but I thought it well to remind them who and what I was.

"Remember, Inspector," I said gently, "I have certain skills when it comes to the rough-and-tumble of life." I waited until I saw the recollection dawn in a familiar male look of quizzical half disapproval, and then I did laugh. He looked abashed, then chuckled unwillingly.

"You're right, I was forgetting. That lad with the knife—two years ago was it? You broke his arm well and truly."

"It was his elbow, and I didn't break it; he did it himself."

"Still could have been dangerous," he said, referring to the more recent escapade. "I mean to say, what if young Edwards had been able to, you know . . ."

"Meet me on my own ground? I was quite certain he could not. One can tell, something in the way a person walks." I dismissed the topic. "At any rate, now you have my story. Colonel Edwards had a motive to kill Dorothy Ruskin and the organisational skills and experience to seize an opportunity and carry it out. He had the means, with both a driver and a son available to him; he was in the area when she was killed; he has no firm alibi for the period after her death, when her room was searched, or for the following night; and his son was not only not in Scotland, he was actually in the south of England the morning after our home was ransacked. Furthermore, the person who searched our papers was interested primarily in those written in foreign alphabets and those taken up with chemical and mathematical symbols, which to the uninitiated may resemble a language. The Greek was then discarded, but the pages they took away with them include a seventeenth-century fragment of the Talmudic tractate on women, a sixteenth-century sermon in old German script, a sampler or, more probably, practice page from some Irish monk's pen, which was Latin but so ornate as to be illegible, a Second Dynasty Egyptian hieroglyphic inscription—a copy, actually, dating from no later than the middle of the last century—and half a dozen pages of a Coptic text. As none of them were of any great value, and in fact several were my own transcriptions, I believe we can leave out the question of a mad collector of rare manuscripts. I only note that Gerald Edwards reads Greek and, I should think, Latin, but not Hebrew, certainly not the old German script, and I doubt that he has ever heard of Coptic."

"You are discounting the evidence they left behind, then, Russell?" Holmes asked quietly.

"Holmes, even twenty years ago the hairs you found would have been very near to a sure thing. Now, however—well, there's just too much common knowledge about detecting techniques to make me happy about having a case rest on five hairs and some mud. These days, even the butcher's boy knows about fingerprints and tyre marks and all those things that you pioneered—this lot certainly did, as they never took off their gloves. You've been too successful, Holmes, and what the police know, the criminal and the detective-story writer pick up very soon. Those hairs could conceivably have been put there for us to find."

"My dear Russell, as you yourself have admitted, I am not yet senile. It is obvious that those hairs could have been put there as red herrings. It is an attractive theory and even possible, but I fear I deem it unlikely." He dismissed it with a wave of his hand. "Now, if you are finished, I believe that Inspector Lestrade's shining eyes and position on the edge of his chair indicate a certain eagerness for the floor. What have you for us, Lestrade?"

"We've had an interesting week, Mr Holmes. First of all, we managed to find a nurse in the hospital where Mrs Edwards died. She had a clear memory of it for the simple reason that she was newly qualified, and it was her first death. It was childbirth that brought Mrs Edwards there. The baby, a girl, lived for less than an hour, and the mother followed her two days later. However, the man who brought her in? He was not a man, but a woman. The nurse remembers her very well, because 'she dressed and talked like a man, but wasn't,' in her words. She seemed very nervous, but she stayed to help Mrs Edwards in her confinement. The nurse had the impression that the stranger was an actress or a singer, and the reason she had to leave the next morning was that the show was moving on. She telephoned several times and talked to the nurse, seemed satisfied with her friend's progress, but suddenly Mrs Edwards took a turn for the worse, and she died that night of childbirth fever. The nurse was off duty when the woman next rang, and she was never heard from again."

"Did Colonel Edwards know all this?" I asked.

"Exactly my question, and the answer is yes. The nurse wrote a short report for the file, which the colonel read, and she later spoke with him about it when he went to see her in early 1919."

"So he knew that his wife had miscarried his baby while off with a mysterious female theatre person, had been with her for some time, in fact. Also that there was a file describing it all, which later conveniently disappeared."

"There's more. The nurse well remembered the baby—she was holding it when it died—and finds it hard to believe that its, er, gestational age was more than five months, six at the very most."

"And the colonel had been back at the front since the autumn," I remembered.

"November. Slightly over eight months."

"He couldn't have had a leave and the records lost?"

"Unlikely."

"How very sordid and ugly. One can't help wondering—"

"If he drove his wife to it, or if she drove him to what he is now?" interjected Lestrade with unexpected perception.

"Mmm. I'll have some brandy now, please, Mycroft. I feel rather cold." My shoulder ached, too, from the horse's strong mouth on the reins and the succession of long days, but I ignored it and concentrated on what Lestrade was saying.

"Next, we started working our way through all the travelling entertainers who were in York at the time, beginning with the legitimate theatre players and working our way down to the dancers in the nightclubs. Pretty close to the bottom, we came across an all-woman troupe that specialised in rude music-and-dance versions of Oscar Wilde and Shakespeare. Yes, and it seems to have been as dotty as it sounds. People were hard up for entertainment during those years, but still. . . . Any road, the old, er, bat who managed it—Mother Timkins, she calls herself—is still alive by some miracle, running a, er, a house in Stepney."

"A 'house,' Inspector?" I asked. "Of ill repute?"

"Er, yes. Precisely. She did remember Mrs Edwards, though not by that name. The colonel's wife was with the Timkins troupe for five or six months, we finally determined. Joined at Portsmouth, was sick mornings for a couple of months, and had just started to, er, to 'show' when she died in York. The woman dressed as a man who took Mrs Edwards to hospital was probably Annie Graves, stage name Amanda Pillow. She and the Edwards woman were close."

"Lovers?" I asked bluntly. His delicacy was becoming irritating. He turned scarlet and consulted his notes furiously.

"Er, the Timkins woman seemed to think it possible, although there were a number of men, as well. Obviously, there had to be at least one." He cleared his throat again. "The, er, the interesting thing is that she told Colonel Edwards the two women were, as you say, lovers, when he went to see her in March of 1919. A month after he received his demob papers, that was."

"Four months before he was hospitalized for drink," I commented. "What happened to the Graves woman?"

"She was killed." We all looked up. "In June of that same year. She went off with someone after a performance, and she was found at four the next morning on a country lane thirty miles away. Dead about two hours. She'd been walking, stinking drunk and in five-inch heels, and was run over by a vehicle. Her body was down among the weeds in the verge, but it was quite visible as soon as it became light. They never found the car. Never found the person she'd gone off with."

Throughout my report Holmes had appeared to listen politely, which I knew, to my severe irritation, meant that he was taking in perhaps one word in three. With Lestrade's last revelation, however, he began to pay attention, and he was now looking affronted, as profoundly taken aback as if he had just discovered a distorting flaw in one of his instruments that threatened to cast doubts on the results of an experiment. He did not say anything, merely ground out his cigar and then tried to relight it.

"Furthermore," Lestrade continued, with a glance at his notebook, "there may be a slight discrepancy between when the colonel says he arrived home and when he actually did so. I say 'may' because the one neighbour who saw the car drive in has a most unreliable clock, which may or may not have been ten minutes slow or fast that night. According to both Colonel Edwards and the headwaiter at the restaurant, he left in his car just before midnight, no more than three or four minutes before. At that time of night, it takes eighteen minutes driving slowly and roundabout or eleven minutes direct and briskly to the Edwards home. The neighbour thought it was closer to twelve-thirty when he came home, but as I said, it's unreliable."

"Why did Miss Ruskin walk?" Mycroft asked. "Granted, it's not the worst area of London, but I should have thought a gentleman would have insisted on driving her, or at least have arranged a taxi."

"According to the restaurant's doorman, there was some disagreement outside the restaurant about just that, which ended with the lady simply walking off."

"Could you go over the maître d's story again?" I asked Lestrade.

"I was going to do that. He seems to have spent a couple of days thinking, and when I went back Thursday, he had a lot more to tell me. Remember, he told Mr Holmes there was some disagreement between Miss Ruskin and the colonel? Well, it occurred to me that for a headwaiter he was very unaware of what was going on in his restaurant, and I mentioned at our first interview that I might find it necessary to ask the local PC to patrol the area more closely, stick his head in occasionally."

"Coercion, Lestrade? Tut-tut," said Holmes in mock disapproval.

"Not coercion, just encouragement. It did serve to boost his memory, and he managed to give me a more detailed account of the three hours the colonel and Miss Ruskin were there, with certain gaps where he, the waiter, was off elsewhere, though it was not a busy night. The first half hour, he said, seemed pretty heavy going, long silences, much studying of menus.

He got the impression that the colonel had been expecting her to be a man, remember, and that he was not at all happy about having to deal with Miss Ruskin. She, however, seemed to find it funny. Things did settle down, and they spent the next couple of hours going through a pile of papers she had with her. By this time, about eleven-forty, they'd both had a lot of wine and the colonel had drunk three g and t's besides. Unfortunately, this was one of the times when the waiter was out of the dining room, some kind of hubbub in the kitchen, apparently, and when he came back about ten minutes later, the two of them were staring each other down across the table, furious about something. He says he was worried because the colonel looked like a gentleman they'd had die in the restaurant four or five years ago, his face dark red and his eyes popping in his head. He was gesturing at some papers Miss Ruskin was holding, and was, in the waiter's words, 'considerably upset' over them. She seemed to be very sure of herself, and he heard her say a number of times something like 'Yes, it's possible.' A few minutes later, the colonel's chair fell over and the waiter looked up, to see him, I quote, 'standing over that old lady, looking for all the world like he was going to grab the papers away from her, or hit her, or something, but she just sat glaring up at him like a banty, and halfway to laughing. He stood there almost shaking, like he was about to explode with anger.'

"That's when he asked to use the telephone. He had the waiter bring him a double brandy in the manager's office and was closed up in there with the telephone for about ten minutes before he came back. He was calmer then, sat down and talked to her for another twenty minutes or so—uncomfortable talk, very stiff, and they seemed to be working themselves back up to the state they had been in before when all of a sudden, Miss Ruskin put her papers back into her briefcase, got to her feet, and left. Outside on the street, he offered to drive her to her hotel. Which offer she refused, and she died perhaps fifteen minutes later."

"Those words of hers—'Yes, it's possible'—are just what she told me that afternoon when I doubted the manuscript's authenticity," I said. "It sounds fairly conclusive that she showed him a copy of it."

"I agree," said Lestrade, then stifled a yawn that left his eyes watering. "Sorry. Haven't had a solid eight hours for two weeks."

"The Kent murders?" asked Mycroft with sympathy.

"That, yes, and yesterday I was down in Cornwall, where the child was killed. Nasty piece of work, that. Still, there was a witness, which should help. And as for your witnesses, Miss Chessman and Mr O'Rourke were no help at all. He had his back to it the whole time—climbing a drainpipe to nick a flower from a window box for his lady love—and she draws a blank and starts crying when it comes to details. Says she saw the old beggar sitting and Miss Ruskin walking up to the street corner, but after that, all she remembers is shiny black paint and the blood. She was pretty hysterical, I gather, by the last time I sent someone round, and worse than useless at the inquest. You saw we got an adjournment, did you?"

We had.

"Now, about Mrs Rogers. You'll understand, I hope, that this case has pretty low priority compared with two women knifed in Kent and a little boy horribly dead in Cornwall, which means that information is slow in coming in. All I have to add concerning Mrs Rogers is that her two sons have greying hair, since you asked, Mr Holmes. One is a sailor, like his father. He is not married—in this country at any rate—and has been out of the country since March. The other is married to an Italian woman; they have four sons and three daughters, ages fifteen to thirty-two. The two youngest and an unmarried daughter and her child live at home still, but the others are scattered from Lincoln to Bath. I had already begun to look at them before I got your telegram," he said with a faint touch of reproof, acknowledged by Holmes with a gracious nod.

"Three members of the family have criminal records, for what it's worth: The sailor son bashed someone over the head with a bottle in a brawl a few years back, got four months; a granddaughter, Emily, aged thirty now, was done for shoplifting seven years ago; and a grandson, Jason, age twenty-six, seems to have spent his youth with a bad crowd—housebreaking, picked up for passing stolen goods once, petty stuff, not brutal and never for bodily harm—but either he decided he wasn't much good at it and went straight or else he suddenly got much better, because he hasn't been touched in four years. And before you ask, Mr Holmes, most of the crew have dark hair.

"Finally, the ibn Ahmadi family and their grudge against Miss Ruskin. Preliminary reports—"

I interrupted him. "Who?"

"Ibn Ahmadi," he repeated, doing his best with the strange pronunciation. "Oh, sorry, I forgot what a solid week it's been. That's the family Mr Mycroft Holmes mentioned, who were done out of a piece of land in Palestine."

"Muddy," I offered, to his momentary confusion, the homophone suggested by Erica Rogers in the letter to her sister—a name foreign, multisyllabic, and sounding like *mud*. Before I could go further, he was nodding.

"Yes, muddy, like she said in her letter. There are no less than twenty-four members of the clan, if I may call it that, here in Britain at present, all but four of them male, every one of them, I'd wager, having black hair, with the possible exception of one old auntie of sixty-three years who was thoroughly draped and hidden. Questions are being asked concerning whereabouts, but it will be slow, I'm afraid, and less likely to be fruitful as each day passes."

"I fail to see any connection between the Ahmadi family and the ransacking of the cottage," growled Holmes. "Her death, perhaps, but could she have had something they wanted? Mycroft?" He seemed curiously uninterested in the question, merely as it were playing out a part written down for him.

The large figure of his brother stirred and leant forward in his armchair, his grey eyes on the balloon glass of brandy cradled in his enormous hand.

"I fear that I shall have to throw yet another scent in our paths by answering that in the affirmative." Holmes made a sharp, impatient motion that amounted to a derisive snort. His brother ignored him. "One of my . . . colleagues succeeded in identifying the taxi driver who picked Miss Ruskin up from her hotel that Tuesday morning."

"No easy matter, that, in this city," I commented. His fat face took on a satisfied look, like a cat full of warm milk.

"I was pleased with that piece of work, true. Very fortunately, Miss Ruskin was not taken to a railway station or to the underground, but to a specific address here in London—a house. I had become interested in this case, so I went there myself, only to find that the family who lived in that house had no knowledge of such a woman. Nor did the four houses on either side. I was even more interested by now, and I took a leisurely stroll up and down, until I came across a house on the next street over that had all the signs of being other than a family dwelling: curtains tightly shut, signs of somewhat greater foot and bicycle traffic than the other houses, no wear on the front door at child level—all those small indications—you know them as well as I. The address was one which I recalled from a report that came across my desk a few months ago, minor organisations in London that in themselves seem harmless but which might nonetheless become linked with difficulties in the future. I knocked on the door and asked the man who answered if I might speak to whomever had been seen by Miss Dorothy Ruskin that Tuesday.

"He was, shall I say, hesitant about letting me in, and I was forced to make a few unfriendly and authoritative noises at him. After much dancing about, he went off and returned with the gentleman who seems to be in charge of the house, which is, as you might have foreseen, a unit of Weizmann's Zionist organisation. I will not trouble you with the whole of the following lengthy and highly interesting conversation. I will merely say as a précis that we found ourselves to have a number of mutual friends, and when eventually we returned delicately to the topic of Miss Ruskin, my new friend the rabbi was happy to admit that she had indeed been there, had brought with her a thick manila envelope containing a number of letters and papers from Palestine, and had, among other things, told the rabbi that the business of the ibn Ahmadi family's land was far from over and that she foresaw an escalation of hostilities, both within Palestine and without. She was concerned that this might become a ready rallying cause for a variety of unrelated grievances, and she wanted to warn her friends to be, as the saying goes, on the lookout."

"Inconclusive, but suggestive," commented Holmes grudgingly. "How long was she there?"

"Approximately two and one half hours. One of their men was going into town, and they shared a cab as far as Paddington, where she left him just before noon."

"Oxford," I cried at the name of the train station. "I told you she went to Oxford. Did you have any results with those names, Inspector?"

"None at all. The old man at the library was gone part of that day, and he didn't see her."

"Jedediah out sick? The place will collapse—he's been there practically since Thomas Bodley married Mrs Ball."

"His mother's funeral, I believe. She was one hundred and two."

"Ah, good. For a minute, you had me worried."

"Was there any more, Mycroft?" asked Holmes, as scrupulously polite as a concert pianist at a children's music recital.

"Just that I was allowed to examine the envelope of papers, and they were as they should have been, no personal documents, no will. That is all, Sherlock. The floor is yours."

Up to that point, I had immersed myself in the charade. I had stated my evidence factually, listened to Lestrade's contribution as if it were of some importance, and noted Mycroft's rumblings, but before Holmes opened his mouth, before he so much as sat upright, I knew what he was going to say. I could see all my hard-won efforts tumbling down, and I knew that it was an emptiness. I saw the body of the case against Colonel Edwards flash up and crumble away into a drift of ashes like the walls of a wooden house in a fire: Holmes had the case in his hands, and there was nothing for it. The rest of us—even Mycroft—were left scrambling on thin air, and I was suddenly furious, seized by a pulse of something disturbingly near hatred for this superior prig I had so irrevocably attached myself to. It lasted for only an instant, before common sense threw a bridge out across the morass of tiredness, resentment, and uncertainty, of the awareness of urgent work undone and the remnants of shame and confusion from the afternoon, and I stood again on firm ground. I only hoped that neither pair of all-knowing grey eyes had witnessed the moment's lapse. Holmes was completing the motion of sitting upright.

"Thank you," he said. "Lestrade, would you mind pulling that crate over from the corner? Just put it here, thank you." He leant forward, untied the grubby string, and removed the top with the flourish of a conjurer. Inside was a jumble of chromium-plated bits of metal, hunks of broken glass, a large slab of dented mud guard, and a sheaf of the inevitable evidence envelopes. My heart twisted at the sight, then started to beat heavily. I must have moved or made a sound, because Holmes looked at me.

"Yes, Russell, the murder weapon. Or rather, portions of it. I knew it would be there, once I knew that Miss Ruskin had been killed by a motorcar, and particularly when the machine was not found nearby, stolen, used, and abandoned. Why a motorcar, a method which took at least two persons to arrange and had all the attendant danger of the telltale damage? The person who thought of it had to have the vehicles both ready to mind and near to hand; plus, the means of repairing damage must be available to him. I knew I should find some such facility as a garage, and the only danger was how thoroughly they had covered their tracks. In this case, they were too sure of themselves—Jason Rogers had rid himself of the pertinent sections in a load of other scrap metal sold to a local dealer, from whom I retrieved them.

"Unfortunately, their carelessness went only so far. They did quite a thorough job of washing the wreck down before they set to repairing it. There are only three small deposits of what may be dried blood, the largest being here, inside the broken headlamp. Samples of black paint from the side of the mud guard are in the envelope—to be matched up against whatever you may find on the button and her hairpins in your evidence envelope—as well as several hairs and one tiny scrap of fabric that resembles closely Miss Ruskin's coat, all of which I found among the débris. Fingerprints were useless, all of them from people who work in the shop, and as Inspector Lestrade notes, most of the Rogers grandsons have black hair, including Jason and his younger brother Todd, who occasionally works in the shop. I did take samples from the back of Jason Rogers's chair, though, as you know, the most one can hope for is a probable match. I have been working on different tests for matching hairs, but I have yet to come up with the definitive one."

Four sets of eyes scowled down into the box of mechanical jumble, wishing with varying degrees of intensity for the evidence to be there. Finally, Lestrade folded up his notebook and took up the piece of string.

"I'll give it to my lab people, Mr Holmes, with thanks. I don't think I'll ask how you came to have the stuff, though."

"Oh, it's all quite legal and above board, Lestrade, I assure you, part of a shipment of scrap purchased by a newly formed company called Sigerson Limited. You shall receive the billing invoice in the morning. You may be less happy with my methods of obtaining a certain letter. Do you have it, Russell?"

I had worn the letter in my undergarments most of the day, but now I took it from my handbag and gave it to Lestrade, who raised his eyebrows at its gouged, ink-splattered appearance. His eyebrows nearly disappeared beneath his overly long hair as he read it, and he whistled softly and handed it to Mycroft.

"Seems to me that Colonel Edwards is less and less likely, wouldn't you say, Mr Holmes?"

"It looks that way, I agree." His voice was bland, and he did not look at me. I felt another irrational and momentary surge of irritation, as if someone had dismissed my prize thoroughbred as being not quite up to the rest of the field.

"Mycroft's Arabs strike me the same way," I said, sounding regrettably peevish. Holmes glanced at me then, amused, and rose to his feet.

"I think that brings us up-to-date. When shall we four meet again?"

"If it's in thunder and in rain, I'm going to throw Miss Small's accursed shoes out the window and wear my Wellingtons," I grumbled. "Not tomorrow—I'll be back late. Tuesday?"

It was agreed, and we dispersed.

Holmes and I drove back with few words. He had to return the cab to its owner, and as it was still raining hard, he stopped in front of the boardinghouse to let me out. I looked out the window at the unwelcoming door, with my fingers on the car's door handle.

"You won't be long?" I asked. It would be just like him to disappear again for some days.

"Twenty minutes. If he's there, I'll have him drive me back."

I nodded and moved to open the door. His voice stopped my hand.

"You know, Russell, one of the damnable things about working in partnership is that one has to take the other person's proprietary feelings into account—*Russell proponit sed Holmes disponit.* It's not everyone who will put up with being run roughshod over in the course of the chase and then be willing to brush himself off and set to again as if nothing had happened. It was one of Watson's most valuable strengths as a partner, his doglike devotion. However," and here he turned his face towards me, though there was not enough light to reveal his expression, "you will no doubt have noticed that I did not consider this a strength when it came to a permanent partnership."

It was a generous apology, for Holmes, and I grinned at him.

"Woof," I said, and ducked out into the rain.

# PART FIVE

## Monday, 3 September 1923– Wednesday, 5 September 1923

*The poet's pen . . . gives to airy nothings a local habitation and a name.*

—Shakespeare

# NINETEEN

T

*tau*

I never tire of Oxford. Cambridge is stunning, of course. Cambridge is sweet and ethereal, and the air in Cambridge bubbles in the mind like fine champagne, but I cannot imagine getting any work done there. Oxford is a walled city still, and within her black and golden, crumbling, scabrous, aged, dignified, and eternal walls lie pockets of rarefied air, places where, turning a corner or entering a conversation, the breath catches and for an instant one is taken up into . . . if not the higher levels of heaven, at least into a place divine. And then, in the next moment, there comes an eddy of grit, and the ghostly echo of mediaeval oxcarts is heard rumbling down past Christopher Wren's bell tower on their way from Robert D'Oilley's castle to his grand bridge over the river. Even in Oxford University's holy of holies, the Bodleian Library, there comes an occasional grumble and whiff of the internal combustion engine.

The grit that morning was palpable, for the haze that softened the sunlight of what might otherwise have been a shimmering morning was the result of burning stubble in the surrounding countryside, and even at the early hour of my arrival, the black skeletal remains of the hard stalks rained gently onto the city, forming drifts that swirled up at the passing of motorcars. I saw no washing hung up to dry that Monday morning as I walked into town from the train station, along the sluggish canal, under the shadow of the otherworldly castle mound, looking in its vernal leaf more like a setting for Puck and Titania than it did a hillock for undergraduate picnics overlooking the prison, then past the decrepit slums of Greyfriars and out onto the deceptive everyday face of the most beautiful high street in any city I have seen, dodging carts, autos, trams, and bicycles, the town centre strikingly incomplete without its normal complement of fluttering black gowns, like a friend with a new and extreme haircut. Up the High towards the tantalising curve, but before entering it, at the very foot of St Mary's wise divinity, I made an abrupt turn north, and there, oddly satisfying in its scorn for a deliberate and formal perfection, was the quadrangle with the rotund earthiness of the Radcliffe Camera in its centre, bounded on its four sides by the tracery of All Souls on my right, the height of St Mary's at my back, Brasenose College on the left giving nothing away, and before me, where there should rightly have been trumpets and gilt, the unadorned backside of the Bodleian and the Divinity School. I was home.

I had come here for three purposes. The first, I dispatched within two hours: Although modern Egyptian history is not my field, once one knows the basic techniques of research, no field's fences or unfamiliar terrain make much of a barrier. I skimmed half a dozen books and brought the colonel's wavering scholarship back to earth, noted two contrary arguments and a nice apothegm I would steal for him, and then abandoned Egypt, to proceed with my own, considerably more appealing projects. I began in Duke Humfrey's.

My tools were a broad-nibbed pen, an unlined notebook, and a page with twenty words written on it. On a quick tour of the room, I spotted three familiar heads: a good beginning. I gathered up two of my fellow students, approached the third figure, a don whose subject was church history, and explained my need.

"I wonder if I might ask your help with a little project of mine," I began. "There's this fairly old piece of manuscript that I think may have come from a woman's hand. I have a friend who's something by way of an expert on handwriting—you know, he can tell you whether the person is right- or left-handed, old or young, where and how much he was educated, that sort of thing—and he said that if I were to collect some samples of men and women writing Greek and Hebrew, which is what the manuscript is in, it would give him a paradigm for comparison."

"What great fun," the don exclaimed, his eyes sparkling through bottle-glass lenses. "Do you know, just the other day I dug up a sheaf of letters in Bodley, and as I was reading through them, two of them struck me as some-how ineffably feminine. They're Latin, of course, but if you do come up with anything on your project, you might be interested in seeing these others. Any particular phrase you want written?" he added, reaching for his pen.

"Yes, here's the list, and do use this pen—it'll keep the samples uniform." His eyebrows rose at the selection of words, but he wrote them neatly and handed back the pen and book. The other two did the same. I made note of their identities on each page, thanked them, and left them to their books.

Academia being what it is, the reactions of everyone else I approached during the course of the day's investigations were quite predictable. Intensely curious and intellectually excited, particularly over my chosen words (which in Greek included *Jerusalem, Temple, Rachel, madness, confusion,* and *Romans,* and in Hebrew the words for *day, darkness, land,* and *wilderness*), they were nonetheless loath to trespass on my personal research. As a result, all helped, except one ancient of days who was having a flare-up of arthritis in his writing hand, and all demanded to see the results of my little project as soon as it was published. By early afternoon, I had a filled notebook. Furthermore, by late afternoon, I had a clear idea of what Dorothy Ruskin had done on the missing Tuesday, and by evening, when I prepared to turn my back on the town centre, I had a vastly renewed sense of vigour and purpose. For all of those things, I felt profoundly grateful.

I made my late supper of a meat pie and half a pint of bitter at the Eagle and Child, and took the train back to London. It was nearly eleven o'clock when I said, "Evening, Billy" into the empty corridor and heard his reply through the door. I was hardly surprised that the room next to mine was empty. It had taken me some days to get back into the rhythm of a case, but I had now remembered it, and I no longer expected Holmes to appear but for brief snatches of consultation, reflection, and sleep.

I went down the hallway to the bathroom and washed away the day's grime, checked to see that I had an ironed frock for the next day, and settled down at the little window table with a lamp and the notebook. Shortly after midnight, I heard a key in the door of the adjoining room, and a moment later the grizzled, disreputable face of my husband leered at me from the connecting door, one eye drooping and sightless, teeth stained brown and yellow, lips slack.

"Good evening, Russell, hard at work, I see. I'll be with you in a moment." He pulled back into his room. I closed my notebook and walked over to the doorway to lean against the jamb with my arms crossed, watching him as he discarded the disguise. There was a lift to his shoulders and a gleam in his eyes that I rarely saw at home, and he looked and moved like a man twenty years younger as he tossed his clothing into an untidy heap in the bottom of the wardrobe, replacing it with his usual spotless shirt and soft dressing gown, then bent over the mirror to remove his eyebrows and scrub off the makeup. He was back in his own proper element.

My face must have reflected my thoughts, for he caught my eye in the mirror and began to smile.

"What amuses you, my wife and colleague?"

"Oh, nothing, Holmes. I was just wondering about the bees."

He looked startled for a moment, and then he began to laugh softly.

"Ah, the bees, yes, and the pottering beekeeper. Even an old hound occasionally stirs to the sound of a distant horn. I do wish you would not snort, Russell; it is really most unbecoming. I suppose you would like me to shave," he added, examining his chin thoughtfully.

"I only snort at snortworthy statements, Holmes, and yes, please do. Unless you intend to spend the night on the streets."

"There has been quite enough of that in the last week, thank you. I have been very cold without my Shunammite."

I studied him as he stropped the ivory-handled cutthroat, with a jaunty flick of the wrist at the end of each stroke.

"You must have been heartily sick of that snowstorm, Holmes. From Genesis to First Kings, just to escape the missionaries."

"Oh, no, I only reached the twenty-eighth chapter of Leviticus on that occasion. I appropriated a pair of skis as soon as the snow stopped." He reached for the shaving mug and began to whip the brush furiously about.

"I didn't know you could ski."

"I learnt. It was less hazardous duty than the missionaries."

"Coward. You might have learnt something from them, such as the fact that Leviticus has only twenty-seven chapters. Now, if you will excuse me, I shall go and warm the bed."

Sometime later, I thought to ask what he had been doing that day.

"I have been reading my Bible."

"I beg your pardon?"

"Sorry, was my arm over your ear?"

"It must have been—I could have sworn I heard you say you were reading your Bible. You don't even own one."

"I did, I was, and I do. Now. Thanks to your friend the colonel."

"Holmes—"

"Do not ruffle your feathers; I shall explain. I have spent the evening in the company of a number of unfortunate gentlemen who, like myself, are willing to participate in a rudimentary Bible study, provided their stomachs are not empty at the time."

I sorted this out.

"The colonel's church runs a soup kitchen."

"Got it in one. There seems to be a certain degree of affection on the part of the unfortunates towards their benefactors, judging from the way they lowered their voices for the more ribald of statements concerning King David and Abishag, his human hot-water bottle."

"That doesn't surprise me. But how did you find him? Did you follow him all day?"

"Hardly. I began in the bookstore-cum-printshop that produced the tract on women you found on the colonel's bookshelf. In the course of our conversation, the owner told me of a lecture being given in the afternoon on the topic of 'Women in the Church.' I went and sat two rows behind Colonel Edwards."

"Not dressed as one of the unfortunates, I think."

"By no means. I was a highly respectable gentleman with a neat little beard. A most informative lecture, Russell. You would have found it quite stimulating."

"No doubt," I agreed politely. "So, you followed him to the church, changed yourself into that character with the eye, and allowed him to serve you soup and try his best to save your soul."

"Essentially, yes. It was truly a most amusing day."

"Amusing, but was it absolutely necessary to douse yourself in the scent of cheap gin? It is very off-putting."

"I apologise. It was a means of adding corroborative detail and artistic verisimilitude to an otherwise bald and unconvincing narrative."

Before I could decide whether or not to pursue this obvious conversational red herring, he picked up the questioning himself.

"And you, Russell. How was your day?"

"Highly satisfactory, thank you, from beginning to end. Despite the fact that it's between terms in Oxford, I have sixty-seven writing samples. I also picked up the information the colonel wanted. Bought two books, one of them out of print since 1902. Had a nice chat with a few friends over a pie and a pint, and met an odd man named Tolkien, a reader in English literature at Leeds who has a passion for early Anglo-Saxon poetry and runes and such. And, oh yes, I found where Miss Ruskin was on that missing Tuesday afternoon."

His reaction was gratifying, and he was no longer relaxing towards sleep.

"Well done, Russell. I hoped you might dig that one out. Wait, let me get my pipe."

He came back, wrapped himself in his dressing gown, and pulled the chair over next to the bed, settling down like a cat, with his legs tucked beneath him.

"Once I knew her college, it didn't take long," I told him. "The dean was in, and I just asked her if there might be any particularly close friends of Miss Ruskin's about. She knew Miss Ruskin herself and was surprised that I should be asking. 'Isn't that a coincidence,' she said. 'I saw her only, oh, less than two weeks ago. I happened to be heading down the Corn-market and I looked up and there she was. I couldn't stop to talk, unfor-tunately, but it was she. Her sight is getting very bad, poor thing, isn't it?' No, she didn't know. I told her, and she was rather upset, but not shocked. I suppose hearing that one of the older alumnae had died must be a com-mon enough occurrence for her. At any rate, she gave me the names of five people whom she knew to be friends of Miss Ruskin—three in the Oxford area and two in London. I was lucky—three of the five were on the tele-phone. One said she had spoken with Miss Ruskin but hadn't seen her. An-other was in Canterbury, and the third was not aware that Miss Ruskin was in the country. That left one in Oxford and one in London. I took a taxi up the Woodstock Road to the fourth friend, but I found her house shut up tight. I stood about scratching my head and looking lost until one of those nosey neighbours with see-all lace curtains at the windows came out to tell me that dear, sweet Miss Lessingham was in hospital with a broken hip, had been for three weeks now, though she was doing considerably bet-ter. So, I backtracked to the Radcliffe Infirmary and found that yes, indeed, 'dear Dorothy' had spent some hours with Miss Constance Lessingham, her onetime tutrix and lifelong friend. Had, in fact, spent the entire afternoon there at her side, reading to her and helping her write a number of letters, before leaving to catch the eight-ten to Paddington.

"You should have seen her, Holmes, lying there in that hospital bed in her mobcap, like a thin Queen Victoria, regally accepting the ministrations of nurses, doctors, friends, grandchildren of her old students, you name it. She must be ninety-five if she's a day, but completely aware, not in the slightest fuzzy. I told her about the manuscript, and she was fascinated. Nothing would do but that I should recite it to her—twice: once in the original, then in translation. I felt like I had just been through a viva voce when she finished with me. It must have tired her, too, because she fell asleep for about ten minutes.

"When she woke up, I told her that Miss Ruskin had died, and how. At first she didn't say anything, just stared out the window at the clouds, but then two tears came, just two little drops on that tiny wrinkled face, and she said, 'That makes seventy-one of my students who have predeceased me, and at every one, I've thought that it just doesn't seem right. They were my children, you see, and a mother should never have to outlive her ba-bies.' She was quiet for a minute, and then she sort of chuckled and said, 'Well, that's what I get for being too stubborn to die, I suppose,' and she returned to the manuscript. I asked her several questions, on the chance that Miss Ruskin had told her something, but so far as I could tell, they had just talked about archaeology and mutual friends. Sorry there wasn't more to the missing afternoon."

"At least it fills in a distressingly large hole in her schedule. I assume that her departure from Oxford and her ten o'clock return to the hotel match up?"

"They do, I'm afraid."

"Never mind. Tomorrow is another day."

"Are you returning to Cambridgeshire tomorrow?"

"No. The work there is finished." He did not mean the wallpaper.

"Good."

"Go to sleep now. I shall finish this pipe, I think."

"Stay here."

"I won't disturb you?"

"To the contrary."

"Ah. I have felt your absence as well, Russell. Sleep well."

I drifted away into confused thoughts of indomitable old ladies and monocled young aristocrats, and the heavy pipe smoke seemed to tingle on the inside of my right wrist. In the muzziness that comes just before sleep, the incongruous statement Holmes had made earlier came back to mind, and I knew where I had heard it.

"Good Lord, Holmes!" I exclaimed, brought up out of sleep.

"Yes, Russell?"

"Since when do you go in for Gilbert and Sullivan?"

"Of all the unpleasant acts I have been forced to perform in the course of an investigation, trailing a suspect who was addicted to light opera and vaudeville was one of the most depraved. I might ask the same of you, Russell."

"The girl who lived down the hall had a beau in a D'Oyley Carte production of the *Mikado* when it came to Oxford, and she dragged me along."

"Was that the hypochondriac whose bandages we stole?"

"No, the one with the brandy that tasted of petrol."

"That explains it, then."

"Good night, Holmes."

"Mmm."

# TWENTY

## υ

*upsilon*

The following morning, I woke at first light, to find Holmes still curled up in the chair, his eyes far away. The only signs that he had moved during the night were the saucer on the arm of his chair (heaped with burnt matches and pipe dottles), the faint stir of the curtains (where he had thoughtfully cracked open the window to prevent our suffocation), and the small notebook of writing samples on the bedside table (which I had left in the chest of drawers). I could almost see the thin film of greasy smoke on the walls, and I shuddered as I pulled the blankets back over my head in protest.

"You look like a vulture sitting there, Holmes," I growled. Four hours' sleep makes me irritable. The last of the objects I had noticed galvanised a faint activity in my brain cells.

"What is your judgement on the writing?" I asked with eyes firmly closed.

"Your papyrus is definitely from a woman's hand."

"Good. Wake me at seven."

There was no answer, but a minute or so later, a horrible, cold, bristly male person insinuated itself into my cozy nest, stinking faintly of cheap gin and strongly of stale tobacco.

"My dear, sweet wife," it murmured into my tightly blanketed ear.

"No!"

"Russell, my dear."

"Absolutely not."

"Wife of my age, I am going to give you another opportunity to solve this case of yours."

"At this very moment?"

"This afternoon."

I pulled the bedclothes down a fraction and eyed him. "How?"

"You will go to see Miss Sarah Chessman."

"The witness?" The blankets fell away. "But she's been questioned a number of times. She can't remember a thing."

"She couldn't remember for the police, no." His voice was curiously, ominously gentle. "Perhaps she needs to be asked by someone who knows how best to release answers that lie buried deep in the mind."

I knew instantly what he was talking about, and a cold finger trickled up my spine.

"Oh no, Holmes," I whispered. "Really, no. I couldn't. Don't ask that of me. Please."

"I am not asking anything of you, Russell." His voice was steady and soft, and he knew precisely what he was doing. "I simply thought that if it helped her remember what happened that night, you might think it worthwhile. It is your decision."

"You—Holmes, you utter bastard. Goddamn it, why don't you do it? All you do is play dress-up and prune roses and root around nice tidy automobile salvage yards while I vamp that man and dodge his son's slimy hands, all for nothing, and then you tell me to go mucking around in someone else's nightmare and—oh God." I sat back against the head of the bed and took a deep breath. "Sorry. I am sorry, Holmes. You're right. You're always right, damn you." I turned to him, and lay listening to the steady rhythm of his heart and lungs. "We're down to very little else, aren't we?"

"I honestly do not know. I ought to have kept the evidence I gave Lestrade and worked on it myself. I am seized by the idea that they will make some terrible missteps. Police laboratories can be either as inexorable as doomsday or as flighty as a cage of butterflies, and one never knows. We can wait and see what they produce with those bits of chromium and enamel. Juries do so like motives, though. I cannot escape that thought. But you are right, Russell, there is no reason to rush into the interview with Miss Chessman. No reason at all. And even if the laboratory finds nothing concrete enough to convict on, there is still a choice. Always we have the choice of turning back. The woman is already dead, and I cannot see anyone else being killed if her murderer isn't caught."

I raised up and looked at him, and I saw myself reflected in his grey eyes.

"I can't believe I heard that," I said. "You must believe me fragile indeed to have even thought of it. Of course we go on. We have no choice. The choice was made weeks ago, when we invited her to Sussex. That doesn't mean I have to like it, though."

"No, it does not mean that. You'll think about seeing Miss Chessman?"

"I'll go this evening, when she gets home from work."

He said nothing, just warmed me until it was time for me to leave for work. Why I was returning to the Edwards house, I was not certain, as it was fairly obvious now that the trail led elsewhere. Partly, it was that I had said I would be there, and explanations on the telephone might prove difficult. There was also the fact that I did not wish to waste the work I had done in Oxford the day before, and I felt some responsibility to the book. Mostly, though, it gave me something to do to take my mind off of the cold pit in my stomach. I dreaded my own past and the pain that could well be dredged up while helping Miss Chessman recover her memories of Dorothy Ruskin's death. Coping with Edwards and son would keep the cold sweats at bay.

I determinedly kept the colonel to the book all morning, and by the time Alex rang for lunch, I had given him the outline, two sample chapters, and the name of an editor whom a friend in my college had recommended for the purpose. Over lunch, I told the colonel that I was being called back home and would have to leave London by the end of the week, most terribly sorry. I was glad that young Gerald was not around.

"Mary, look, is it because—"

"No, Colonel, it is not because of anything you have or have not done. Or your son, for that matter. I have enjoyed working here, and I hoped more would come of it. In fact, I think we could have become friends." A statement, I realised, that gave a half truth, an emphatic truth, and, to my own surprise, a further truth. "I did not realise that my prior commitments would return to claim me quite so soon, and I'm sorry about it all."

"No apologies necessary, Mary. You are a most mysterious lady, though. I wish I had come to know you better. Would that be possible, do you think?"

"Colonel, I doubt that you'd like what you learnt. But, yes, perhaps I shall reappear, mysteriously, if you like. Now, I wanted to talk to you about that fifth chapter. I really do think you should consider a few pages on family structure and the subtler powers of the woman in Egyptian society. . . ."

# TWENTY-ONE

*phi*

A t 5:20, my week's pay in my handbag, I stood outside the building where Miss Sarah Chessman lived. Seven minutes later, I saw a woman matching her description alight from a crowded omnibus and clack purposefully down the street towards me, a small woman with glossy shingled hair, wearing clothes that had been carefully tailored for a woman who weighed a few pounds more than she did just now. The deliberate set to her jaw and shoulders made me wonder how long she could stretch her reserves, and as she drew near, I could see the pallor of her skin and the tautness next to her eyes and the slightly haunted look I had often, in the past, seen in my own mirror. She took out her key, and as she moved past me to the door, I held out a meaningless but official-looking card which Lestrade had prepared for me.

"Miss Chessman?" I asked politely.

She jumped as if I had screamed at her, and when she looked up from the card, she had on her face a look of pure loathing.

"Oh, bloody hell, not again!"

She jammed her key into the lock, slammed the door violently open, and stalked into the building.

"Miss Chessman?" I called after her.

"Come in, for Christ's sake. Let's get it over with. But it's the last time, do you hear? Absolutely the last time."

I followed her up to her tiny flat and closed the door behind me. The room was painfully neat, and the way in which she went automatically to the wardrobe to brush her coat and hang it up and to place her hat on the shelf told me that it was not a temporary tidiness, but a permanent state. Like its occupant, the room was glossy, smooth, and designed to allow no one entrance without permission. Both room and woman were very different from the teary, newly affianced flosshead I had expected to find. This was going to prove even more difficult than I had anticipated.

She was, however, nervous and could not quite hide the fact. She went to a cupboard and poured herself a drink, straight gin, without offering me anything. She took a large swallow, went to a table near one of the two windows, took a cigarette from a japanned tin box, and made a great show of inserting it into a holder and lighting it. She stood and puffed and drank and looked down at the passing cars, and I waited motionless, hands in pockets, for her to gain control of herself. Finally, she stubbed the cigarette out in a spotless ashtray and went back to the drinks cupboard. She spoke over her shoulder.

"I've already told you people everything I can remember. Three nights last week and once on the weekend, one bloody set of police after another. You'd think I'd run her down, the way the questions come."

"I'm not from the police, Miss Chessman." The mildness of my reply turned her around, and she ran her eyes over me as I stood there patiently. "The card was given me so you would know I was here with their permission."

"Then who are you? The newspapers?"

"No." I had to smile at the thought.

"Who, then?"

"A friend."

"No friend of mine. Oh, you mean a friend of hers, that woman?"

"Of that woman, yes."

I thought for a minute she would tell me to go, but abruptly she threw up one hand in a lost little gesture, and seemed even smaller.

"Oh, all right. Sit down. Can I give you something?"

"A small glass of the gin would be nice." I did not intend to drink it, but it established the community of the table. She brought it and her own refilled glass and sat opposite me. I thanked her.

"Really," she said, subdued, "I cannot help you. I've told everyone everything I can remember. You're wasting your time."

"She was my friend," I said simply. "You were the last person, aside from her murderers, to see her alive. Do you mind awfully, going through it again? I know it must be very painful for you, and I'll understand if you can't bring yourself to do it."

Her face softened, and I caught a glimpse of the person her friends saw, when her formidable defenses were down. She would have few friends, I thought, but they would be lifelong.

"Do you know, you're the first person who has said that to me? Every other one acted like I had all the feelings of a phonograph record."

"Yes, I know. I should hate having to be a policeman, having to grow all hard and impersonal to keep from being eaten up by it all. I'm sorry they were so awful to you."

"Oh, well, it wasn't that bad, I guess. The worst of it was the way they wanted every last detail, where was I standing, and where was the beggar sitting, and did the screeching sound come after she fell or as she was falling, and all the time all I could think of was the sound of—" She stood up and went for another cigarette, then pulled the harshness back up around her voice. "It's stupid, really, but I keep thinking of the time when I was nine and I saw my dog get crushed under a cart. Try telling a Scotland Yard chief inspector that." She laughed, and I knew that she would not help me, not in the way I needed her to help me, unless I could shatter that smooth surface. It would cost me a great deal to buy her cooperation, and there was no guarantee that the results would be worth the expense. I studied her glossy, smooth hair and well-cut clothes, and felt too tall and unkempt and poorly clothed, and I knew again that I had no choice. I exhaled slowly.

"May I tell you something?" My soft question brought her attention around to my face, and what she saw there brought her, wary, back to the chairs. I told her then the story I had given to only two other people in my life. It was a simple story, a terrible story, of an automobile that strayed from its side of the road and what happened when it met another automobile at the top of a cliff overlooking the Pacific Ocean, and what happened to the only survivor, the child who had been the cause of it: me.

It was a cruel thing to do, telling her that tale with the hideous, ever-fresh guilt lying naked in my face and voice. My coin was pain, my own pain, and with it I bought her. By the time I finished, she was, unwillingly, in my debt, and I knew that the drained starkness in her face was a reflection of my own.

"Why are you telling me this?" It was almost a whisper. "What do you want from me?"

I answered her indirectly but honestly.

"You have to remember that I was only fourteen. For several weeks, I ranged from states of near catatonia to violent fits of self-destruction. And amnesia. I could not remember the accident at all, not while I was awake, until a very good and amazingly sensitive psychiatrist took me on. Yes, you begin to see the point of it now. With her help, I learnt to get it under control, at least to the point that I could take it out and look at it. The

239

nightmares took longer, but then I . . . didn't have her help for more than a couple of months."

"Do you still have nightmares?" This was more than idle curiosity asking.

"Not of the accident, not anymore."

"How did you get rid of them?"

"Time. And, I told someone who cared. That took a long time."

"To tell?"

"To work up to the telling."

I waited while she fussed with another cigarette. Her short hair fell perfectly from the razor-sharp line down the centre of her scalp.

"What did she do to make you remember? The psychiatrist?"

"A number of different things, many of which would be inappropriate here. Are you by any chance expecting your fiancé this evening?"

My question confused her, but she answered willingly.

"Yes. He said he'd be here at six-thirty." It was five past.

"After he gets here, with your permission and his, I'd like to think about something, a little experiment. Have you ever been hypnotised?"

Her eyes grew slightly wary.

"Hypnotised? Like with a swinging watch, 'you are getting sleepy,' and that? I was at a party once where someone was doing it, making people walk through the fountain and such, but they were all pretty tipsy to begin with."

"What I'm talking about is quite different, and that's why I'd like your friend here before we make any decisions. I don't want to hypnotise you, and I certainly don't want to make you jump into a fountain or bark like a dog. What I should like to do, with your full cooperation, is to help you hypnotise yourself, so you can root around for any minor details you may have forgotten about that night. You know, sometimes the mind works a bit like those straw Chinese finger tubes, where the harder you pull against them, the more difficult it is to get loose. Having the police hammering away at you has only made the mind put up a wall to protect itself, and the idea of hypnotism is to allow you to relax and see through some peepholes in the wall." This was an entirely inadequate explanation, but its homeliness would satisfy and reassure. "You would be in charge, not I, though I'd like to have Mr O'Rourke here so that you feel perfectly safe about it."

"You won't make me do anything I don't want to do?" She didn't like the idea of relinquishing control any more than I would.

"I'm not certain I could, even if I wanted to," I lied, and then I returned to the truth. "You'd be aware and in control at all times, you could stop whenever you want, and Mr O'Rourke would be there to make certain of it."

"How long would it take?"

"Between one and two hours, I should think. If you are interested in doing it tonight," I said, shifting gently from the conditional and vague to a future and definite, "you ought to have something to eat first, and use the lavatory." I could see the simple details reassure her further.

"Tommy—Mr O'Rourke—is bringing some sandwiches. We were going for a picnic supper," she said noncommittally.

"I could come back tomorrow, if you like."

"No, it's all right. Actually, you've got me interested in it."

Mr Tommy O'Rourke arrived early with sandwiches and fizzy lemonade and an expression of deep mistrust when he saw me. By this time, Miss Chessman's apprehension had given way to a degree of enthusiasm, and she explained and chattered in between bites. I turned down the offer of food, took some coffee when it was made, and then sat down to explain the process so they would both know what to expect. When I had finished, Miss Chessman excused herself for a moment and left the room.

"How do you feel about all this, Mr O'Rourke?" I asked.

"D'you know, I think it may be a good idea. She's in a real state about it all, and I think . . . well, if she could feel she had helped some, instead of blaming herself for not being able to help, she'd feel . . . I don't know. She hasn't been sleeping at all well, I don't think." He was incoherent, but his concern was unmistakable.

"You understand that she may, to a certain extent, relive the accident? That she may go through the horror again, but I'll help her to lay it to rest, and you mustn't interrupt? It could be hard on her to be interrupted just then."

"I understand. Do I need to sit in the corner or anything?"

"Small noises and movements will not distract her, but please don't address her directly unless I ask you to.

"So, Miss Chessman, all ready? You will need to be comfortable. Lie down if you like, or sit in a chair that supports your head fully. Yes, that should be fine. A pillow, perhaps? Good. Shoes off? No? Very well." My voice became gentle, unobtrusive, and rhythmical.

"As I said, Miss Chessman, the idea of the exercise is to allow you a certain amount of distance between the world around you and the world you carry within you. We do this by steps, ten of them, by counting backwards from ten. Each of the ten steps takes you a bit further down into yourself, and when we come back up, we reverse the process. At ten, you are fully alert, relaxed, your eyes are open, and you can talk normally. Further down, between approximately six and three, or two, you may find speech inconvenient, distracting. In that case, if I ask you a question, I should like you to raise this finger, just slightly, to indicate yes"—I touched her right forefinger—"and this finger, just slightly, to signal no." I touched her left forefinger. "Do that now, please, for yes. That's right. And for no. Good. We are at ten now, all ten fingers relaxed and warm. You may leave your eyes open if you wish, or close them at any time. It does not matter in the least, though many people find it helpful to concentrate on a single object" ( . . . *one pink plaster rose on a pale yellow ceiling* . . . ) "as they walk down the ten steps. Noises from the room or your body's little reactions will not distract you, just nudge you a bit further towards the next step. We are at ten now, like your ten fingers, I want you to feel them one at a time as I count them, beginning with one." I touched the last knuckle of each finger in a slow cadence, numbering each one in turn, but I broke the rhythm after nine. An instant after I should have touched the last finger, it twitched ever so slightly, and I smiled to myself. This lady would not only walk through a fountain; she would probably undress first if I asked her. Intelligent, well-defended people are often the easiest to manipulate. I made a mental note to add a caution before I brought her back up from the trance.

"Very well, you are now fully relaxed, and you understand what we're doing, and in fact, when we're finished, you'll be able to do it all yourself. It's actually a very useful thing to know—for when you're going to the dentist, especially. I once had nine teeth worked on, and by walking down the steps first, I didn't have to be bothered by the discomfort; I could answer the dentist's questions, and afterwards I didn't have any pain, because my body had already acknowledged it. So you can see what a useful thing it is, and very easy, really, you've already made the step to nine, a small step, very easy, wasn't it? Just that bit more relaxed, your hands feel a bit heavier—feel your thumb joint, how heavy it is?—heavy and warm, even the tips of your fingers, down to nine, just under the surface now, and your face is beginning to relax now, your eyes and your mouth, like the feeling you get after a day of physical work, when you can sit back and relax, very tired, but a good tired, a satisfying tired, a tired that you feel at eight o'clock at night, in front of a warm fire with a hot drink, after eight hours out in the fresh air, but it's evening now, and you can relax and be satisfied."

Hypnotism is all rhythm and sensitivity, and I guided her down, never taking my eyes from her, never mentioning the night we were aiming for, always building her confidence and relaxation. In twenty minutes, we had passed through the yawning and twitching phases and were at four. Her eyes had fluttered closed. Tommy O'Rourke had not moved.

"Four, a nice balanced number, four limbs, four corners to a square. A dog has four legs, and I'd like you to do something in a minute, with your right hand, as we move down to three, only three steps now, three points in a triangle." I talked about three for a while; then, when she was firmly settled, I said, "I'd like you to make your right thumb meet your right middle finger in a circle, but you don't want to rouse yourself to do it; you want to let the two fingers do it, let the two tips of the two fingers come together all by themselves because it's the most natural thing for them to do. You can feel how they want to touch, can't you, if you just allow them. Just think about how it would feel to make a circle with those two fingers."

I spoke very slowly now, increasing the silences between the phrases. I was myself more than halfway into a trance, and as I spoke, I could hear another voice in my ear, saying the words I was about to pronounce, a woman's light voice with a slight German accent, speaking to a severely traumatised adolescent whose problems were considerably greater than those of Sarah Chessman's. The voice in my mind fell silent, and I stopped talking for a minute and watched the beginnings of the involuntary muscle control in her hand, jerky at first, as her unconscious mind took control of the muscles of the thumb and finger and brought them together, slowly, inexorably, into the light joining that would be like an iron link to pull apart. O'Rourke watched the eerie movements, and I felt his eyes on me, but I had no attention to spare him, and he subsided again into his chair.

"There is now a circle, one circle, and you can feel it now, one deep, quiet circle of now and then, and you can look into this circle because you are in it, and it is in you, this one circle, and you are on the bottom step, and that is as far as we can go now, and you are free to talk as you want and think as you want, and whenever you are here, you need feel only safe and sure of yourself, and nobody can touch you here; no one can ever ask you to do anything you don't want to. It's your step, Sarah, yours alone, and now you've found it, you can come back to it anytime you want, but just now, let's explore a bit, if you want to, and you can tell me all about the dinner you ate two weeks ago, on Tuesday night it was, you remember. It was a nice dinner, wasn't it, and if you want to tell me, I'd like to hear about it."

Her mouth made a kind of chewing motion two or three times, as if tasting the words, and then she spoke, her voice low and flat, slow at first, but quite clear.

"Tuesday night, we went to Matty's house for dinner. I wore my blue dress and we took a taxi because it isn't far and it was raining." She was launched, and she continued on in monotonous detail until I finally eased her out of Tuesday night into Wednesday morning, then the afternoon.

"And now it's Wednesday evening. You've come home from work, and Tommy's coming to pick you up at—what time did he say?"

"Half seven. We're going to a posh restaurant to celebrate our six-month anniversary, and there's a flaming pudding at the next table, so I order that, and Tommy orders champers." I let her go on again for some time before giving another touch to the reins of her narrative.

"And now it's later, and you're leaving the restaurant, and you're full of lovely food and happy with Tommy, and where do you go?" My voice was light and calm. O'Rourke, across the room, was beginning to tense up, but she was not; deep in the hypnotic state, she did not anticipate anything.

"We walk to the pub where we met, back in February, and we see some friends who got married in June and we go to their house and laugh and drink and Solly has some great new records from America and we dance and then the neighbours pound on the floor and we have to leave."

"And you set off walking and you're humming the music, aren't you? And you're still dancing along, and you love Tommy and the feel of your arm in his, and you cuddle a bit here and there because there's no one on the street, and in the light from the streetlamp Tommy sees a pot of red flowers up under somebody's window. . . ."

"And he starts to climb up the drainpipe to get me one, and I say, 'Oh, Tommy, don't do that, silly boy. Stop it. There's somebody coming and she—' "

It came upon her as suddenly as it had that night, and she went rigid, her mouth and eyes staring wide, and I went down beside her and spoke forcibly (*The sound of the voice with the German accent was deafening. Surely she couldn't hear me over it; surely O'Rourke would stand up and come over and demand to know who it was saying, "Mary, your clever eyes can remember—"*), into her ear.

"Tommy can't see, Sarah, but you can; your clever eyes can remember—it's like something in a cinema house, isn't it, on the screen, but slowed down, no more real than that, a car on the screen, coming out of the darkness and hitting her and tumbling her around, and it drives around the corner and then that dirty-looking beggarman stands up and he moves and he does something. He does something; he bends down and he is doing something with his hands. What is he doing, Sarah?"

"He . . . He . . . stands up. He isn't old. Why did I think he was old? He stands up like a young man and he goes to the pillar-box and he has . . . he has something in his hand. He has a pair of scissors in his hand, and he bends down, and then he . . . he's winding yarn into a ball, and he picks up his briefcase that's lying on the street and he turns his back on the . . . on that . . . She's not dead; she just moved. Tommy, she just moved, and the man walks off. He turns and sees us and he starts to run and the car is waiting for him and the door is open, someone in the front seat is leaning back to hold it open, a small person, wearing . . . I can't see, but he falls into the car, the back seat, and it starts driving away while his leg is still out of it, and then the door swings shut and the car is gone around the corner, and we go and see, but she's dead now. Oh God, how horrible, she's dead, oh God."

"Sarah," I interrupted, "The car, Sarah, look at the car going around the corner. What are the numbers on the registration plate at the back of the car?"

"That's funny, isn't it? There aren't any numbers on the back of it."

"All right, Sarah, look back at the beggarman. He's standing up now, Sarah; he's standing up and taking a step toward the pillar box, and he's wearing a hat, isn't he, a knit cap, and it's dark on the street, but the street-lamp lights up his face from the side. See how it hits his nose? You can see his nose clearly, the shape of it. And his chin, too, against his coat, and when he turns his head, the light falls on his cheeks and his eyes. You'll never forget the shape of his eyes, even though you can't see the eyes themselves. They're in the shadows, but his face, Sarah, you can see his face, and you'll never forget it. You'll remember him even when you've walked back up the steps, won't you, Sarah, because you're a clever girl, and Tommy's here to be with you, and that was a good woman who shouldn't have died, and you want to remember everything. Even if it hurts, like a sad movie, you can remember."

Her face was faintly surprised as she stared into the room, and slightly relieved, but not afraid or horrified. I continued, "You have it now, the moving picture of the beggar standing up and the people inside the car, and you can hold on to it now, like a clear cinema film. You can run it any-time you want; you can bring it back up the steps with you. Shall we go, then? One step now. You want to turn around now, and step back up onto step number two. It's as easy as breathing, slow and steady, taking that one section of the circle with you, up to number two, and then to three, the third step." I watched to see when she was firmly on each level before proceeding. "And to four, four steps up, you feel like you're waking up, though you haven't been asleep. You're halfway back now, at five."

She took a deep, shuddering breath at six and stretched at eight, and her eyes found Tommy and she smiled at ten. I sat back, limp, and closed my eyes. My blouse was clinging to my back with the sweat, and my neck and shoulder throbbed with fire.

Miss Chessman, in contrast, looked better than she had three hours before. Her eyes were clear, and she seemed rested. She smiled tentatively at me.

"Is it still clear in your mind?" I asked her. The smile faded, but her answer was even.

"It is. Funny I couldn't remember it before."

"Shock does that. I'd like to telephone a friend from Scotland Yard. He'll listen to your story without making you feel like a gramophone record, and he'll bring some photographs to see if any of them match the man you saw. Is that all right? I know it will be late when you finish, but it's best to do it while you're fresh, and he can fix it with your employers so you don't have to go in early."

"I don't mind. It would make me feel good to be doing something to help that woman. I mean to say, I know it's too late to help her, but—"

"Fine, then. Is there a telephone?"

"Down the hallway to the right."

I slumped against the wall as I waited for the connexion to Mycroft's number. Holmes answered it at the first ring, and I tried to keep the exhaustion from my voice.

"Hello, husband. Would you please ring Lestrade and tell him to bring his photographs along? I'll wait for him, then get a taxi back to Mycroft's when they're through with me."

"You got it?"

"As you say, I got it."

"It was hard?"

"In my humble opinion, psychiatrists are not paid enough. I'll be back as soon as I can."

But Holmes arrived even before Lestrade, and we left them to it, and I stumbled off to Mycroft's guest-room bed without even waiting to see which of Lestrade's sheaf of portraits Sarah Chessman picked out.

# TWENTY-TWO

*chi*

It was light in the room, despite the curtains, when a small noise woke me. After a moment, I spoke into my pillow.

"It occurs to me that I am condemned rarely to awaken normally under this roof. I am usually disturbed by loud and urgent voices from the sitting room, occasionally by a particularly horrendous alarm clock at some ungodly hour, and once by a gunshot. However," I added, and turned over, "of all the unnatural noises which serve to pull me from slumber, the rattle of a cup and saucer is the least unwelcome." I paused. "On the other hand, my nose tells me to beware a detective bearing coffee, rather than the more congenial beverage of tea. May I take this as a wordless message that my presence is required, in a wide-awake state?" I reached for the cup.

"You may. Lestrade is sending a car for us. He has made an arrest. Two arrests."

"The Rogers grandsons?"

"One Rogers grandson, and one friend of a Rogers grandson. A friend who has been known to carry a long and unfriendly knife, whose taste in clothing is towards the extreme, and who has in the past had contact with the long arm of the law over such varied disagreements as stolen property, driving a car in which a pair of unsuccessful bank robbers attempted to make their escape, and an argument over a lady in which blood was shed, but no life lost, at the end of the aforementioned knife."

"And Erica Rogers?"

"She has been brought down from Cambridgeshire for questioning. It took some time to arrange a nursemaid for the mother."

"Why, what time is it?"

"Five minutes before eleven o'clock." I'd slept for twelve hours.

"Good Lord, the colonel will think I've walked out on him. I told him I'd stay until Friday."

"I took the liberty of telephoning him at eight o'clock, to tell him you would not be to work today. He wished you well."

"Yes. I have some explanations to make there, I fear. But why the coffee?"

"Your presence is requested by Mrs Erica Rogers."

"Mrs Rogers? But why?"

"She told Lestrade that she would not make a statement without you present. My presence, though not required, is to be permitted."

I shook my head in a futile attempt to clear it.

"Does she know who you are, then? That her gardener and the hero of 'Thor Bridge' are one and the same?"

"It would seem so, although I could have sworn she did not know while I was there."

"But why me?"

"She did not tell Lestrade why, just that you must be there."

"How extraordinary. And Lestrade didn't object?"

"If it persuades her to make a statement, no. She's a stubborn old lady, is Mrs Erica Rogers."

"So I gathered. Here, take my cup. I must bath if I'm to deal with her."

Inspector Lestrade's office was not the largest of rooms, and with seven people seated there on that warm morning, all of whom were to some degree anxious, it became a claustrophobe's nightmare and stifling besides. Not everyone present had bathed that morning, and the windows were totally inadequate.

On closer inspection, two people presented a front of cool composure. One was Holmes, inevitably; the other was Mrs Rogers, who shot us a glance that would have stripped the leaves from an oak tree before turning back to face Lestrade. Her solicitor was red-faced and damp-looking, and I thought that his heart was probably not in the best of condition. Lestrade was without expression, but the furtiveness of his eyes and the nervous way his small hands shuffled his papers made me think that he was apprehensive about the coming interview. The young uniformed policeman to his side held his notebook tightly and clasped a pencil as if it were an unfamiliar weapon—recent graduate of a stenographer's course, I diagnosed, and fished my own pad out of my bag to hold it up unobtrusively, raising an eyebrow at Lestrade. He nodded slightly, looking marginally relieved. Holmes and I took the last two chairs, next to a stiff police matron who looked anywhere in the room except at Mrs Rogers. When we had seated ourselves, Lestrade began.

"Mrs Rogers, I asked you to come down here today so I could take a statement from you concerning your movements on Wednesday the twenty-second of August, the night your sister, Dorothy Ruskin, was killed by an automobile, and on the night of the twenty-fourth, when the house belonging to Mr Holmes and his wife was broken into and certain objects were stolen."

"Inspector Lestrade." The corpulent solicitor's voice informed us that he was a busy man and found this unnecessary intrusion on his time rather annoying. "Am I to understand that you are charging my client with murder and theft?"

"Suspected murder and burglary are being investigated, Mr Coogan, and we have reason to believe that your client may be able to assist us in this investigation." Lestrade was cautious in his choice of words, but he would make a poor poker player. Everyone in the room knew what a sparse hand he held. Erica Rogers, on the other hand, was completely inscrutable.

"Inspector, my client has no objection to helping in a criminal investigation, so long as she is not the subject being investigated. As far as I can see, you have little to connect her with Miss Ruskin's death, save their blood relationship. Is that not the case?"

"Not entirely, no."

"Then what evidence have you, Inspector? I believe my client has the right to know that, don't you?"

"I'll tell you what evidence they have, Timothy: They have nothing, nothing at all." Mrs Rogers's voice was as hard and as scornful as her old vocal cords could make it, and I saw the young constable go white and drop his pencil, while my hand scribbled automatically on. "They have a box of wrecked parts from the front of some motorcar that was brought into my grandson Jason's shop for repair, and they have the story of a woman who was drunk at the time but miraculously recovered her memory after being mesmerised, who described a person fitting Jason's general description. That is nothing, Chief Inspector. I had no reason to kill my sister, now did I? Yes, I thought her digging holes in the Holy Land was a waste of time, but I can't see you taking that in front of a judge and jury as some kind of a motive for murder. And as for the two of you"—she swung around to where Holmes and I sat and stabbed at us with her eyes—"I wanted you here so you could see just what your prying and nosing about get you: nothing. You, young lady, though I don't know that *lady* is the right word for you, you come poking your nose into my sitting room, pretending to be all sympathetic and helpful. You should be home scrubbing your floors or doing something useful.

"And as for you, Mr Basil, or Sherlock Holmes, or whoever you are, I hope you're proud of yourself, the way you wheedled your way in my door, ate my food, slept in my shed, took my money, and then used my generosity to spy on me. Can you imagine how I felt when Mr Coogan here shows me a photograph of Mr Sherlock Holmes and I see it's old Mr Basil, who's been working in my potato patch? Inside my house? It made me feel dirty, it did, and I have half a mind to have you arrested for it."

"I beg your pardon, madam," broke in Holmes, in his most supercilious manner, "but with what do you imagine I could be charged? Impersonating an officer, in my ancient tweeds? Hardly. Fraud? With what did I defraud you? You hired me to do work; I did the work, at, I might say, considerably lower wages than I generally pay my own workers and in considerably poorer conditions. No, madam, I broke no laws, and had you consulted your expensive legal counsellor before threatening me, he would have told you that." His voice turned cold. "Now, madam, I suggest that you stop wasting the time of these officers of the law and continue with your statement."

Her eyes narrowed as she realised what she had been harbouring in the unshaven person of Mr Basil. She glanced at Lestrade and Mr Coogan, then down at her hands, which held no knitting.

"I have nothing to say," she said sullenly.

"I'm afraid I shall have to insist, Mrs Rogers," said Lestrade.

"Then I want them out of here," and she jerked her head at us.

"Mrs Rogers, you asked for them to be here," protested Lestrade. "You insisted on it."

"Yes, well, I've had my say, and now I want them gone."

Lestrade looked at us helplessly, and I folded my notebook and stood up.

"Don't worry about it, Chief Inspector," I said. "You can't be held responsible for the whims of other people. Or for their lack of manners," I added sweetly. "Good day, Mrs Rogers, Mr Coogan. I shall be down the hall, Chief Inspector, borrowing a typewriter."

As we went through the door, Mrs Rogers fired her final peevish shot at Holmes.

"And you made a rotten job of the wallpaper, too!"

\*   \*   \*

It took only a few minutes to type a transcription of my shorthand, and it took Lestrade only slightly longer to receive Mrs Rogers's statement. He was sitting slumped at his desk, staring at it morosely, when we returned to his office. He straightened abruptly, glanced at Holmes and away, and fumbled with unnecessary attention at lighting a cigarette.

"How could she have known our evidence? Or lack of it?" He said finally.

"Did you leave her alone with that young constable who was taking notes?" enquired Holmes.

"He sat with her on the way down from Cambridgeshire, but—Good Lord, he told her? But how could he be so stupid?"

"With Mrs Erica Rogers, I shouldn't wager that you wouldn't have told her yourself, if she started in on you. She's a very clever woman. Don't be too hard on him."

"I'll have him back on the streets, I will." He seized his anger like a shield and would not look at us.

"What of the two men?" I interrupted impatiently. "Holmes said you had arrested them. What were their statements like?"

"Actually, we, er, we've decided not to arrest them just yet. Yes, I know, I thought we would, but we've let them go for the time being. Maybe they'll get cocky and hang themselves. There was nothing in those statements, nothing at all. The two of them were out both those nights, testing the engines on two cars. No alibis whatsoever, but they shut their jaws like a pair of clams after they recited their story, and they'll say nothing more."

"That doesn't sound like the Jason Rogers I met," commented Holmes.

"It's the old granny's doing, I'm sure of it. She's a cunning old witch, is that one, and she's put the fear of God into him to shut his trap. She was right about the need for a clear motive, though how she figured it out, I cannot think. Must have been her— Coogan didn't seem to have brains enough to pound sand down a rat hole. Without either a motive or harder evidence than buttons in a burn pile, five hairs that bear a passing resemblance to theirs, some smashed auto parts with a tiny bit of dried blood, and the fact that she got rid of a shelf full of murder mysteries, we'd be fools to give it a try. The only thing that's the least bit firm is the mud on your ladder, which matches the wet patch outside her potting shed, but even Coogan wouldn't have much trouble making a jury laugh at that. I'd rather go for Miss Russell's colonel, or Mr Mycroft's Arabs. I won't make an arrest yet, but we'll keep a very close eye on those boys. They may try to sell the stuff they took from you. If granny keeps an eye on them, they won't, but we can always hope. We'll get them, Mr Holmes, eventually. We know they did it, and we'll get them. Just, well, not yet." He ran out of words, then looked up from the intent study of his hands like a schoolboy before the headmaster, mingled apology and dread on his face, and shrugged his shoulders. "Without a motive, we'd be fools to make an arrest, and we've been over the inheritance with a nit comb—no insurance, no big expenses to make anyone need cash now. Wouldn't seem to make any difference if Dorothy Ruskin died now or twenty years from now. Her stuff from Palestine should arrive in the next week; we'll go through that. May find a new will or a handful of diamonds in there." His attempt at laughter trailed off, and Holmes stood up and clapped him on the shoulder with an uncharacteristic bonhomie.

"Of course we see that, Lestrade. Never mind, you'll get them eventually. Patience is a necessary virtue. Keep us informed, would you?"

We collected our possessions from Mycroft, and we slunk home.

# PART SIX

# Wednesday, 5 September 1923–
# Saturday, 8 September 1923

*The letter kills, but the spirit gives life.*
    —The First Letter of Paul to the Corinthians 3:6

# TWENTY-THREE

*psi*

$I$t was a sorry pair of detectives who rode the train south towards Eastbourne. I felt dreary and drained and utterly without interest in matters criminal or academic. Holmes, controlled as ever, looked merely determined, but there lay about him the distinct odour of brutally quenched campfire.

With an effort, I pulled myself out of this stupor. Oh goodness, Russell, I expostulated, it's hardly the end of the world, or even the end of the case. A temporary check in the hunt, no more. Lestrade will surely . . .

I had not realised I was speaking aloud until Holmes shot me a frigid glance.

"Yes, Russell? Lestrade will surely what? Oh yes, he will surely keep his ear to the ground, but he will also certainly be caught up in these other cases of his, and time will pass, and if he does lay hands on the link of evidence he so desires, it will be only through sheer luck."

"For heaven's sake, Holmes, she's just an old granny, not a Napoléon of crime."

I should have known that the phrase would tip him over the edge into an icy rage.

"It's a damned good thing for Lestrade's lot that she's too much a middleclass English woman to turn her hands to crime. Napoléon went to war, but she's satisfied herself with one brief, self-righteous campaign, and now she's captured her goal—whatever the deuces it might have been—she's entrenched. The police will never prise her out on their own. No, I ought never to have listened to you and Mycroft. If we'd kept Scotland Yard out of it, I might have got to her without giving warning, but now it's going to mean weeks, months of delicate, painstaking, cold, and uncomfortable

work, and I tell you honestly, Russell, I'm feeling too old and tired to relish the thought very much."

His last bleak phrase deflated any reciprocal anger I might have summoned. I sat while he fished a crumpled packet of Gold Flakes from his
pocket and lit one. He looked out the window; I looked at the cigarette.

"Since when have you taken to gaspers again?" I asked mildly, more
mildly than I felt, seeing the sucks and puffs of nervous anger.

"Since I first laid eyes upon Erica Rogers. She's not the only one with
premonitions." That cut it. I took a deep breath.

"Holmes, look. We will get her. Give me a week to tie things up in Oxford, and then we can go after them. Or to Paris, or Palestine, if you think
there's anything there."

He snatched the cigarette from his lips and dashed it to the floor, ground
it under his heel, and immediately took out the packet again.

"No, Russell, I'll do this myself. I can hardly expect you to sacrifice your
firstborn for the cause."

I was furious and crushed and obviously superfluous in the compartment,
so rather than making matters worse, I left and walked up the train to stand
staring out the window at the gathering clouds and sea drizzle.

This was by no means the first failure Holmes had had, but it rankled
to be defeated by a woman of no great wits, her lumpish grandson, and a
small-time crook. Holmes, too, had been touched by Dorothy Ruskin, and
it was hard not to feel that we had let her down. The dead have a claim
on us even heavier than that of the living, for they cannot hear our explanations, and we cannot ask their forgiveness.

I knew, however, that what disturbed him most was the thought that he
had failed me. He knew the affection and respect I had had for Dorothy
Ruskin, and it could only have been devastating to know that all his skills
were not enough. I did not hold him to blame, and I had tried to make it
clear that I did not, but nonetheless, for the first time he had on some level
failed me.

However, I had to admit that he had been right, yet again, back there
in the compartment: Were I to lay down my academic career, even temporarily, in order to expiate my guilt and bolster his ego, it could well prove
damaging to the strange creature that was our marriage. On the other
hand, were I to lay the books aside out of my own free choice—well, that
was another matter entirely.

I had known Holmes for a third of my life and had long since accustomed
myself to the almost instantaneous workings of his mental processes, but
even after two years of the intimacy of marriage, I was able to feel surprise

at the unerring accuracy of his emotional judgement. Holmes the cold, the reasoner, Holmes the perfect thinking machine, was, in fact, as burningly passionate as any religious fanatic. He had never been a man to accept the right action for the wrong reason, not from me, at any rate: He demanded absolute unity in thought and deed.

Oh, damn the man, I grumbled. Why couldn't he just be manipulated by pretty words the way other husbands were?

The train slowed. I climbed down and walked back along the platform to help Holmes with the bags. We got the car running, I drove back to the cottage, and we went about our separate tasks, with barely a word exchanged—not in anger, but in emptiness. He went out late in the afternoon. After an hour or so, I laced on my boots against the wet grass and followed. I found him on the cliff overlooking the ocean, one leg dangling free, the smell of a particularly rancid brand of tobacco trailing downwind. We sat in silence for some time, then walked home.

That evening, he picked at his dinner, drank four glasses of wine, and ignored the accumulation of newspapers spilling from the table near the door. Later, he sat staring into the fire, sucking at an empty pipe. He had aged since that fragrant August afternoon so long ago, when we had drunk tea and honey wine and walked the Downs with a woman who would be dead in a few hours.

"Have we overlooked anything?" I had not meant to speak, but the words lay in the room now.

For a long moment, he did not respond; then he sighed and tapped his teeth with the stem of the pipe.

"We may have done. I don't know yet. I begin to doubt my own judgement. Not overlooking things used to be my métier," he said bitterly, "but then they do say it's notoriously difficult to see what one has overlooked until one trips over it."

Like a taut wire on a street corner, I thought, and thrust it away with words.

"She told me that afternoon that it was the most pleasurable day she could remember for a long time, coming here. At least we gave her that." I shut my eyes, encouraging the brandy to relax my shoulder and my tongue, to push back the silence with a tumbling stream of reminiscence. "I wonder if she knew it was coming. Not that she seemed apprehensive, but she mentioned the past several times, and I shouldn't have thought that like her. She used to come here as a child, she told me. She was also fond of you. Perhaps *fond* is not the right word," I said, though when I looked, he didn't seem to be listening. "Impressed, perhaps. Respectful. She was intrigued by you. What was it she said? 'One of the three sensible men I've ever met,' I think it was, grouping you with a French winemaker and a polygamous sheikh." I smiled to myself at the memory.

"I'll never forget meeting her at her tell outside Jericho, coming up over the edge and there's this little white-haired English woman glaring up at us from the bottom of the trench, as if we had come to steal her potsherds. And that house of hers, that incredible hotchpotch of stone and baked-earth bricks and flattened petrol drums, and inside a cross between a Bedouin tent and an English cottage, with great heaps of things in the process of being classified and sketched and a silver tea service and a paraffin heater and block-and-board shelving sagging with books and gewgaws. She had a handful of exquisite pieces, didn't she? Like that ivory puzzle ball." I sipped my brandy, so lost in the memory of those exciting few weeks in Palestine that I could almost smell the dusty night air of Jericho.

"Do you remember that ball? Odd, wasn't it, that she should have a Chinese artefact? Such a lovely thing it was, with that pearl buried in it. She mentioned it, come to think of it, when I was driving her back to the station. You made quite an impression on her, the way your hands seemed to figure it out by themselves while you carried on with some story about Tibet. I wonder what happened to it? It looked so incongruous on those bare planks, like the silver tea set complete with spirit burner pouring Earl Grey tea through the silver strainer into rough clay—"

I stopped abruptly. Something had changed in the room, and I sat up startled, half expecting to see someone standing in the doorway, but there was no one. I pulled out my handkerchief and wiped the spilt brandy from my hand and the knee of my trousers, then took up the glass again to settle back into the cushions, but when I turned to my companion to make some sheepish remark about the state of my nerves, the words strangled unborn. Meeting his eyes was like brushing against a live electrical wire, a humming shock so sudden, my heart jerked. He had not moved. In fact, he sat so still in his chair that he looked as if he might never move again, but his eyes glittered out from the hardened brow and cheekbones, intent and alive.

"What did you say, Russell?" he asked quietly.

"How incongruous the ball and the tea set looked—"

"Before that."

"How she saw your hands as an extension of your mind when—" I stopped. The barest beginnings of a smile lurked in the grey eyes opposite me, and I continued slowly, "when you opened the ball."

"Yes."

"Dear God in heaven. Master of the Universe, how could I have been so unutterably dense?"

"Bring the box, will you please, Russell?"

I flew up the stairs to the heap of bags I had thrown in a corner and returned with the gleaming little depiction of paradise that was the Italian box. I held it out to Holmes. He took up his heavy magnifying glass, and after a minute he shook his head in self-disgust and handed both objects to me. Once I knew to look, I could easily see that the decorative carved line forming the lower border was not just a surface design, but a crack, no wider than a hair. The box had a secret base, but there was not the remotest hint of a latch or keyhole.

"I'm not going to tear this box apart, Holmes," I said, though we both knew that it might come to that, and the realisation brought a sharp, almost physical pain.

"I shall endeavour to prevent that from becoming necessary," Holmes said absently, absorbed in the box.

"Do you think you can open it?"

"Dorothy Ruskin thought I could. She may have been impressed by my parlour trick, but I doubt that it led her to endow me with godlike abilities. I don't suppose she made offhand mention of any of the box's attributes, as a help?"

"Not that I remember."

"Then it should not be terribly difficult. Ah, here. May I borrow a hair-pin, Russell?"

He found the tiny pressure points fairly quickly—two of the giraffe's jet spots and one of the monkey's eyes had infinitesimal and unnoticed dents in the adjoining wood—but beyond that he was wrong, it was difficult, extraordinarily so considering the age of the thing. After two hours, he had found that by pressing in a certain sequence with varying pressures, he could loosen the bottom, but it would not come free. I went to make coffee, and when I brought it in, he was looking as frustrated as I have ever seen him.

"Leave it for a while," I suggested, pouring.

"I shall have to. The nearness of it is maddening." He stood up, stretched the kinks from his back, placed his right hand gently on the box, and leant forward to take his cup. We both heard the click, and we looked down at the thing, every bit as astonished as if it had addressed us. He gingerly spread his fingers around it and lifted the top and sides away from the base. A clockwork intricacy of brass latches and gears lay revealed and, pushed down between the works and the wooden side, a tight roll of paper resembling a long, thin cigarette, tied in the middle with a length of black thread. Holmes picked it out with a fingernail and held it out to me. I rubbed my suddenly sweaty palms on my trousers, then took it.

It was a letter, tiny, crowded words on half a dozen small sheets of nearly transparent onionskin paper, and I had a sudden image of Dorothy Ruskin bent over her hotel table with the magnifying glass. I read her words aloud to Holmes.

"Dear Miss Russell,

Were I not blessed with the ability to appreciate the humour in any trying situation, this one would verge on the macabre. I sit here at my shaky desk in a distinctly third-rate Parisian hotel, writing to a young woman whom I met but once—and that several years previously—in the hopes that she and her husband will choose to make enquiries should I die a suspicious death whilst in my homeland, despite the fact that I will have given them no hints, no clues, no reason to believe that someone wants my death. Indeed, I am not at all sure that I do have reason to believe it.

A peculiarly amusing situation.

I have spent several days trying to imagine the circumstances under which you will read this, if indeed you ever do. Are you investigating my death? What a queer sensation comes with writing those words! And if your answer is in the affirmative, how might I respond? 'I'm pleased to hear that' seems inappropriate, somehow. And yet, if that is what you are doing, if that has led you to this letter, it would give me the—surely *satisfaction* is not the right word?—of knowing that my inchoate, illogical fears were entirely justified.

Again, a most peculiar situation.

But, enough meandering. I intend to visit you in your Sussex home and leave with you this box, the manuscript, and, incidentally, these contents of the secret compartment. I shall have to find a means of planting in your mind the possibility that the box can be opened and do so casually enough to be natural, yet firmly enough that you remember it later if the need should arise. If I have failed in the first instance,

264

and your curiosity has led you to open the box while I am still alive, then I beg you, please, to replace the following document in the box and have a good laugh over the imagination of an old woman. If I fail in the second instance and you do not remember my dropped hints, well, then, I am writing this for the chance, future amusement of a total stranger, and my precautions have been for naught.

It is ridiculous. It is foolish of me, and I am not accustomed to doing foolish things. I have no evidence that I will die, no signs or portents or threatening letters in the post. And yet . . . I am filled with a strange dread when I think of crossing the Channel, and I want to turn for home, to Palestine. I cannot do that, of course, but I also cannot ignore this odd, compelling feeling of menace and finality. It is not death that I fear, Miss Russell. Death is a person with whom I have some passing acquaintance, and if anything, it is a motherly figure who holds out forgiving, welcoming arms. I do, however, dread the thought that my work, my life, will die with me. If I return to Palestine, I intend to work out more fully the details of how my estate, minor as it may be, might best be put to support the archaeological effort there. This letter is merely insurance. I have no time to have a proper will drawn up, so I have written and signed a holograph will, witnessed by two of my fellow guests in this hotel. It clearly states my wishes and intentions regarding the disbursement of my estate. You will please take it to the appropriate authorities, whom, no doubt, you know better than I.

As I said, I have no evidence whatsoever that anyone seeks my death, other than this persistent, irrational hunch. It may be that I will succumb to illness or an accident. It is also quite possible that I may survive England to return home, have my solicitor in Jerusalem draw up a new and complete will, and write to tell you of the box's hidden opening, feeling foolish when I do so. In any case, I will not accuse anyone from beyond the grave, as it were, and even the enclosed will can hardly be used to indict a person who otherwise appears blameless. If it points a surreptitious finger, so be it.

You will no doubt ask yourself why, if I intend to change my will, I do not do so openly. I have asked myself the same question, and although there are several valid reasons for it, they boil down to two: First, I need to witness the state of my family's affairs before I can make any final decisions; second, I am quite honestly torn between the absurdity of my premonitions and the urge to action. This is a compromise, and puts it into the hands of God. That I say this would certainly amaze some of my acquaintances, but I think that you, Miss Russell, will understand when I say that faith in a divine force and the ability to think intellectually are not necessarily incompatible. I am tired, I am uncertain, and therefore I will arrange this all so that God can make the final decision.

I should dearly love to see your reaction to that, and I admit to a sense of frustration and regret when I realise that I will not witness the machinations by which this letter again sees the light of day. However, the pleasures of imagination will fill the spare moments of my next days.

Thank you, Miss Russell, Mr Holmes, for your faithfulness to me, a near stranger. The box and the manuscript are not to be regarded as payment, for I would have given them to you in any case, and I know that payment would be neither required nor accepted. I hope that Mary's graceful hand brings you as much pleasure as it has me.

Yours in friendship,<br>
Dorothy Ruskin"

The will began: "I, Dorothy Elizabeth Ruskin, being of sound mind and body," then went on to state simply that the entirety of her estate was to go to support the archaeological effort in Palestine, with specific names and locations given.

When a copy of the will was shown to Erica Rogers, she said nothing, but that night she suffered a massive seizure and spent the remaining months of her life in a nursing home, next to her mother. When agents from Scotland Yard went to arrest the grandson and his accomplice, Jason Rogers escaped. His body was found the following day by two hikers, in the wreckage of a very expensive car that did not belong to him. The problem of Erica Rogers's apparent alibi was solved during the subsequent interview with Jason's wife, when she confessed tearfully that she had taken Erica's place in the home for the two nights Mrs Rogers was away, caring for old Mrs Ruskin and turning the lights on and off at the appropriate times. She, however, was not charged with participation in the actual murder, as it became obvious that she had been accustomed to do just as her husband ordered.

The other partner in the killing, whose name was Thomas Rand, never confessed his part in the murder, but he was eventually brought to trial, convicted, and hanged.

Lestrade came down from London himself to tell us about Rand's arrest, wishing, I think, to remove the aftertaste of failure from his mouth in front of the headmaster. He came for tea, looking more dishevelled than ever and yet oddly more competent for it, and he recited each detail of the evidence against Rand, up to and including the man's possession of my camera, my odds and ends of manuscripts, and Mrs Hudson's jewellery.

"Only one thing I can't figure," he said finally. Holmes shot me a sardonic glance.

"Glad you've left me with something to explain, Lestrade," he growled, which remark alone put half an inch on Lestrade's stature.

"It's Mrs Ho—Miss Russell's papers. If they weren't looking for the manuscript, the pie—what'd'ya call it?"

"Papyrus," I said.

"Right. If they weren't looking for that, why cart about all the things written in a foreign alphabet and steal half of them? You can't imagine Jason Rogers or his friend would know Greek, or know about the value of that letter, and I wouldn't have thought it was the old lady's style, either."

"Ah," said Holmes, "but there you would be wrong. What Erica Rogers was looking for was very much in her, as you say, 'style.' The day Miss Ruskin was here, she happened to mention that in their childhood she and her sister—the daughters of a minister, remember—used to play a game of hiding coded messages in a place they called 'Apocalypse,' because the top came off. The verb *apocalyptein*, I believe Russell could tell you, is Greek for 'uncover,' " he added helpfully. "It's very likely that the 'code' was simple English written in the Greek alphabet. I recall doing just that myself, with Mycroft. Did you play that game with your brother, Russell?"

"Yes, though we used Hebrew, which was a bit trickier."

"Remember, too, that Erica Rogers was an enthusiast of Watson's thrilling nonsense. When she heard that her sister was coming to see me, her suspicions must have positively erupted. It was indeed very much in her 'style' to believe that her sister would write an encoded will, or a will written in one of the several foreign languages she spoke, and then lodge it with the Great Detective for safekeeping."

"But that's absurd—beg pardon, Mr Holmes."

"Elaborate and ridiculous and utterly unlike something Dorothy Ruskin might do," he agreed. "But very much in Erica Ruskin's style. A woman who would arrange an elaborate murder involving a beggar disguise and an automobile, who would anticipate the possibility that the death might not be accepted as a road accident and move to cloud any investigation by arranging to make it appear that she had remained at home, and then even think to plant a letter to her sister implicating an imaginary but plausible group of Arabs named Mud—a woman with a mind like that would not hesitate to believe that her sister could write a will in Serbo-Croatian and lodge it on the top of Nelson's Column. Real penny-dreadful stuff, and not, I think, completely sane. Scotland Yard is going to have to look into the influence art has on true crime one of these days, Lestrade, mark my words."

Lestrade wavered, decided to take the remark as a joke, and laughed politely.

"Inspector," I asked, "have you an idea of the value of the Ruskin estate yet?"

He told us, and Holmes and I glanced at each other.

"Yes," said Lestrade, "more than you'd have thought, and taken as a whole, an amount worth fighting for. When Dorothy Ruskin came back here from Palestine, she must have told her sister, either directly or by something she said, that she had decided to make a new will and put the money into her archaeological projects. Erica Rogers might have put up with seeing the third part of their father's money that had already been divided up poured into a lot of holes in the ground, but she drew the line at having half of old Mrs Ruskin's money follow it. If the old lady died first, Dorothy Ruskin would inherit her share and it would be gone. Therefore Dorothy Ruskin had to die before their mother. I imagine Mrs Rogers said something to that effect to her grandson Jason, and he then brought in a friend who was experienced at this sort of thing. And," he added thoughtfully, "they then decided to retrieve the money Dorothy Ruskin already had, by finding and destroying the new will. If they'd been satisfied with just the old lady's money, we'd never have got on to them."

"Greed feeds on itself," commented Holmes.

"I'm not sure, though, why the three of them thought the will was here."

"Miss Ruskin probably hinted that it would be," I said. "According to her hidden letter, that is what she planned to do to us, bring us the box and drop hints that it had a secret. I expect she did the same thing to her sister, trailing her garment to tempt her and point her at Sussex. Had Erica Rogers been honest, she'd have ignored it completely."

"Miss Ruskin laid a trap."

"You could say that. A trap that could only be sprung by the presence of criminal intent."

"Not very nice of her, neglecting to mention your part in the arrangements."

"The woman had an incredible faith in us, I agree. And not an entirely warranted faith, at least when it came to me. Her sister's ears were much sharper than mine at hearing nuances."

"The search of our cottage did catch our attention, though," said Holmes benignly.

Lestrade shook his head.

"So elaborate. And almost suicidal. Why not come to us in the first place, or even to you, bring it out in the open? As mad as her sister, in a way."

"I think it began simply—in a conviction—and grew. And yes, immensely single-minded, practical people do seem mad. But, you may be right about one thing: I don't think she much cared for the chance she had of living blind."

A short time later, Lestrade's local police driver arrived to take him to the train. Before he left, Holmes congratulated him, so that going down the drive to the waiting car, his shoe leather was floating several inches above the gravel. Holmes shook his head sourly as we watched the driver negotiate the ruts and stones and peace began to settle again onto our patch of hillside.

"What is wrong, Holmes? I'd have thought you would be as cock-a-hoop as Lestrade, snatching a solution from the jaws of befuddlement as you did."

"Ah, Russell, I had such hopes for this case," he said mournfully. "But in the end, it all came down to greed. So commonplace, it's hardly worthy of any attention. Do you know, for a few days I allowed myself to hope that we had a prime specimen among cases, a murder with the pure and unadorned motive of the hatred of emancipated women. Now, that would have been one for the books: murder by misogyny," he drawled with relish, and then his face twisted. "Money. Bah!"

Two days later, I took the train to London to see Colonel Edwards. I dressed carefully for that meeting, including my soft laced-up boots, which brought me to well over six feet in height. I arrived back late in the afternoon, and while Mrs Hudson went to heat more water for the teapot, I walked over to stand at the big south window that framed the Downs as they rolled towards the sea, to watch the light fade into purples and indigo and a blue in the heights the colour of Dorothy Ruskin's eyes. Small noises behind me told of Holmes filling and lighting his pipe—a sweetly fragrant tobacco tonight, an indicator of his temper, as well. Mrs Hudson came in with the tea. I accepted a cup and took it back to the window. It was nearly dark.

"So, Russell."

"Yes, Holmes."

"What did your colonel have to say?"

I took a contemplative sip of the steaming-hot tea and thought back to the man's reaction as he saw his gentle, hesitant, stoop-shouldered secretary climb out of the taxi as Mary Russell Holmes. I could feel a smile of pure devilment come onto my lips.

"He said, and I quote, 'I always felt there was more to you, Mary, but I must say I hadn't realised just how much more.' "

I grinned as I heard the sounds behind me, then turned, finally, to take in the sight of Sherlock Holmes collapsed in helpless laughter, his head thrown back on the chair, pipe forgotten, uncertainty forgotten, all forgotten but the beauty and absurdity of the colonel's elegy.

# PART SEVEN

*A woman seldom writes her mind but in her postscript.*
—Richard Steele

# POSTSCRIPT

*omega*

The letter that lay at the heart of our investigation, the little strip of stained papyrus that was written in a hurried moment some eighteen and a half centuries before I first laid eyes upon it, preserved by simple peasants in a vague awareness of its importance, passed within its clay amulet during the formative years of Islam into a branch of the family that followed the Prophet, kept in the heart of generations of believers over centuries of war and wandering until a simple act of generosity on the part of an Englishwoman brought it to light, is still in my possession. In the decades since it came to me, the scientific study of documents has made huge strides, from the chemical analysis of writing materials to radiocarbon dating to the grammatical analyses of the words themselves. Not one of these tests has taken me substantially further than Holmes' graphological conclusion or my own intuitive conviction that the thing was real. Certainly none of the tests that I have thus far been able to conduct or oversee has cast any degree of doubt on Mary's letter. As yet, I have found no indication that it is other than what it seems: a hasty, affectionate letter written by a woman of considerable wisdom and strength to a bewildered but much-loved sister, at a moment when the writer realised that her world was coming to a violent, catastrophic end.

It pains me, even now, to know that I have failed Mariam; I feel I have betrayed her trust. Rational factors count for little, and the promise I made to Colonel Edwards on that final afternoon all those years ago, a promise to delay publication of Mary's letter, need not have been said; the fact is, sheer cowardice kept me from revealing the letter Dorothy Ruskin gave into my keeping, abject terror at the thought of the battle I should be in for, a battle that would have consumed my entire life and all my energies. I have kept it safe in a bank vault; I shall hand it over to another, but I am not proud of my actions.

I admit, as did Dorothy Ruskin, to a degree of frustration in knowing that I will never witness the reaction when Mary's letter comes to light. It will not be released until a minimum of ten years after my death: I gave that promise to Col. Dennis Edwards to atone for my actions against him, and although the temptation to break my word has been great, I shall not. I do, however, like the previous owner, receive a great deal of amusement when I picture the results of the letter being made public.

I suppose that the Christian world at the close of the twentieth century will be better equipped to deal with the revelations contained in Mary's letter than it was in the century's earlier decades. As Miss Ruskin noted, presupposed notions of the rôle of women in leadership during the first century need to be discarded before the idea of Mary of Magdala as an apostle of Jesus and a leader of the Jerusalem church sits easy in the mind. Archaeologists, male and female, are pointing us inexorably in that direction, and presuppositions are teetering: We know that women were heads of synagogues in the early centuries of the Common Era and that adaptations to the Roman expectations concerning the Godhead were considerable as the nascent Church moved away from its troubled birthplace and struggled to carve a place for itself in the empire.

Perhaps before too many years, my heir will judge the world ready to see Mariam's letter. I do not know if I envy her, or pity her.

Death, and life, and the written word that binds them. The first letter to hit my desk brought with it an all-too-brief refluorescence of a friendship and led to the deaths of four people. The next letter gave life to a voice which the world had lost for more than eighteen hundred years. And a last letter, reaching out from the grave to assert the will of its writer and ensure the continuance of her life's work, coincidentally condemned those who would have brought that work to an end. The hand of bone and sinew and flesh achieves its immortality in taking up a pen. The hand on a page wields a greater power than the fleshly hand ever could in life.